Stubborn Hearts

Carol Ritten Smith

CRIMSON
ROMANCE

Avon, Massachusetts

This edition published by
Crimson Romance
an imprint of F+W Media, Inc.
10151 Carver Road, Suite 200
Blue Ash, Ohio 45242

www.crimsonromance.com

Copyright © 2012 by Carol Smith

ISBN 10: 1-4405-5412-9
ISBN 13: 978-1-4405-5412-4
eISBN 10: 1-4405-5413-7
eISBN 13: 978-1-4405-5413-1

This is a work of fiction.

Names, characters, corporations, institutions, organizations, events, or locales in this novel are either the product of the author's imagination or, if real, used fictitiously. The resemblance of any character to actual persons (living or dead) is entirely coincidental.

Dedication

THIS BOOK IS DEDICATED WITH LOVE TO MOM FOR ALWAYS BELIEVING IN ME AND MY DREAMS. THANK YOU FOR YOUR INSPIRATION AND ENCOURAGEMENT.

Acknowledgments

Stubborn Hearts would not exist if not for the help of many.

My heartfelt gratitude goes to my family and friends who read the manuscript and offered great advice; and to everyone at my writers' group, Red Deer and District Writers Ink, for their helpful critiques and insights.

Also, a big thank you goes to my editor, Jennifer Lawler, for her guidance and patience.

And I would be remiss if I didn't thank my husband, Denis, for his love and support and for never saying, "You haven't started supper yet?" You're my hero.

Chapter 1

Tom Carver pulled his coat up around his neck and leaned into the night's hard rain. Streams of muddy water coursed down the street, and the downpour had already submerged portions of the boardwalk. Though he didn't relish getting soaked to the bone, he welcomed the deluge needed to douse the possibility of any prairie fires. As he passed the doors of the Star Saloon, the jovial brouhaha reaching his ears told him he wasn't the only one relieved to have the rain.

He should have known that this storm was coming. Old Jack seemed extra stiff today. Had Tom been as smart as his dog, he'd have stayed home too. He'd have been cozy and dry instead of suffering the drizzle down the back of his neck. But then, it wasn't raining when he'd left to see Abigail.

Another bolt of lightning struck and the buildings on either side of the street shone ghostly white in its light. Almost immediately, a crack of thunder resounded, and the boardwalk reverberated beneath his feet.

Damn! That was close.

He broke into a run, hoping his barn hadn't been the target. A lightning strike could set an old barn ablaze as quickly as a spark to dry kindling. When he arrived out of breath, everything seemed fine, but to be safe, he jogged a circuit around the barn. At the far side he stopped short. The door was ajar. He distinctly remembered closing it, which meant someone had opened it. He crept inside.

Tom stood dead still, ears straining to hear footsteps. There. The steps came closer. He waited until the intruder passed in front of him, then tackled him from behind. They landed with a hard thud on the packed dirt floor, the prowler flattened under Tom's weight.

"Ow! You're hurting me! Get off!"

By the small body size and high voice pitch, Tom concluded he had caught a young boy. "Quit your damn squirming," he growled. "It won't do any good."

But the struggle continued, and Tom pinned the boy's arm back between his shoulder blades and applied moderate pressure. The scuffle ceased immediately.

"All right, that's better. Now I'm going to let you up and you can tell me what you're doing in my barn. It better be good, because I've a mind to take the reins to your backside for trespassing." Tom eased off his weight, but as soon as he did, the youth scrambled forward on all fours. Tom lunged, grabbed him by his belt, and yanked the intruder to his feet by wrapping a free arm around the lad's front.

Tom stopped short when his hand grasped something soft and malleable. Intrigued, he tested the shape again, this time more gently. A rounded breast settled pleasantly into his palm. Hmm, nice, he thought, sorely tempted to fondle it longer. Curbing his lusty urge, he moved his hand to the lady's shoulder.

By now, he was downright curious as to her identity. "Ma'am, I'm gonna let you go and you better not move. Hear me? I won't hurt you." He loosened his hold, and when she didn't try to escape, he reached for a match in the tin holder on the wall behind him. "I hope I didn't harm you none, but in the dark I thought you were a boy." He flicked the match with his thumbnail and held it high, clearly illuminating a long coppery braid. It was still dripping, indicating she hadn't been out of the rain very long. "Now turn around so I can see who you are."

Tom's eyebrows lifted in recognition. "Well I'll be . . . Miss Patterson, you're the last person I expected to find sneaking around my barn."

The town's new schoolteacher remained silent.

Tom gave her a quick once over and decided he had seen scarecrows better dressed. An old jacket hung from her shoulders and her frayed trousers were so covered with mud, it was difficult to distinguish where the trousers ended and her equally muddy boots began. A pocketknife lay close to her boots.

Tom picked it up. "This yours?"

She snatched it from him and, having found her voice, snapped, "It must have fallen out of my trousers." Considering it took some effort for her to shove it into her front pocket, he suspected she was lying, but he couldn't fathom why.

She sidestepped around him. "Thank you and goodnight," she said, as if she'd been his invited guest.

Tom stepped in front of her. "Hey! Not so fast. What were you doing in my barn?"

Her large eyes glanced at the door and Tom expected her to bolt. But suddenly and completely, her fear seemed to vanish. "I was looking for my cat. He wandered away a few days ago. I thought I saw him come into your barn."

Tom couldn't hide his disbelief. "Are you telling me you're looking for your cat in the middle of the night in this downpour?"

She straightened her shoulders and lifted her chin as if daring him to call her a liar.

Having occasionally played poker, Tom was a good judge of when someone was bluffing and he was tempted to call her on it. Instead, he chose to see how this farce would end. "Did you try calling him?"

"Of course, but he didn't come."

"So you figured you could just sneak into my barn to look for him."

She puffed up with indignation, reminding Tom of a little Banty hen. He fought to keep a straight face.

"For your information, Mr. Carver, I did not sneak and I resent your saying that. If *anyone* was doing the sneaking it was you! Are you in the habit of jumping on women in your barn?"

Her question begged a salacious comeback and Tom couldn't deny himself the fun. "Sadly, I haven't jumped a woman in this barn for a while." Even in the soft lantern light he could see her face turning red, whether in outrage or embarrassment, he wasn't certain.

"I never meant it that way and you know it!"

"Oh, sorry, I guess I misunderstood." He tried to look

remorseful but did a damn poor job of it. "Hey, why don't I call my old dog? Jack hates cats. He'll find him."

As he raised his fingers to his mouth to whistle, she grasped his elbow. "No! No, that's fine. You're right. Why on earth *would* my cat be out in this weather? I must have been seeing things."

"Tell you what. Give me a description of your cat and if I find him, I'll bring him back."

"Um, well," she stammered, "he's white with some orange and some black on him."

"He's a calico?"

"Yes, that's right and his name is . . . Cally."

"You don't say!" Tom studied the small-framed woman before him. He thought everyone knew that calico cats were female, one of those interesting quirks of nature. Apparently, Miss Patterson either didn't know that fact and was too dim-witted to tell a male cat from a female . . . or she was lying. Tom leaned heavily on the latter explanation. "I'll keep an eye out for Cally."

"Thank you. I won't bother you any longer."

"No bother. Wouldn't you like to wait until the storm lets up?"

"I don't mind a little rain."

Tom stepped aside to let her pass. Right, he thought, a little rain. He watched her slog through the deepening mud. "Oh, Miss Patterson?"

She turned. Wet strands of hair plastered her face. "Yes?"

"You should take those britches over to Abigail Craig's and have her let them out a bit. They're a tad snug through the hips." Seeing the fury on her face, Tom expected her to fling a gob of mud at him or blast him with a few caustic remarks. She simply clenched her fists, tightened her lips, and turned on her heels, nearly toppling over into the mud.

As Tom did a quick check on his horses, he chuckled. As if he was going to believe her cockamamie story about a cat! But why on earth would she lie?

*

Once the boardwalk ended, the streets of Whistle Creek were nothing but mud and rivers of muck. With every step, the mire sucked at Beth Patterson's boots. By the time she got home, her legs were wobbly and her muscles ached. She was soaked through and her teeth chattered uncontrollably. This was all Bill's fault. She'd throttle him when she got her hands on him.

She never thought he'd be home, sitting at the table. Globs of mud settled underneath his chair. "You idiot!" she yelled. She wrestled the pocketknife from her trousers and flung it at him. It bounced harmlessly off his chest. "What were you thinking, trying to steal Mr. Carver's horse?" She hung her drenched coat on a peg.

"I had it all planned, and if you hadn't come along, I would have been on my way to Tannerville by now."

"On your way to jail," she countered, removing her muddy boots and shaking as much sludge from her trousers as she could. "You're lucky he caught me and not you. I had to lie through my teeth to explain what I was doing in his barn."

Bill shrugged. "I knew you'd think of something. When I saw him coming, I snuck out the door on the other side." Then, as if first noticing her garb, he asked, "What are you doing in my clothes? You look stupid."

"When I went in to kiss Davy goodnight, I saw you weren't in bed. It wasn't difficult to put two and two together, you with your grand ideas of owning a horse. I was in such a hurry to stop you, I grabbed whatever was handy."

"Davy told you whose place I was going to, didn't he, the little snitch."

"No. I had to pry it out of him. You're lucky I did." She went to the dry sink and washed her hands and face in a basin of cold water before sitting at the table opposite him. "Honestly, I can't believe you, trying to steal the most recognizable horse in town. You must have rocks for brains."

Bill rose from his chair.

"Sit down!" Beth ordered, and for once her brother did as he was told. "You could have jeopardized our safety. You know we can't risk drawing attention."

"Yeah, yeah. I know."

She slapped her hand down on the table. "No, I don't think you do. We need to—"

Bill jumped to his feet, nearly knocking over his chair. "Shut up! I'm sick of you bossing me around. Just 'cause you're three years older than me don't mean you're smarter, 'cause you're not. You don't know squat about nothing. I'm gonna get me a horse. You'll see." Bill slammed the door behind him.

She yanked it opened. "Where are you going?" He didn't give a reply.

She ached for her bed, but, since she was too upset to sleep, she set to work cleaning up the mess. She filled a bucket from the copper boiler on the stove and began to mop up the mud.

"Beth?"

Taken by surprise, she jumped, nearly dropping her mop.

Davy stood in the bedroom doorway, holding the front of his nightshirt away from his skinny body. "I wet the bed. Please don't be mad. I tried, but I couldn't hold it any longer."

"Oh, Davy."

"When you went after Bill, you made me promise to stay in bed. Remember?"

"I didn't mean you couldn't use the pot under the bed." If she hadn't been so emotionally and physically spent, Beth might have seen the some humor in the situation. Instead she wanted to sit there and have a long cry. Digging deep, she summoned one last bit of patience. "Change into another nightshirt, and crawl into my bed. I'll wash your bedding in the morning."

A few minutes later, dressed in dry bedclothes, Davy padded from his room to Beth's. "You coming?" he asked.

How she wished she could. "I'm going to wait for Bill. Then I'll come." While she rinsed out her mop, she wondered if Mr. Carver believed her story. Probably not. Unbidden, the memory of their few minutes in the barn returned in vivid detail. Bad enough to be caught in his barn, but the rough treatment, his falling on top of her, and then . . . Her cheeks heated at the memory of his recent manhandling and she slapped her mop hard against the wooden floor and swished it around with vigor. She refused to give him any latitude because he thought she was a boy. *Slap. Swish. Swish.* And the audacity of him, making that lewd comment about her "britches" being too tight through the hips! *Slap. Swish. Swish.* Shame on him for looking. What sort of man was he? A scoundrel! She ceased mopping as she searched for a better word. A reprobate? No, worse than that. A defiler of women! Yes, that's what Tom Carver was.

Slap. Slap. Swish. Swish. She scrubbed the floor with a fervor, conjuring up reasons to dislike him, while at the same time desperately trying to ignore her conscience niggling at her. Fine! All right, she admitted grudgingly. He wasn't *all* bad. When she had arrived at Whistle Creek's train station with her two brothers, the school committee almost turned them away. But Tom Carver believed her sob story about their parents' untimely deaths and how she couldn't leave her siblings behind. Tom was the one who had convinced the other committee members to let the three of them stay.

Beth threw the muddy water outside and refilled her bucket. She bent to work, mopping up the remaining mud. She still couldn't quite believe how lucky they had been. Though she had no formal training as a teacher, she relied on her years of attending a one-room school to get by. Soon she was taking attendance and assigning lessons as if she'd been doing it for years.

Then Bill got a job at the livery. Sadly, working with horses spurred his idea of owning his own horse, despite the fact they couldn't afford one. They had several arguments, but there was no reasoning with him. At sixteen, he was increasingly difficult for her to handle. Oh, who was she kidding, she thought. She had no control over Bill whatsoever.

She shuddered to think of the consequences had he been caught stealing Carver's horse. Details of their dreadful past would surely be exposed. Best case scenario, they'd be run out of town. Worst case, Beth would hang for what she had done.

*

Bill returned home late the next afternoon. He looked as though he'd been on the losing end of a fist fight. His cheek was abraded, his left eye was all but swollen shut, and his chin was caked with dried blood from a bloody nose.

"Where have you been?" Beth grilled. "And what happened to your face?"

Giving no explanation, Bill tramped into his room and slammed the door.

*

Monday, Beth ushered her students outside to eat their lunches. She wanted to utilize the quiet time to mark their spelling tests. Freddie North's spelling was dreadful and it wasn't only the big words that were giving him trouble; even words that the first graders could spell stumped him. Beth resolved to spend extra time with him. The thought annoyed her, not because she begrudged the time or work, but because Freddie didn't care one bit about his studies. He would rather pester the other children. He was the biggest, the oldest, and by far her most challenging student in the classroom.

Something hit the roof and Beth knew a noisy game of ante-I-over had been initiated. It was difficult to concentrate on paperwork with the ball thumping on the school roof, and children screaming as they chased each other around. Ten minutes later the racket stopped, indicating that the children had moved on to some other entertainment.

Soon thereafter blonde-headed Inga burst into the classroom. "Miss Patterson, the boys were throwing Penelope's hat and now it's in the tree and they can't get it down."

"Oh, for heaven's sake!" Beth often wished the large spreading maple in the corner of the schoolyard wasn't there, and if it hadn't been such a beautiful old tree, she might have chopped it down herself.

She followed the girl outside to the maple where everyone stood gazing upwards. High above their heads, lodged in the crook of a branch, sat Penelope's bonnet decorated with feathers and bows, looking like a fancy bird's nest.

Beth berated herself for not having the foresight to put that hat safely in her closet until classes were dismissed. Something that garish was bound to be too tempting for any boy to leave alone.

"Who started this?" she demanded.

No one confessed.

"I'm going to close my eyes. Whoever started this foolishness had better step forward by the time I count to three . . . or every single student will have to write lines. One . . . two . . ." Before she got to three, there was a scuffle. "Three," she said and opened her eyes. Standing before her was Freddie North, no doubt pushed front and center by his fellow classmates.

It didn't surprise Beth in the least he was the culprit. But today of all days, why couldn't it have been someone else? Freddie's father was Raymond North, the owner of North's Bank. Beth planned to go to the bank this afternoon for a loan so Bill could buy a horse. Punishing his son would not go in her favor.

Beth felt sick. "Did you take Penelope's hat from her, Freddie?" *Please say no.*

Freddie gave her a belligerent look. "What if I did?"

"You should not take someone else's property without their permission. Did you ask Penelope if you could have it?"

"Yeah, I did."

"He did not! I would never let him have my bonnet!"

Freddie turned on her. "We was just playing a little game o' keep away. Ain't no harm in that."

Beth interceded. "The *harm* is that Penelope's hat is now in that tree with no way to get it down." She knew she was committed to follow through with some form of discipline. "Fred, I want you to go into the school, and write fifty times on the chalkboard, 'I will show restraint when tempted to do wrong.' And be sure to use a dictionary."

Freddie groaned. "But—"

"Make that seventy-five times." She stared him down, knowing that if he openly disobeyed, she would have no way to enforce her discipline. He wasn't much taller than her, but he was far stronger. Her heart thudded erratically. When Freddie stomped toward the schoolhouse, she slowly released her breath. "I will show restraint when tempted to do wrong," she hollered after him.

The remaining boys stood, hands in pockets, looking guilty and likely thanking their lucky rabbit's foot they hadn't thought of grabbing Penelope's hat first.

This was Beth's first major disciplinary action. She hoped the other students took note that Miss Patterson was not a teacher to push about. She was in control of what happened on the school grounds and they had better remember it!

"Teacher, how are you going to get the hat down?"

Beth felt her control blow away like a leaf in a tornado. What *was* she going to do? It was obviously too high to reach with a broom.

"I can climb up there and get it," an older boy volunteered.

"No, you most certainly can not. No children are to climb this tree. That's the rule."

Davy shot his hand straight into the air. "I know! You could climb it, Beth. You're not a kid anymore. You're all growed up. And you used to be real good at climbing tr . . . " His voice petered out when Beth glared at him.

"Oh, please, Miss Patterson," Penelope begged in a fresh rush of tears. "Mother will be so upset if she finds out I wore it to school. Auntie sent it all the way from Toronto."

"Hush. Let me think." Absurd as Davy's suggestion may have been, Beth decided the only viable solution was to climb the tree herself. She looked over the maple's structure. When she was younger, she'd shinnied up trees a lot trickier. "Very well, I'll do the climbing. Everyone stand well back."

Immediately, the class backed up several paces. Turning to the maple, Beth lifted one leg and settled her foot firmly in a waist high crook. For once, she was thankful for the many layers of concealing petticoats dictated by fashion. She looked up, reached for a branch above her head, grabbed it, and pulled herself up. She reached for the next limb. Despite the branches snagging her bulky skirt and petticoats, Beth climbed with confidence until she reached the branch cradling the hat. Its feathers fluttered in the gentle autumn breeze.

She looked down. The class had moved forward again. "Everyone back!" she commanded. "I don't want you hurt if I fall."

She inched out along the limb. It creaked under her weight. She carefully shifted herself further along and stretched forward with her arm. The bonnet was at least ten inches out of reach. If she just budged a little bit more . . . Suddenly the branch dropped six inches and Beth nearly fell.

The girls below screamed.

"It's okay. I'm fine." Beth wondered if she was reassuring herself or her students. She decided it was unsafe to continue and started back down. "The branch isn't strong enough," she explained. A short wispy stem caught a strand of her hair and pulled it from the tidy knot at the back of her head.

"Still looking for Cally, Miss Patterson?" a deep voice asked.

Chapter 2

Lord love a duck! Beth looked down through the branches. There stood Tom Carver, his head cocked back, gazing up at her. He sported an exceptionally wide smile. Beth could only imagine how she must look with her petticoats draped on either side of the branch, her hair a mess. She scrambled down from the tree.

"That was a pretty sight."

Beth glanced to see if any of her students overheard his comment. She couldn't tell. "Mr. Carver. A gentleman would have averted his eyes."

"I tell you what, the next time you're up a tree, I promise to look away." He grinned.

She wondered how many times he had used his swarthy good looks to get out of trouble. Well, it wouldn't wash with her! "The wind carried Penelope's hat into the tree. I was merely trying to retrieve it for her."

"Seems to me, you might do better if you were wearing those britches again," he said in a low voice.

The nerve of him! "Mr. Carver," she retorted, her whisper seething with outrage, "it is none of your business what clothes I do or do not wear."

Tom shook his head. "Oh, trust me, Miss Patterson, if you chose to wear no clothes, I'd make it my business."

Beth gasped and hot color poured into her cheeks. How dare he be so crass, once again warping her words into something crude! She presented her back to him and clapped her hands. "Children, lunch break is over."

"But what about my hat?" Penelope cried.

"You will just have to wait for the wind to bring it down."

Tom tipped his head back to peer through the leafy branches. "I haven't climbed a tree in a long time . . . oh, what the heck! I'll give it a go." He whipped off his leather blacksmith apron and dropped it in the brittle grass. Stepping up to the maple's trunk, he reached high above his head for a secure hold and started climbing. He rapidly ascended the maple and moved along the branch beyond the point where Beth had stopped. It groaned under his weight, but dropped no further.

Beth hoped the branch would break. Nothing would please her more than to see that scoundrel flat on his back. But the branch held and with the agility of a cougar Tom stretched out on the limb and retrieved the bonnet, then descended with it perched at a jaunty angle upon his head. He jumped the last few feet to the ground, removed the bonnet, and bowed low. The children applauded exuberantly.

"You just have to know how to distribute your weight properly." Tom turned the hat over and inspected its plumage. "If you ask me, this thing looked more at home in the tree. Surely women don't wear hats like this. Those feathers would make any person look bird-brained."

Several boys snickered. Beth snatched the hat from Tom and handed it to Penelope. "Mr. Carver, this bonnet is of the latest fashion back East. All proper women wear them."

"Yeah? Judging by your get-up the other night, I guess *you* would know."

It took a great deal of restraint to resist kicking him in the shin. "If you will excuse me, I have classes to teach." She marched to the school steps. "Come along, children. Line up, please. Tidy rows now."

She stood tall and straight as each student filed past her into the school. Before she could follow them inside, Tom hollered, "One other thing, Miss Patterson."

"What now?"

He ambled over to her. "Got so distracted with you in the tree and all, I almost forgot why I came over in the first place. Mr. Hoosman had a mare stolen late Friday night. You remember Friday night? We met in my barn."

She could tell he was watching for a reaction and she was determined not to give him one.

Tom continued, "He asked me to come out to his place to have a look around. You know, to see if I could find any clues. And guess what I found?"

"Really, Mr. Carver, I don't have time for guessing games. What did you find?"

From inside his trousers, Tom withdrew something small. "Your knife. Right there in Hoosman's corral. Now how do you suppose it got there?"

"I have no idea." She kept her face void of any emotion. "But thank you for returning it."

"No problem. But be careful with it. I sharpened it for you."

She refused to thank him for his trouble. She entered the school, gripping the pocketknife until her knuckles were white. She tossed it into her desk drawer, propped her elbows on the desk and leaned her head into her palms. Her head pounded. Had Bill decided after his unsuccessful foray at the Carver place to try to steal Hoosman's horse?

Probably, and now his foolish actions had roused suspicions and she was left to deal with that contemptuous blacksmith. Beth massaged tiny circles along the sides of her tight neck.

"Is everything all right, Beth?" Davy asked, standing in front of her desk.

Oh yes. My one brother is a would-be thief, I'm a murderer, and we're trusting a six-year-old with our secrets. Things couldn't be better. "Go back to your seat, Davy. Children, get out your slates."

*

Freddie North remained after dismissal to complete his lines, but the moment the final word was written, he cleared out. "You're going to be sorry," he threatened over his shoulder before leaving.

Beth had no doubt he'd go straight to his indulgent father and give him a woe-be-gone story about his unjust punishment. Sighing, she grabbed her sweater off the back of her chair. "Come on, Davy."

"Where're we going?" he asked, retrieving a marble from under the washstand at the back of the classroom.

"To the bank."

"For money for Bill's horse?"

"That's right. Now, when we get there, I want you to wait outside. I won't be long."

"Would it be all right if I go to Betner's store to look around?"

"I suppose, but don't be a pest. And don't touch anything!"

"I won't."

*

Mr. North's office was a small cubicle partitioned off by a three-foot high wall, and just as Beth had predicted, Freddie was expounding to his father. Turning her back to them, she marched directly to the first wicket.

"Good afternoon, Miss Patterson. How may I help you?" the male clerk asked.

"I'm here to see about getting a loan."

"Oh, then you'll need to talk to Mr. North. Please have a seat. I believe Mr. North is engaged at the moment."

The uncomfortable wooden chair did little to ease Beth's nervousness, nor did watching Freddie gesticulate wildly as he related the incident. Every so often she'd catch a word or two, and Mr. North would frown. She forced her attention elsewhere.

The bank was finished with rich, dark walnut paneling. Above the clock on the back wall hung a portrait of a prominent man bearing a remarkable resemblance to Mr. North, no doubt Mr. North Senior and likely the bank's founder. Beth fortified herself with the realization that if the bank had been in business that many years it was because of sound business management. Surely Freddie's sniveling would not thwart her chances of getting a loan.

Still, when Freddie sauntered past her on his way out, looking smug and satisfied, Beth worried.

After the teller advised him of Beth's presence, Mr. North came forward and opened the gate to his cubicle. "Good afternoon, Miss Patterson. Please, come in."

Reassured by his professional manner, she took the seat he indicated while he circled around the desk to his leather-padded chair. "Now, what can I do for you today?" he asked as he braced his elbows on the desktop and steepled his fingers.

"I'd like a loan to buy Bill a horse."

"A horse." He nodded. "Let's see what we can do."

Beth felt better.

North opened his top drawer and pulled out a form, then picked up his pen and dipped it in his ink well. "All right." He smiled at her, putting her completely at ease. "Let's see what you have for collateral. First item, property. You're living in the old Grant place, aren't you?"

"Yes. We're renting. The school board made all the arrangements."

"Ah, yes. I remember hearing about that. You have no other property?"

"No."

North scratched a zero in the box beside the word *property*.

"How about livestock?"

"Oh, we have a few laying hens."

Mr. North smiled in an overly solicitous manner, as if Beth were a senseless child. "I'm sorry, but we don't accept poultry as collateral. They die too easily. I was thinking more in the line of cattle, or pigs . . . or horses." Then he laughed. "Oh no, of course you don't have any horses or you wouldn't be here for a loan, now would you?"

"No," Beth replied, sinking slightly in her chair.

With a satisfied smirk much like Freddie's, Mr. North filled in another zero on the form. There was no mistaking the enjoyment he derived from humiliating her, but Beth was willing to be humbled if it meant getting the loan.

After scribbling several more zeros, North put down his pen, and scratched his balding, aged-spotted scalp as if pondering the situation. He sighed in exasperation. "As you can see Miss Patterson, you are what we bankers call a high-risk applicant."

"I understand," Beth replied, understanding only too well. "But what about the money Bill and I make? Couldn't we take a loan against that?"

"It is quite obvious that you and your brother's earnings are barely sufficient." He stared at her, as if waiting to see if she'd grovel for the money. Finally he inked his pen nib. "I'll tell you what. Against my better judgment, I'll lend you the money." He scratched a few numbers on a slip of paper and slid it across the desk to Beth. "That should be enough and I think the interest is fair."

Fair! At first she thought he was joking, but the look on his face told her he was dead serious. She fought to keep her anger in check. "Mr. North, this is far higher than the prime lending rate."

"Yes, I realize that. But the bank is sticking its neck out. That should be worth something." North clasped his hands together on his desktop. "That is the term of this loan. Take it or leave it."

Beth rose from her chair, no longer able to contain her mounting frustration and anger. "But that's unfair!"

North also rose from his seat to meet her eye to eye. "Miss Patterson, kindly show restraint," he said, flinging at her the very words she had Freddie write on the blackboard. "Now, if you are unwilling to accept these terms, then please leave my office. I don't have time to waste with you or your brother's petty wants." He dropped into his cushioned chair and tossed Beth's loan application in the wastebasket, indicating that he was quite finished with her.

Tears threatened, but she would not give North the satisfaction of knowing how upset she was. She picked up the paper he had written the figures on, tore it up and dropped the pieces. They floated down to his desk like bleached autumn leaves. "You may have the only bank in Whistle Creek, Mr. North, but there are other towns and other banks . . . with owners who would never permit their personal grievances to get in the way of their business dealings. They are far too professional. Good day!"

The bank was silent, so silent that when Beth accidentally knocked a pen onto the floor, she heard it bounce. Everyone stared at her as if stunned by her outburst. Holding her head high, she exited the bank and strode across the street to Betner's store to find Davy. She marveled that her trembling legs could hold her up since her confrontation with Mr. North had sapped most of her self-confidence.

Inside she saw Tom Carver leaning against the back counter, visiting with Earl and Mary Betner. *Great. Him again.* A few feet away, Davy stood on tiptoe, peering into the glass jars filled with jawbreakers, all-day suckers, saltwater taffy, and licorice pipes.

Beth summoned forth the last of her poise as she approached the counter. "Come on, Davy, it's time to go home." She deliberately stood with her back to Tom. She was shaking and it wouldn't take much to make her melt into a puddle of tears.

"Did you get the money?" Davy asked.

"We'll talk about it when we get home." She kept her voice low, hoping Davy would take the hint and drop the subject.

"But what did the loan man say?"

"Davy! Enough! We'll talk about it later." This time her voice held a stern warning.

"Oh, all right. Can I get a licorice pipe?"

"No."

"They're not real. They're pretend. Those are just tiny red candies on the end to make—"

"Davy! I said no!"

"But why not? I didn't break nothin', did I, Mister Betner?"

Without waiting for a reply, Beth grabbed Davy's hand and dragged him outside.

*

Tom plunged the red-hot iron into the nearby bucket of water and, while waiting for it to cool, looked out the smithy's wide open doors. Sure enough, the younger Patterson boy was sitting on the boardwalk across the street, tossing pebbles absentmindedly into a mud puddle. His narrow shoulders were slumped as if the weight of his plaid shirt was too much for him.

This was the third consecutive afternoon the kid had been there. On a nice autumn day like today he ought to be ripping around, getting into mischief with other boys his age. Tom considered going over to talk to him, then shook his head. *Mind your own business, Carver. The boy is none of your concern.*

He shoved another piece of iron into the forge's red coals. Blacksmithing was hot work and salty sweat ran down past Tom's brows. He went to the water bucket and drank deeply from the dipper, then poured a second dipperful over his head. He flipped his wet hair from his face. Despite his resolve to ignore the boy, Tom dropped the dipper back into the bucket, and strode across the muddy street. He stopped directly before the lad, squatted down, and peeked at the forlorn face hidden under the mop of orange hair.

"Hey," Tom said, "I've seen a happier face on a fishing worm."

Davy shrugged his shoulders.

"Something bothering you?" Tom sat beside him on the boardwalk.

Davy shrugged again.

Tom hadn't spent much time around kids, and since the boy wasn't adding much to the conversation, he wasn't sure what to say next. He grasped at an idea. "Would some candy cheer you up?"

Seeing a flicker of interest in the boy's eyes, Tom stretched a leg out and reached his hand down his front pocket, fishing for a penny. "Here, take this and get yourself a couple of licorice pipes."

"No thanks. My sister won't let me."

"Then get something else."

Davy eyed the coin suspiciously as if he'd never known a stranger to be so generous.

"Go on, take it before I change my mind."

The lad delicately extracted the penny from Tom's palm, politely saying, "Thanks," before racing to the general store.

Tom returned to work, soon forgetting all about the boy. A few minutes later, when he spied Davy standing just inside his shop door, he wished he'd left well enough alone. Last thing he needed was a pesky kid under foot. "Did you get your candy?" he asked at length.

Davy, fascinated by the forge and the glowing coals, stepped closer. "Yessir, jawbreakers. Want one?"

"No, you keep them."

"You're Mister Carver, aren't you?"

"So they tell me."

"I'm Davy."

"I know who you are."

"Whatcha doing?"

"Sharpening this plough share." Tom withdrew the iron strip from the forge, examined the color and thrust it back into the forge again. He cranked the handle on the blower.

"Why are you turning that thing?"

"To get the coals glowing hot." While Tom worked, he explained the process of heating and hammering the metal. He couldn't help being impressed by Davy's myriad of intelligent questions.

"It looks like fun."

Tom had never thought of his job as being fun, but he did find it rewarding. He looked up from his work long enough to smile.

Davy came closer to watch. "I could turn that handle for you if you want. Beth always says I'm a good help—" Davy stopped mid-sentence, apparently having just spotted the dog sleeping behind the forge. "Oh boy! A dog! What's his name?"

"Jack."

"Can I pet him?"

Tom didn't have the heart to refuse. "All right, come around this side, but don't touch the forge. It's hot."

Davy tiptoed around the equipment and bent down to pet the dog.

"He's getting old," Tom explained, "and he doesn't move about much anymore. He spends most of his time sleeping. Old dogs are kind of like old people. They need their naps."

Davy lay down on his side near the dog, and stroked its silky head. Jack woke and licked the boy's hand.

"Did you see that? He likes me! I wish I could have a dog. I never had a pet before."

"Never?" Tom asked casually, remembering quite clearly Beth Patterson's night-time venture into his barn. "Not even a cat?"

"Nope. But once I kept a pet mouse in a jar until Beth made me let it go. She said mice were dirty and I couldn't keep it. Anyhow, I'd rather have me a dog."

"Well, Jack will be your friend so long as you don't play him out."

"I won't," Davy vowed.

Tom expected the boy to be bored in short order, but Davy talked and petted Jack for some time. He was distracted momentarily by the hot metal sizzling and popping in the cold water.

"Wow!" said Davy. "Know what that reminds me of?"

"No, what?" Tom really didn't care but he found himself unable to ignore the boy's questions.

"Once, me and Bill had a fire going outside behind our old place, and Beth told us we had to put it out 'fore we burned the house down. So when she went back inside, we peed on it." Davy giggled behind his cupped hands. "It sizzled just like that . . . only not so loud. Have you ever peed on a fire, Mister Carver?"

At first, Tom wasn't sure he'd heard correctly, but when he decided he had, he fought to maintain a straight face, "Nope, can't say that I have."

"Don't do it. It stinks." He pinched his nose and made a sour expression. "Real bad!" After sharing the wisdom he gained from his experience, he continued petting Jack.

Tom laughed aloud. Darned if he wasn't enjoying the kid!

Davy had been at the smithy for well over half an hour when it struck Tom maybe he should ask, "Does your sister know you're here?"

"Nah, she's too busy with that stupid Freddie to pay any attention to me."

Tom knew all about the conflict between Freddie North and Miss Patterson. Mrs. North had given him an earful about how that young upstart schoolteacher didn't know the first thing about teaching, how she favored the girls and picked on the boys, especially her Freddie. Just to shut the woman up, Tom had promised to talk with Miss Patterson.

"Is your sister keeping him after school again?"

Davy nodded. "More lines."

"How come you don't go visit Bill?"

"Shucks, he don't want me hanging around. Says I'll get him fired."

Tom laid down his sledge and took off his heavy apron. "I tell you what. I've got to go over to the school and talk to your sister about something, so why don't you stay here and keep Jack company. I'll let her know where you are."

Davy jumped to his feet. "Oh boy!"

"But you've got to promise not to touch anything."

"I promise." Davy spat on the dirt floor and, with the toe of his scuffed boot, drew a cross through it.

Smiling, Tom reached for his hat hanging by the door.

Chapter 3

Beth was vigorously erasing the blackboard at the front of the classroom when Tom entered. "Did you forget something?" she asked tersely, not bothering to turn around.

"Nope. Don't think so."

Startled by the deep voice, she spun about. "Oh, I thought you were Freddie North." She set the brush on the blackboard's narrow ledge and wiped her chalky hands on her skirt. "Please, Mr. Carver, come in." As much as she disliked him, she strove for an air of professionalism. "How may I help you?"

Tom removed his hat and came forward, stopping in front of her desk, and for a moment she thought he might have come to apologize for his rude behavior toward her.

"I'm here to see you about Freddie."

"Oh?" An alarm sounded inside her head.

"Mrs. North came to see me today. Seems she thinks you're picking on her son."

Beth bristled. Her heart pounded and her face felt flushed. To calm herself she set about gathering up the books and worksheets on her desk.

"Actually, I'm glad she brought this to my attention. As one of the school trustees, I need to know what's going on in the classroom."

No longer able to contain herself, Beth spoke up in self-defense. "Mr. Carver." She succeeded in making his name sound like a vile expletive. "What is *going on* in this classroom is learning. I believe that is why the school board hired me. Freddie North is a troublemaker and if you're here to tell me I should ignore his disruptive behavior, then you're wasting your time." She slammed the books down to emphasize her position.

It would have been so much more dramatic if a loose sheet of paper hadn't floated off her desk to land at Tom's feet. He picked it up, a half smile playing on his lips and definitely on her nerves.

"If you would let me finish." He placed the paper squarely on top of the books. "I don't expect you to let him off the hook. Rather, I would like to discuss your disciplinary actions."

"I assure you, there is nothing excessive or unduly cruel with insisting a student write lines."

"I didn't come here to criticize, Miss Patterson, just to offer some advice. Maybe you should consider giving Freddie the strap. That straightens most kids out."

Beth was certain Mr. Carver had had more than his fair share of strappings, and she wondered if corporal punishment had done him any good. But the thought of administering the strap caused her to blanch. Her voice became quiet when she spoke. "I prefer not to use the strap. In fact, I threw the old one away." She straightened as if her spine were a yardstick. "I am quite positive Freddie has had enough of writing lines and this will be the end of it."

"Well, let's hope so. I hate to think that the other students are suffering because of one troublemaker."

Her green eyes flashed. "Rest assured, Mr. Carver, none of my students are suffering in any way, but if they were, then by all means I would administer the strap."

"Good," Tom said, "then you won't mind me bringing by a new one." He set his hat back on his head. "By the way, Davy is at my shop. I told him I'd clear it with you."

"That boy! He supposed to be playing outside, not traipsing around town by himself."

"Now don't get all riled up. He just dropped in for a visit. Seemed a little lonely, what with you spending so much time with Freddie. You know, a little guy like that can't be ignored for long or he's going to get into trouble."

Beth had just about all she could take from this man. She came around to the front of her desk and faced off with him as best she could since he was a good foot taller than her. "Really, Mr. Carver, I was not aware you knew so much about children."

Tom shrugged. "It's just plain common sense. Don't need to be an expert to figure that out. He's kind of a cute little tyke, quite infatuated with my old dog." Then eyeing her intently, he added, "Instead of trying to find your cat, maybe you should consider getting him a dog."

Beth forced a smile. "Thank you. I'll keep that in mind." When Tom closed the door, she threw a piece of chalk at it. *Arrogant jackass!*

*

Beth found the strap on her desk the next morning and though she was dead set against any sort of physical punishment, before the day was out she was forced to use it. Apparently writing lines was no deterrent for Freddie. All day long he moved from one infuriating prank to another, most of the time victimizing the girls. To make matters worse, the other, normally well-behaved boys had begun to emulate Freddie's behavior. Before things got any further out of hand, Beth needed to take control, so when Freddie dipped Inga's beautiful blond pigtails in ink, she took immediate action.

"Class is dismissed early today."

The children immediately cheered and books slammed shut.

"But not you, Freddie. You are to stay behind."

Freddie groaned. "What, more lines?"

"No," Beth replied, displaying a calm demeanor, one she wished she possessed. She pulled open the center drawer of her desk, reached far to the back and retrieved the strap. She placed it with purposeful precision along the front edge of her desk.

The strap might as well have been a corpse stretched across her desk. Students filed quietly past as if paying their last respects. At the cloakroom door, they gave Freddie a final glance, somehow sensing that from this moment on he would never be the same.

Beth could hear the scuffle outside the school windows as students vied for the best viewing position. *Why did it have to come to this?* She was certain Freddie didn't want to be on the receiving end of the strap any more than she wanted to be on the giving end. Regardless, the inevitable had arrived.

"Come forward, Freddie," she demanded, suddenly very angry to be forced to do something so against her grain. "Hold out your hand."

*

Freddie left the school holding back tears. Beth slowly and weakly made her way around to her chair and dropped into it. Through her own tears, she stared at the flat brown strap still in her hand. It sickened her to think she was no better than her abusive aunt and uncle. In a blind rage, she yanked open her desk drawer, grabbed a pair of scissors and began hacking savagely at the strap. The scissors twisted and hurt her hands, but they did little harm to the vile piece of rubber. Finally, she flung them both and they skidded across the wooden floor, stopping against a desk.

She dropped her head onto her folded arms and began to cry. Soon she was weeping great heaving sobs that squeezed her chest and wrung the breath from her. Why did she ever think she could teach?

Outside, when the students saw Freddie's red hands shaking and tears rolling down his face there was a new reverence for the teacher, albeit one earned by fear rather than respect. They followed on Freddie's heels, barraging him with questions about the strapping.

Davy made a bee-line to the smithy after leaving the rest of his classmates.

Tom glanced up from his work. "School out early today?"

"Guess what? Beth gave Freddie the strap!"

Tom raised his eyebrows. Somehow he never thought she'd

have the gumption to use it. "You look pleased."

"Yup," Davy answered honestly. Tom smiled.

"So, how's your sister doing?"

"I don't know. If she's in that bad of a mood, I'm not going near her."

Tom nodded. Freddie must have pushed the young teacher far beyond her limit for her to have administered the strap. Because he suggested the punishment, he felt obliged to see if she needed any bolstering. "I think you'd better head home. I'll check on your sister. She might be upset."

When he arrived at the school he decided that "distraught" would have been a better word. A big lump of compassion stuck in his throat. If he had known she was going to take it this badly, he never would have suggested the strap. Hell, as a school trustee, he probably could have booted Freddie out of the classroom or strapped him himself for that matter. He wished now he had.

He placed his hand on her shoulder and she lifted her head at the gentle pressure.

Beth turned in her chair, presenting her back to him. "If you came to gloat, just go away and leave me alone."

"Davy told me what happened and I just came to see if you are okay." Tom stepped around in front of her and squatted on his haunches. "Don't beat yourself up over this. Freddie got what he deserved."

"Why did you have to bring that stupid strap over anyhow? I was doing just fine without it." It was obvious to both of them she wasn't. "Freddie just kept pushing and pushing—" She covered her face with her hands and resumed sobbing.

In all the time Tom had been courting Abigail Craig, he'd never seen her cry like that. A tear maybe, but nothing near as heart wrenching as Beth's anguish. "Now, now," he said awkwardly, "no more crying. You did what you had to do."

She nodded and managed to get her sobbing under control. She looked at him, her eyes red. When a single tear rolled down her cheek and sat at the edge of her pretty little mouth, Tom wondered if she would lick it. Shocked by his untimely and inappropriate thought, he stood and took a step back. "You know, if you're going to be a teacher, you better toughen up." His words came out more harshly than he'd intended.

But at least they got a rise out of her. "What do you mean, if?" She stood nose to chest and glared up at him. "I *am* a teacher, a good teacher!" She fished a hankie from her pocket and blew her nose loudly. "You have no right to criticize. And one spoiled brat isn't going to stop me, thank you very much!" Slamming her books closed, she gathered an armful and headed out the school, her head held high and skirts swaying confidently.

That a girl! Tom nodded his head. He closed up the school behind him.

*

At six o'clock, Tom locked up the smithy for the day and headed to Abigail's. Ahead Tom saw Miranda Parsons coming his direction, her mother following closely. Tom cursed silently. He could come up with a number of unflattering descriptions for Miranda, but the kindest—though not the most accurate or colorful—was "hussy." Rumor had it that she kept a list of all the men she had bedded and the list was growing faster than fleas multiplying on a mutt. It was beyond him why any man would be the slightest bit interested in her. Catching her affection was no more challenging than stirring up an anthill and seeing if any ants climbed the stick.

Acting nonchalant, Tom strolled toward mother and daughter, intent upon walking straight past them with only a nod of his head. Not surprisingly, Miranda grabbed his shirtsleeve.

"Oh hello, Tom," she gushed. "What a surprise."

Tom politely tipped his hat. "Mrs. Parsons, Miss Miranda."

"Momma and I thought we'd go for a walk down by the creek. It's such a lovely day. Would you care to join us?"

Mrs. Parsons scowled at her daughter.

"Sorry," Tom said, "I have other commitments."

Miranda pursed her lips into a practiced pout. "What a shame. Maybe some other time then?"

Tom made no reply. He tipped his hat again, then stepped aside to allow them to pass.

As they continued on, Tom could hear Mrs. Parson scolding her daughter. He figured the dear woman might as well save her breath. Miranda was too far gone for any morality lecture.

Across the street, Earl Betner swept the wooden step in front of his store as was his habit every morning and night. He paused long enough to call to Tom, "You're still coming for supper Sunday night?"

"I'll be there."

"Come hungry. You know how Mary loves to cook."

That he did.

When influenza orphaned Tom at age twelve, Mary and Earl took him in as though he was one of their own. They loved him, fed him, and disciplined him right along with their other five boys. With seven males in the house to feed, Mary had needed to be an excellent cook.

"My stomach's growling already." Tom waved at Earl.

*

Abigail Craig's place was a tiny, white, single-story, clapboard house. Colorful pansies bordered the walkway that led up to the front door. A wooden sign—Abigail Craig, Seamstress—hung by two short chains from the awning above the door, and it creaked as it swung in the wind.

Tom stepped up to the door, pressed his hands and face against the screen and peered into the kitchen. Abigail was standing at the wood stove with her back to him, and from the swaying movement of her body, Tom knew she was stirring something, something that smelled mighty good.

Silently, he opened the screen door, careful it didn't slam shut behind him, then tiptoed up behind Abby and tapped her on the shoulder. She gasped and spun about, nearly smacking him with the large wooden spoon in her hand. The contents of the spoon continued its forward motion and splattered across Tom's cheek.

"Tom Carver! You took ten years off my life!"

"Meaning now you're only twenty-five. You should be thanking me." With his wide, flat thumb, he scraped some food off his face and tasted it. "Hmm. That tastes like more." He grabbed the towel that hung beside the wash basin and wiped his face clean before peering into the pot. "What are you cooking?"

"Just never you mind. Here." She handed him a jar of beet pickles to open.

Tom unscrewed the sealer ring, then popped off the lid using the blunt edge of a knife. Before setting the jar on the table, he slid a pickled beet slice into his mouth, then sucked the red juice from his fingertips.

"Could you wait at least until everything is on the table!"

Uh, oh. Abby only snapped when something was bothering her and he knew from experience that it would be foolhardy to ask her what was wrong. Besides, he had a hunch as to why her back was up. There had been a tea in town. No doubt some old biddy had snubbed Abby because of her relationship with him. Why couldn't women mind their own business?

Abigail sawed into a fresh loaf of bread. "I got a letter from Auntie Bets today. She wants me to go back East. Help with her millinery business."

"For how long?"

"Permanently."

Not in the least expecting that, Tom was taken aback. "What

did you tell her?"

"Nothing. I haven't decided yet."

And he knew exactly why. She was wondering if he ever going to propose and give her a reason to remain in Whistle Creek. They'd been seeing each other for well over a year, enjoying all of the privileges that a marriage would bring. But their so-called *union* was very different from that of married couples. They were together only on Fridays nights. They began dating on a Friday night and because neither of them had other commitments on that night they continued meeting every Friday night. Somehow before they knew it, they had evolved into this one-night-a-week pretend marriage. And though Abigail often asked him to stay the night, Tom never did. He could tell himself it was only to quell the gossip for Abby's sake, but regrettably, Tom had another reason to turn down Abigail's invitations, one far less altruistic. He knew that staying one night would eventually lead to staying for another, and then another, and in no time at all they'd be kneeling before an altar. That was a commitment he didn't want to make. Not yet.

Still, the time had come for him to make a decision, but because he didn't know what to say, he changed the subject. "Did you hear that one of Carlson's granaries burned to the ground?"

*

Beth decided the only good thing about that day was that it was Friday, which gave her a reprieve from planning the next day's lesson. Drained from the day's ordeal, she retired to bed early. She dropped immediately off to sleep and likely would have slept through the night if not for the loud voices in the kitchen.

For a few seconds she was disoriented, but then she realized that Bill was arguing with someone and it wasn't Davy. Quietly she rose and donned her robe, pulled the sash tightly around her waist, and went to the door to listen. She groaned when she recognized the blacksmith's deep voice. She had no choice but to open her bedroom door and face her nemesis.

"Good, you're awake," Tom said, coming to his feet when he saw her.

"How could I not be awake with all the racket? Is there a problem?" The wall clock said two-thirty in the morning.

Tom sat again at the table opposite Bill. "If you call stealing horses a problem, I guess there is."

Beth tried to act calm despite her heart beating so wildly she thought it might explode. "I assume you think Bill is involved?"

"He's involved, all right! I caught him red-handed, coming out of my barn with one of my horses. He sure as blazes wasn't looking for stray cats!" Tom's voice rose with every word, as did he, and when he finished, he was standing with both hands gripping the pine table's edge.

Bill slapped his hands flat on the table. "I already tried to explain."

"Be quiet, Bill, let me handle this," she said firmly. "Please, Mr. Carver, sit down so we can discuss the matter calmly. And please keep your voice lowered. There is no need to wake Davy."

Repressing his anger with a growl, Tom sat again.

"Now what do you propose to do?" Beth asked him forthright.

"Well, the way I see it, I have two choices. One, I contact the authorities and let them decide the punishment." Beth felt her knees go weak and she sank into the nearest chair. The law would surely uncover more than Bill's attempt at stealing a horse. If both she and Bill were sent to prison, what would happen to Davy? Her hands began to shake so she hid them in the folds of her robe.

Tom continued. "They might go easy seeing as he's young. Then again, they might not. Just last month, over in Clapton County, they hung a fellow for the very same thing."

Beth felt ill. She glanced at Bill. He looked like a wild animal ready to tear the blacksmith to shreds. "And the other alternative?" Beth asked, her voice squeaking.

Tom eased forward and clasped his hands on the tabletop. He stared at Bill. "I take him out back and give him some belt-driven logic. I prefer this option myself, but maybe Bill has something to say about it. Which should it be?"

"Surely, Mr. Carver—" Beth started.

"Let the boy speak for himself," Tom commanded. "Well, Bill, which will it be?"

"I already told you. I was walking by your barn and I thought I smelled smoke. I was trying to save your horses."

"How commendable!" Tom replied. "Do you know what I think? I think it's just too much of a coincidence I catch a Patterson in my barn two Friday nights in a row. I think maybe the two of you have yourselves a tidy little business."

"No!" Beth said, and then added with a false laugh, "why, that's ridiculous."

"Really? I have a hunch that if I hadn't caught you in my barn," he said, pointing at Beth, "I'd probably be short one horse. And surprise, surprise, Hoosman lost a horse that very same night." He pointed at Bill. "I think you stole it."

Bill jumped to his feet, and leaned across the table at Tom. "You ain't got any proof."

"I found your pocketknife there."

"That was my knife," Beth interjected. "It has the initials B.P. carved into the handle for Beth Patterson."

"Or Bill Patterson," Tom said.

"But it isn't Bill's. It's mine."

Tom studied Beth and then her brother. "Sit down, Bill. You make me edgy standing over me." To Beth he said, "Bring me the knife, would you?"

"Whatever for?"

"I just want to see it for a minute."

That cockroach. He was calling her bluff, counting on Bill having the knife in his trousers. And it probably was. She glanced at her brother, then excused herself from the table and disappeared into her bedroom. Fuming, she opened and slammed drawers as if searching. A moment later, she returned to the table. "I'm afraid I've misplaced it."

"That's handy." Tom leaned back in his chair, all the while drumming his fingers on the tabletop as he stared at Bill. Finally the finger drumming stopped and he asked, "How old are you, Bill?"

"What difference does that make?"

"I asked you a simple question. The least you can do is answer it."

Bill crossed him arms over his chest. "Don't see as if that's any of your business."

"He's sixteen." Beth provided the information.

Tom nodded. "So, he's a boy really."

"The hell I am!" Bill would have said a mouthful more had Beth not kicked him under the table. Bill clamped his mouth shut, grimacing in pain.

Tom stroked his stubbled chin while his eyes shifted from Bill to Beth and then to Bill again. He seemed to be contemplating what to do with Bill. "I'm trying to remember what sort of trouble I got into when I was sixteen. I guess I did some pretty dumb things in my youth, though I never tried pulling the stunt you did."

Bill opened his mouth to protest, took one look at Tom and wisely clamped his lips together.

"I didn't have much more luck than you, Bill. I always got caught and had to deal with the consequences, and some of them weren't too pleasant. But there was this one time, and I can't exactly remember the circumstances, but I caught hell for something I didn't do. And to this day it sticks in my craw."

"So you believe me?"

"I never said that. I think you're guilty as sin. But I don't have definite proof."

"Then this discussion is over." Beth stood, indicating it was time Tom left.

Tom stopped at the door. "You got off lucky this time, Bill. But a word of warning. I'm going to keep an eye on you, and if I see you riding some horse down the street, you'd better have a bill of sale."

When Tom shut the door, Bill slammed his fists on the table. "I hate that bastard!"

Chapter 4

Beth stayed late every afternoon, grading papers and preparing lessons. When they moved to Whistle Creek, she thought teaching would be an easy charade, never once imagining it would be so demanding to keep ahead of eight grades. At least Freddie no longer posed a problem. His father had pulled him from school, saying he needed him at the bank.

At five-thirty, a stack of papers still loomed before Beth. She sorted through what she would do at home and set the rest aside. She rose from her hard wooden chair and stretched her tired back.

"I'm finished for the day, Davy. Let's go home. I need to get supper started." When he didn't respond, she went outside to see if he was in the schoolyard playing. He wasn't.

That rascal. He was likely at the smithy again, despite her stern orders not to spend so much time there. She feared Tom Carver would press her brother about their past, and though Davy knew the gravity of their secret, he still might accidentally let some critical information slip.

She hurried to the smithy. Davy sat on a wooden workbench, playing with metal filings and a magnet. She glanced about the shop. Good, the blacksmith must be out back. She slipped in and tapped Davy's shoulder.

"Come. It's time to go."

"I can't."

"What do you mean, you can't?"

"Mister Carver asked me to look after the shop for him."

"He left you here alone?" she asked, irritation etching her voice.

"I'm not alone. Jack's here." Davy hopped down from the bench and grabbed Beth's hand, leading her around the forge to where the dog lay. "Shhh. He's sleeping. He sleeps a lot on account of him being so old. But when he's awake, we play fetch."

Beth couldn't imagine such an old mutt being able to get up, let alone retrieve a ball. Her doubt must have registered upon her face for Davy was quick to explain, "I roll the ball across the floor and when Jack wags his tail, I fetch it for him. I could wake him up and show you."

Despite her annoyance, she smiled. "No, let him sleep. Old dogs are like old people. They need to rest."

"Hey! That's 'zactly what Mister Carver said. If he was here, you two could pinkie-wish."

Her wish would be for Davy's friend to drop off the face of the earth, not that she would ever be that fortunate. "Where did Mr. Carver go?"

Davy shrugged, returned to the workbench and began playing with the magnet again. "He'll be back soon. Hey, I know," he said, his face lighting, "while we wait, I can show you around the place." He immediately skipped to the forge, grabbed the crank and gave it a couple of quick turns.

Beth hurried over. "Davy! You shouldn't be touching things in here! It's dangerous."

"Ah, Beth, don't get your shirt in a knot."

She didn't have to ask who taught him that clever saying.

"Every time I turn this crank, oxygen— oh that's Mister Carver's Tom's fancy name for air—anyhow, when I turn the crank, oxygen goes into the coals and then they burn better. It's my job to keep the coals hot."

"Your job? He has you doing jobs while you're here?"

"Uh huh. Mister Carver says idle hands are the devil's workshop." Davy then led her to the center of the dimly lit building. The dirt floor absorbed much of the light that fell through the open door and she wondered how anyone could work in such dark place without tripping over stuff. But as her eyes adjusted to the dimness she realized the smithy was quite tidy.

"This here is an anvil," Davy explained, pointing to the large oddly shaped piece of steel standing on the ground. "Mister Carver pounds iron things on it and it makes a ringing sound, almost like a church bell." Davy picked up the sledgehammer from the workbench. Surprised by the tool's weight, he dropped it, narrowly missing his foot. He glanced up at Beth, as if hoping she hadn't seen.

But she had. "Now do you see what I mean?"

"It's just a hammer, Beth."

"A very heavy hammer and if it had landed on your toe, it would have flattened it."

Not the least bit troubled by Beth's admonition, he pulled her over to the east wall. "You see the horseshoes all along the wall?" Arranged on several wooden pegs were likely two dozen horseshoes of slightly different sizes and shapes. "Mister Carver wants me to make certain they stay straight."

"Oh really," Beth huffed, "how often does *that* need doing?"

"Every day, Miss Patterson." Tom answered, entering the smithy. "Got to keep the place neat."

Beth aligned her back and announced emphatically, "I do not appreciate Davy being left here alone. While you were gone, he almost injured himself."

Tom frowned and glanced at Davy. "What happened?"

"I dropped your hammer."

"It very nearly decapitated his toe."

"Decapitated his toe?" Tom repeated with laugh.

"You know very well what I mean. He could have been badly injured. No six-year-old should be left unsupervised in such a place. This place is too dangerous." Her heart was beating hard and fast. After all his lectures about how to raise her brothers, that insufferable man deserved to get an earful!

Tom glanced at Davy who stood staring at the floor, hands stuffed deep in his pockets. Tom nodded thoughtfully. "Yeah, you're probably right. I'm sorry."

"You should be. And that's not all! You . . . " She stopped midsentence. *He was agreeing with her? How dare he give in so easily!* Beth felt cheated. For once her wrath was completely justified and he backed down before she could really light into him. She felt like a pot of boiling water pulled from the hot stove. All the steam she had built up diminished.

"You were going to say?" Tom urged.

"I . . . I was going to say . . . " What *was* she going to say? He had her so flummoxed she couldn't remember. "It . . . it's time for Davy to get home."

"Ah, Beth," Davy whined.

"Now!" She stomped her foot.

Tom patted the boy's shoulder. "Do what your sister says." To Beth, he gave a nod. "Good afternoon, Miss Patterson." Then he began putting away his tools.

*

"What's the matter with you?" Bill demanded when Davy scratched his head for the third time during breakfast a few days later. "You get fleas from Carver's stupid dog?"

"Jack's not stupid. He's smart!"

"Smart as a two-headed nail."

In a rare show of defiance, Davy jumped from his chair, and began punching and kicking Bill with all the fury his scrawny body could muster.

Bill laughed, easily warding off Davy's feeble blows. "Get away from me, fleabag! I don't want your pets."

"Don't call me a fleabag!"

"Stop it," Beth shouted, but not before Davy gave one last mighty kick at Bill and connected with the sturdy table leg instead. Immediately, he dropped to the floor and wailed pitifully.

"Serves you right, crybaby," Bill taunted. "It's probably broke and Doc will have to cut it off."

"Bill!" Beth had had enough. "Leave him alone! If you're finished with breakfast, go to work."

Bill belched rudely, then pushed back from the table.

"And by the way," Beth said, "plan on being home tonight."

"Why?"

"Because it's Friday, and you seem to have a habit of finding trouble Friday nights." She felt a small amount of triumph when Bill slammed the door on his way out.

Beth turned her attention to Davy. "Let's see your toe."

Davy pulled his foot in closer to his body. "No. I don't want it cut off."

"You know Bill was teasing. Besides, how will you be able to count to ten if you're missing a toe? Come on. Let's see."

Sniffling, Davy presented his foot for inspection, and scratched his head again.

"Nothing serious. You just chipped your nail." Beth went for the nail scissors, and when she returned, Davy was working at a persistent itch behind his left ear. She pulled a chair close to the window where the lighting was best. "Sit here. Give me your foot."

When she was finished tending his toe, she set the scissors down and carefully parted his thatchy hair with her fingertips. Sadly, she immediately found the cause of his itchiness.

"Well, Davy, you don't have fleas. You have head lice."

His face twisted in horror. "Is a licebag worse than a fleabag?" he asked.

Beth laughed, even though head lice was no laughing matter. "There are no such things as licebags or fleabags. Those are just hurtful words. You probably got head lice from another infected student at school."

"What's going to happen to me?" Davy asked woebegone, apparently forgetting completely about his sore toe, now that he was faced with a matter far more serious.

"Nothing. Tonight, we'll wash your hair and treat your scalp with coal-oil." She knew she'd also have to boil all the bedding and disinfect the house and school. She'd been thinking about starting the fall cleaning soon. Now she was forced to do it earlier and far more thoroughly.

"Will the coal-oil hurt?"

"Not one bit. But first thing this morning at school, I'll need to do a careful head check to see who else has lice. They'll need to be treated too." Without proper and quick treatment, the entire class, including herself, could be scratching in no time. Just the thought made her scalp tingle.

*

In the smithy, Tom also scratched his head, not because of head lice, but because he was downright perplexed. Where did he leave his ball peen hammer? He had it just a minute ago.

He was down on his hands and knees, having a gander underneath the workbench when he heard a man say, "What's a person to do to get some service around here?"

Startled, Tom lifted up suddenly and cracked his head on the underside of the bench. He cussed silently. "Be right there," he said, rubbing the back of his head, certain he'd dented his skull. "What can I do for you?"

"I need you to fix the rim on one of my wheels," a man said, pulling out his watch.

Tom carefully surveyed the damaged rim on the buggy.

"Can you fix it or not? I'm already running late."

"I think so. Might take a while though."

"Then get on with it. I've two more schools to inspect before nightfall."

Tom didn't put much stock in a fellow who dressed like a dandy and thought himself superior. This guy wore a double-vested gray suit and derby hat, and looked more like a groom than a school inspector. And those patent leather shoes! Tom hoped he'd step into a fresh horse pucky. The image brought a smile to his face. He extended his hand. "So you're the new school inspector. I'm Tom Carver."

"Martin Glower," the man replied, shaking Tom's hand.

Glower's pudgy fingers reminded Tom of soft cow teats. *He probably hasn't done a lick of hard work in his life.*

While Glower paced back and forth impatiently, Tom began to unharness the horse from the buggy. "Been to see Miss Patterson yet?"

"Is that the new teacher's name? She isn't listed in my ledger."

"No?" Tom ducked under the horse's neck and loosened the other harness strap. "Probably because she didn't start until midway through September. She came with high recommendations."

"Really. Well, I'll be the judge of that." He adjusted his hat with an air of importance. "Which way is the school from here?"

Tom pointed. "You'll see it when you get to the bank corner. But it's almost noon hour. Won't be much to judge when the teacher isn't teaching. Why not eat lunch at Yen's across the street first."

Glower checked his watch again. "How long you say this is going to take to fix?"

"Don't know for sure until I get it off. But I could come over to the school when I'm finished."

"Fine. Do that!"

Tom waited until the inspector entered the Chinaman's cafe, then ducked through the smithy, out the back door and jogged to the school. He only had a minute to warn Beth before Glower would wonder why he hadn't started work on the rim.

He took the steps to the schoolhouse in one leap, barged straight through the cloakroom into the classroom.

Beth nearly used one of Bill's swear words. Regaining her composure, she discretely slipped the fine-toothed comb she'd been using into her pocket. No way on God's green earth would she let him know about the school's outbreak of lice.

"Mr. Carver," she said rather huskily, "it is customary for one to knock before entering."

"I need to speak with you in private." He nodded his head toward the cloakroom.

The words "in private" flagged her attention. *What was Bill up to this time?* Inside the cloakroom with the door closed, she took a defensive stance. "Unless the school is on fire, I can't imagine what would warrant such a rude interruption! Just because you're on the school board doesn't mean you can waltz in anytime you please. It would be far better if you came after school hours."

"But—"

She held up her hand. "I'm certain whatever it is, it can wait until after school. I don't get paid to visit you know."

Tom considered her for a moment. "You're right, this really isn't as important as I thought it might be. I'm sorry to have bothered you."

Finally the victor, Beth nodded smugly.

*

It always took a good five minutes to settle the children after dinner, but eventually the youngsters in Grades One and Two were coloring. Grades Three, Four, and Five worked on their penmanship, while the oldest grades diligently attacked their arithmetic. The lice check was finished and so far it wasn't too serious. She would send home notes with those requiring treatment.

Beth helped Jonah Pickard at the blackboard with a long division problem, and just as he began to grasp the concept, there was a knock at the door.

If it's that blacksmith . . . She never finished her silent threat for when she opened the door, there stood a formidable looking stranger. His hat sat perfectly straight on his head as if God had placed it there Himself.

"Good afternoon, Miss Patterson. I'm Inspector Glower. May I come in?"

No! her mind screamed while her lips said, "Of course, welcome." She turned to her class and wondered if they could read the look of panic on her face. She hadn't even thought to prepare her students for a surprise visit by the inspector. She could only pray the previous teacher had coached them how to behave. "Children, this is Mr. Glower. How do we welcome our guest?" She had hoped for a chorus of "Good afternoons," but instead got an informal jumble of shy "hi's" and bold "howdy's."

Glower sat at the back of the room in the large desk Freddie North had once occupied. "I'm just here to observe. Carry on with your work."

Beth felt the school walls close in around her like bars of a jail cell. How long would it take for him to realize she was a fake? On legs that felt wooden, she returned to the blackboard, printing up several more division problems for Jonah to do before she moved on to help another student.

Bless their souls! Her students bent to work with earnest. She could see they were desperately trying not to scratch their heads. But the more they resisted, the more they fidgeted in their seats.

A sharp cracking sound spun Beth around. Somehow without her noticing, Glower had moved from his desk to the blackboard, rapping it smartly with the pointer stick. "Come on boy, think! How many times does seven go into fifty-nine?" With each crack, poor Jonah cringed.

"Use your times table," Glower commanded.

By then the entire class had abandoned their own studies and were staring at Jonah, who was so rattled he could barely speak.

Eight, Beth's mind urged. *Eight. You know that one.*

"Nine?" the boy answered doubtfully.

The pointer cracked against the board. "Wrong! Eight!" Glower grabbed the chalk from Jonah's hand and scribbled the numbers on the board. Then he slashed a line underneath and subtracted fifty-six from fifty-nine. "The answer is eight with a remainder of three. This is elementary arithmetic. You should know this."

He does, Beth steamed, *but not when someone is standing over him with a stick!*

Glower moved down the aisle toward Davy. "Have you nothing to do but scratch and squirm?"

"No, sir," Davy replied timidly.

"Then get back to work!"

"Yes, sir." He picked up his reader, and even from a distance Beth could see his little hands shake.

Glower marched up and down the aisles like a dictator, slapping the pointer stick against his palm. When he stopped at Penelope Pickard's desk and leaned over her shoulder to inspect her work, Beth knew immediately what would happen. And there wasn't a thing she could do to stop it.

Glower raised his head and listened, then suddenly looked down at his feet. "What on earth!" he uttered, aghast. He was standing in a growing puddle of urine. Penelope, embarrassed and frightened, began to cry.

The boys guffawed. The girls giggled. The inspector growled, "Miss Patterson, have you no control over your class?" He slapped the stick so sharply against Penelope's desktop, the tip broke off, shot across the room like a bullet, and imbedded itself into the wall. The girl ran out the door.

"You," he said, pointing at Norman with the broken stick, "mop up this mess immediately and don't ever laugh at me again or you will face expulsion!"

Beth wanted to take that damnable stick and crack it over the man's head. Who did he think he was? This was her classroom and within five minutes, he had terrified her students. None dared to scratch their heads, but sat on their hands in fear the stick might be used on their knuckles next. She wanted to demand that the inspector leave, but such insubordination would mean her immediate dismissal, so instead she said nothing and allowed the intolerable man to bully his way around her classroom.

"You, how do you spell chrysanthemum?" he demanded. "... Wrong. You, how do you find the area of a cone? Wrong."

Beth went to her desk and began flipping through her manual. Why, that old cur was asking questions that weren't even in the curriculum! Enough was enough!

"Mr. Glower!" she started in, but a knock interrupted her rebuttal.

"Who is it?" she yelled, not bothering to even to open the door, which would have been the proper thing to do. But at that moment, she didn't care.

And she quite honestly didn't know what to feel when Tom poked his head into the classroom.

Before she had a chance to utter one word, Tom said, "Sorry to interrupt, Miss Patterson, but I told Mr. Glower when his buggy was fixed, I'd come and let him know."

"It's repaired already?" Glower asked in amazement.

"I put a rush on it, seeing you said you were in a hurry."

Glower nodded. "Yes. And there's certainly no reason for me to remain here. I've seen more than enough to make my report."

Beth's shoulders slumped.

Tom led the inspector outside, explaining all he had done to make the buggy serviceable.

Beth followed them, but on her way through the cloakroom, she saw the inspector's derby hat. She grabbed it, wishing she could stomp it flat as a cow pie. Then she thought of something even better. She took perverse pleasure in swiping the hat's inside rim with the collar of every lice-infested coat.

When she handed it to him, Mr. Glower placed the hat securely on his head and straightened it precisely. As he climbed into his buggy, he said, "I'm afraid, Miss Patterson, I'm leaving with a rather poor impression of you and your students."

That's not all you're leaving with, she thought with satisfaction as Glower snapped the reins and drove away.

"How did it go?" Tom asked, watching the buggy diminish in the distance.

"Miserably."

"Figures. When he told me he was the school inspector, I knew he'd be a son of a bi—I mean—he'd be difficult to deal with. Don't worry. He may act like he's important, but the school trustees have the final say in what happens in our school."

It surprised her to realize he was trying to make her feel better about the fiasco. And it finally dawned on her why the blacksmith had barged into her classroom just before lunch. If she hadn't been so set on putting him in his place, she would have had prior warning and time to prepare the students.

Beth turned to him, humbled in the face of his kindness. "Mr. Carver, I owe you an apology."

Tom folded and stuffed the inspector's payment into his shirt pocket. "What for?" He crossed his arms and waited.

She could see he wasn't going to make this easy. "For coming to warn me earlier."

"Warn you?"

"You know, about the inspector."

Tom chuckled. "Do you really think I would come all the way over here just to warn you about him? Miss Patterson, you'd best get back to teaching. Like you said, you don't get paid to visit." He walked away, leaving Beth standing by herself.

Deny it all he wanted. She knew the truth. At least she thought she did.

Chapter 5

A few days before the box social, Abigail Craig carried a plateful of goodies covered with a clean tea towel to the smithy. Tom was at the drill press with his back to her. The donkey engine powering the overhead crankshaft, which in turn powered the drill, generated a deafening noise. Attempting to call him would be futile, so she sat on a stool in the back corner and waited.

Tom held up a two-foot length of iron and checked the hole he'd just drilled. Satisfied, he reached over and closed the regulator on the engine. Even after the racket ceased, his eardrums still vibrated. He turned and saw Abigail smiling at him. "Oh, hi. I didn't hear you come in."

"That's not surprising. I brought you some chocolate squares, if you've time to stop." She lifted a corner of the tea towel.

Tom didn't need to see the squares to know he wanted one. "I'll make time." He threw off his leather apron, gave his hands a quick rinse in a tub of water and then dragged over another stool. He leaned in for a better whiff. "Hmm, they smell good!" He popped a whole one in his mouth, chewed for a minute and then said, working his words around his mouthful, "Taste good too." He reached for second one.

Abigail beamed. "I added peppermint oil."

"That's what I thought. Thanks." He bent forward and gave her a peck on the cheek. There was no doubt she spoiled him. Whether he deserved it or not was debatable. Ever since the night that she'd introduced the idea of leaving—was that already more than a month ago?—Tom had been wrestling with his heart and conscience. His conscience said "marry her," but his heart wouldn't let him. And that troubled Tom tremendously. Abigail was a comely woman with a pleasant demeanor. She was an excellent cook, and a satisfying lover—everything a man could want. But after searching his heart, he knew he didn't love her enough to want to spend the rest of his life with her.

But how could he end the relationship without breaking her heart?

Their Friday evenings together were different now. He continued having suppers with her—what single man wouldn't want a sumptuous supper once a week—but he deliberately found excuses to avoid intimacy with her. He said he was too tired after swinging a sledge all day, or he was sore from shoeing horses. These things had never stopped him before, so he made light of it saying he must be getting old, to which Abigail reminded him jokingly that thirty-five was hardly old. But there were occasions when he saw puzzlement or hurt in her eyes and he wondered if it wouldn't be better, kinder, to end the relationship quickly and get the pain over with.

"You're frowning, Tom. Is something the matter?"

He quickly shook his head and smiled. "I banged my leg earlier and it still throbs once in a while," he lied.

"Would another square take your mind off it?"

"That it might." He reached for one but Abby yanked the plate away.

"That's too bad. The only way you can have another one is if you buy my lunch at the box social."

"Oh, I see. That's what this visit is all about." Each fall, the ladies of Whistle Creek organized a box social with the proceeds used to buy candy and small gifts to be given out at the Christmas concert. "When is it?" he asked.

"This Saturday."

"Gee, I'm busy that day."

"Fibber," she admonished. "You haven't missed a box social yet. You like food too much."

"Especially yours."

"If you want, I could tell you how my lunch will be wrapped."

"Abigail!" He pretended to be shocked. "That would be cheating. You wouldn't want me to compromise your principles, would you?"

Her eyes shadowed slightly. "I think it's a little too late to be worried about that."

Damn. Guilt stabbed Tom's gut. She was right. He'd been so unfair to her, their liaison subjecting her to gossip. He needed to stop seeing her. But he couldn't do it now. With most of the community attending the box social, breaking up just before the event would only give the gossipmongers more to talk about and Abigail had suffered enough from their sharp tongues.

No, their break-up would have to wait.

Feeling somewhat relieved the inevitable was postponed, Tom turned the conversation to something lighter. "I hear that Lewie Hanks will be at the social. I bet you'd enjoy sharing lunch with him."

"Lewie Hanks. Isn't he that bachelor who's opposed to bath water?"

"Oh, he's not opposed to it, so long as he's not in it."

She grinned, following his jovial lead. "And I hear that Miranda Parsons will be there. Maybe you're hoping to bid on her lunch instead of mine."

The thought of sharing lunch with that floozy nearly turned his stomach. And if Hanks *did* buy Abigail's lunch—well, he just couldn't let that happen. "You know what? I think we'd better cheat. Describe your lunch and give me details."

"It will be large, and wrapped with pink and white polka dotted paper."

"Pink and white dots. Got it."

"And tied with—"

"Yoo-hoo, Tom. You in here, Tom?" It was Davy.

Abigail immediately tensed.

"Sorry, Abby," Tom whispered. He could see that she was displeased by the boy's untimely appearance. "He comes nearly every day after school."

"You in here, Tom?" Davy called again.

"In the back."

Tom made the necessary introductions. "Abigail, this is Davy Patterson, youngest brother to the new schoolteacher. Davy, this is Mrs. Craig, a very good friend of mine."

"Are you the Widow Craig who sews?"

Abigail forced a tight-lipped smile. Tom knew she hated being called that. "Yes, I am."

"I'm a friend of Tom's too."

"Yes, Tom told me." There was an undeniable coolness to her voice.

"Listen, Davy," Tom said, "would you put some more coal in the forge? I'm talking with Mrs. Craig."

But Abigail stood. "I'd better go. You have lots to do. See you Friday night?"

"I wish I could, but if I'm taking Saturday off, I'd better work late."

She seemed disappointed. "I understand."

*

The day of the social, Beth ticked off the items on her list as she filled the box. Satisfied that everything was packed, she wrote her name on a slip of paper, making certain to sign *Patterson*. She needn't have worried. Accustomed to hearing herself called Miss Patterson at school all day, she seldom even thought of signing Parkerson now. Only once, when they had first moved to Whistle Creek, had she blundered, but quickly caught her mistake before anyone noticed. She merely changed the 'rk' in Parkerson to 'tt' in Patterson.

She set the paper carefully atop the packed food. Mindful to keep the box upright, she wrapped it and then stood back and eyed her lunch, pleased with the results. Once the box was opened, the buyer would pair up with her and they would enjoy the lunch together. She got butterflies just thinking about who he might be.

When Davy exited the boy's' bedroom, Beth's heart warmed at

the sight of him shining like a polished penny.

"Who are you?" she asked as she set the lunch aside.

He looked perplexed. "Davy."

"No, you're not. Davy has a rooster-tail poking straight up right here." Beth tapped her finger gently on her brother's head. "And let me see those fingernails. Ah ha! That proves it! The Davy I know always has dirty nails."

Davy giggled at his sister's teasing.

"There's only one way to tell." She poked him under his arm and in his ribs until he was laughing hysterically.

"Why, mercy, it is you, Davy! I never would have believed it! You look so spit polished."

"So does Bill."

"Does he?" she asked, eyes bright. That was a switch. Dressing up for Bill usually meant making certain his socks matched.

But Davy was right. When Bill came into the room, Beth eyed her brother appreciatively. It had been too long since she'd seen him in good clothes. Heavens, he was even wearing a tie!

"You look handsome, Bill," Davy exclaimed.

"Shut up, twerp," Bill warned, though obviously pleased his groomed appearance had not gone unnoticed. "You ready, Beth?"

"Yes." She carefully placed her wrapped lunch inside a larger box so no one would see which lunch she brought. "Let's go."

"What stinks?" Davy asked.

Bill gave Davy a shove. "It's cologne and it don't stink."

Cologne? Beth wondered where Bill found the money, wishing she had some perfume for herself. Then she had an idea.

"You two go on ahead. I'll catch up in a few minutes." She set the boxed lunch on the table and quickly opened the cupboard, withdrew the small bottle of vanilla and dabbed a few drops behind each ear. For good measure, she dabbed some more at the base of her neck. She grabbed the lunch again and caught up to the boys before they reached the school. They were arguing.

"What's the matter, now?"

"I want to eat with Bill."

"And I said no!" Bill retorted.

Davy kicked at a thistle. "But why not?"

"Because I said so, that's why."

"You can eat with me today, Davy," Beth stated firmly, thwarting any further dispute. If Bill had gone to the trouble of wrestling with a tie and putting on cologne, then someone had caught his eye. Beth was pretty certain that that someone was Annaleese Hewn. Davy would just get in their way.

Several people were already in the school, standing around in clusters, visiting. The students' desks had been pushed to the side, some stacked precariously one upon the other and looking about as stable as a one of Davy's card houses. At the front of the classroom, Beth's desk had been curtained off, allowing the women to secretly deposit their lunches. Beth lifted her lunch from the large protective box and set hers among the others, relieved to find it looked very similar to the other wrapped lunches.

Suddenly she remembered she hadn't packed any cutlery. Racing back to the house, she grabbed the necessary utensils and stuffed them in the large pocket of her skirt. She had just returned to the school when someone called her name.

"Miss Patterson, wait." It was Penelope Pickard, running ahead of her family carrying something large. Perched upon her head was that ridiculous feathered hat.

Immediately the memory of being caught in the maple tree came barging into Beth's mind, but she shoved it aside. There was no way she would let that unfortunate moment ruin this day.

"Would you please take this in for mother?" Penelope thrust a large lunch wrapped in a blanket like an oversized baby into Beth's arms. "I have to go to the privy."

"Oh, of course. Away you go then." She watched her dash to the facility out back. Beth smiled sadly, acknowledging the girl's bladder problem. Before and since the school inspector's visit, Penelope had had several accidents in the classroom.

Down the road a hundred yards, the remaining Pickard children straggled behind their parents, Jonah riding drag. With that many mouths to feed, no wonder this lunch is so enormous, Beth thought. Before her arms were pulled from their sockets, she decided to take it inside.

"Oh here, Miss Patterson, please allow me to take dat from ew." It was Lars Anderstom. "Dis lunch is too heavy for a little voooman such as ew, I tink."

Beth smiled generously at the Norwegian. She'd met him a few times before, usually at Betner's General Store. He had the bluest eyes she'd ever seen. She imagined that they were the color of a deep Norwegian fjord and every time he looked at her, she felt she might drown in their depths. But Lars was shy and didn't often meet her gaze. Today he seemed to be looking at her right ear.

Beth tucked the blanket around the lunch. "It's not too heavy," she lied, shifting the cumbersome lunch to her other arm. "How was your harvest?" she asked, leaning ever so slightly to the right to center herself in his view.

"Ah, da harvest vas gewd."

She liked the way he spoke. His accent had a sing song quality to it.

"And yewr teaching? Dat is going vell?"

"Yes," Beth answered as her arm started to go numb. "The children are wonderful."

Lars nodded.

One more minute and Beth would have no feeling at all in her arm. "I'd better put this inside now," she said reluctantly, wishing she could get one more gaze into those blue pools of his, but Lars had moved to open the door.

"Maybe you'll buy my lunch and we can continue our conversation?" She blushed slightly, never having been so bold with a man before. Oh, but it would be wonderful to sit across from him as they ate!

"Yah, I vood like dat."

*

Tom sat with his back against the old maple in the schoolyard and watched with amusement as Miss Patterson ran back and forth between her place and the school. Sometimes she seemed more like one of her students than the teacher. But what could one expect considering she was so young.

He peered up at the branches and studied the way the sunlight filtered through the canopy of coppery autumn leaves. He closed his eyelids, happily remembering the day he caught her trying to retrieve that fool hat. Hmm, all those ruffles under her skirt. They sort of reminded him of a huge bouquet of carnations.

"I've been looking for you," a soft feminine voice said.

Tom opened his eyes. He scowled as Miranda Parsons settled herself beside him.

"Brrr, it's chilly today." She hugged herself tightly and in doing so, squeezed her breasts together to enhance her already abundant cleavage. "I should have worn my cardigan."

A gentleman would have offered the lady his jacket, but Tom didn't consider Miranda a lady so he felt no need to be a gentleman. Let her go inside if she was so cold.

"Momma didn't want me to come today. She says box socials are nonsense." Miranda twirled her hair around her finger and brushed the ends against her cheek. "She's so old fashioned. I think she was born in the wrong century. I mean, Papa died three years ago and she still wears black. Well, not me. I didn't die. Don't you think my crimson dress is pretty?"

Tom said nothing, hoping she'd leave if he ignored her.

She spread the flounces of her dress around her in a wide circle. "It would be tragic if some old pig farmer bought my lunch. He'd probably stink to high heaven and my delicious lunch would be ruined!" She pouted. "And I baked all my specialties. Why, even Widow Craig's cooking won't be as fine as mine this year."

Tom gritted his teeth.

"Wouldn't it be amazing if you bought my lunch? I wrapped it in a red checkered tablecloth so we could spread it under this tree and—oh my, I've let you know which one is mine. Shame on me!"

Tom could see if anyone were was going to leave, it would have to be him. As he stood, he said, "Actually, it is a shame you let that information slip, Miss Parsons. I wouldn't feel right about bidding on your lunch now. Besides, I'm sure you'd rather share your food with some youngster closer to your own age."

*

Inside, Beth set the Pickard lunch behind the curtained area and rubbed the feeling back into her arms. She whisked off the blanket just as Earl Betner, this year's auctioneer, declared it was time to start the bidding. The adults were called in from outside, and the curtain opened.

The men crowded forward, and the women moved to the back. Beth immediately spotted Tom among the men. He was taller and broader in the shoulders. She noted his dark hair had been freshly trimmed, all except for a small ducktail that curled over his starched white collar. He was likely the best-looking man here today.

She gave herself a shake. What on earth was she doing, comparing him to other men? He could be the best-looking man on earth for all she cared. She reminded herself that she despised Tom Carver. He was a scoundrel, an arrogant rogue who thought nothing . . . "Good afternoon, ladies and gentlemen," welcomed Earl, interrupting her scathing critique of the blacksmith. An expectant hush fell over the school. "It's great to see everyone here today. I hope we have some men with empty stomachs and full billfolds." Everyone politely laughed. "As you can see, there are many pretty lunches to bid on, so let's not waste any time. Mrs. Pickard, I believe you volunteered to be my assistant this year?"

With one child in her arms and another tangled in her skirt, Mrs. Pickard made her way to the front. She handed the first lunch to Earl.

He cleared his throat and began. "Gentlemen, the social is now open for bidding. What am I bid for this delightful box?"

Immediately an arm shot high into the air. "I bid five cents." It was Lewie Hanks. His underarm was stained with sweat and all those near him withdrew slightly.

Earl acknowledged Lewie's bid. "Thank you, I have five cents. Now who will give me a dime? Ten pennies then . . . come gentlemen . . . a pretty little package like this should be worth twice that."

"Fifty cents!" Orville Cook called out. With such a jump in the bid, everyone assumed he was bidding on his wife's lunch. Someone raised it to fifty-five and Orville counter bid with sixty cents.

"Orville knows a good lunch when he sees one. Now, who'll bid sixty-five? Sixty-three then? Going . . . going . . . gone. Sold! Orville Cook for sixty cents! Thank you, Orville. Come pick up your lunch. Just drop your money in the can there. That's right. Remember, gentlemen, no peeking until all the lunches are sold."

The next lunch was a tidy package wrapped with bright green paper and gold ribbon. Beth watched Bill's shoulders straighten when Earl held it up for bid. Lewie Hanks opened with a nickel again, and Bill countered with a dime.

Beth glanced sideways at the women. Annaleese Hewn was nervously biting her lip and Beth could see that, hidden partially in the folds of her skirt, her fingers were crossed. She smiled. Annaleese had been the answer to Beth's prayers. Ever since Bill and Annaleese had started seeing each other, Bill's obsession with having a horse had been completely forgotten. Annaleese had a positive influence on Bill, and Beth was forever grateful. Today she prayed he would have enough money to buy the young lady's lunch.

The bidding went up slowly, and in the end, Bill bought the lunch for two bits. Both he and Annaleese seemed delighted.

Mrs. Pickard slid a large lunch forward to the table ledge.

"Looks like whoever made this lunch packed enough for all of us," Earl joked. Beth recognized it as Mrs. Pickard's. By now everyone expected Lewie to open the bidding, but to their surprise this time a different voice boldly called out, "Ten cents!"

"Lars Anderstom opens with a dime!"

"Fifteen," Mr. Pickard returned and Mrs. Pickard smiled ever so slightly.

"Tew-bits!" Lars jumped the bid.

"Thirty," countered Pickard.

The two men bid back and forth until the bid reached the astronomical price of seventy-eight cents. It seemed obvious to everyone it was Mrs. Pickard's lunch the two men were bidding on, obvious to everyone except Lars. And Beth knew why. When the bidding finally stopped, Lars had bought the lunch, all ninety-six cents worth.

Lars toted the enormous lunch back and set it on the floor beside him. He stole a quick glance at Beth and she gave him a gracious smile. It was the least she could do. Had he glanced at Mrs. Pickard, he would have seen her bubbling with excitement at having brought the highest bid thus far, and from a handsome bachelor to boot.

Beth hoped he was fond of children.

From the far side of the classroom, Tom saw Earl lift Abigail's lunch, a somewhat large box wrapped in pink paper splattered with tiny white polka dots.

Tom's bid of two-bits alerted all the men Abigail Craig's lunch was up for bid and the bidding began again in earnest. Even Lewie Hanks excitedly reached down deep in his pocket and, pulling it inside out, dumped its contents into his hand: washers, coins, chaff and all.

Always a prankster, Ernie Brown palmed some money to Lewie, just to add a little excitement to the bidding. With the added money, Lewie, who had never gone past twenty-three cents, excitedly raised the bid to thirty-five.

"The bid is thirty-five cents. Do I hear more?"

Lewie caught up in bidding fever, raised his own bid. "Thirty-seven!" he hollered.

"Now just a minute. You're getting ahead of yourself, young fellow," Earl said.

Tom could feel Abigail burning a hole in his back with her glare. He had no idea where Lewie's new-found wealth came from, but he did know, no matter what, he'd better out bid him.

"One dollar!" Tom called out and the room buzzed at the exorbitant price.

Lewie's hopes shriveled like a popped balloon.

"Going once . . . twice . . . sold!"

Tom dropped the money into the can on the table and picked up Abigail's lunch. Suddenly a sick feeling washed over him. Sitting farther back on the table, almost hidden from view by other lunches, was a larger box wrapped in pink paper with white polka dots. And he knew without a doubt that one was Abigail's. The lunch he had just purchased was not covered with polka dots at all, but with small white flowers. He stared at it thoughtfully before picking it up. Nothing he could do now but pray Lewie Hanks didn't buy Abby's lunch.

Tom avoided looking in Abigail's direction as he carried his box back with him. And he didn't breathe easy until Mr. Pickard dropped the money in the can for Abby's lunch.

Finally, when all the boxes were auctioned off, Earl announced, "All right, gents, open your boxes and pair off."

When Tom read Beth's name on the slip of paper, he shook his head. *Is there no justice?*

An excited yelp brought everyone's attention around. Lewie was jumping up and down, unable to control his excitement. "I got Miranda Parson's!"

Miranda was so enraged, she marched right past Lewie and out the door. Lewie bounded after her like a dog after a ham bone.

All right, Tom conceded, *maybe there is justice.*

Chapter 6

Tom wove his way through the crowded classroom toward Beth. She didn't look pleased. Too bad. Upsets like this happened all the time at box socials. It was part of the fun. She would just have to put up with him. He had to chuckle to himself. When he thought about it, the entire mix-up was rather humorous. But a glimpse at Abby told him she thought otherwise.

"I believe I have the honor of sharing your lunch, Miss Patterson."

"Yes, I see," she replied curtly, as if it pained her to even be that civil.

Tom handed her the box and then lifted down a set of desks joined in tandem by two planks at the foot of the legs. "How's this?"

"We'll need a chair for Davy."

"Oh good," Tom said, blurting it out almost in relief. At least the boy could act as a buffer between them. "I didn't know he was here."

"He's outside playing. Mrs. Pickard went to call in the children."

Tom brought a chair in from the cloakroom just as Davy appeared.

"Whose lunch did you get, Tom?"

"Your sister's."

"Really? Oh boy! This is going to be fun!"

Tom glanced at Beth's scowl. *Yup. Like a poke in the eye with a sharp stick.* "Are you as hungry as I am?" he asked Davy as they arranged the desks and chair.

"More than."

"I'm hungrier than an elephant."

They volleyed back and forth about their ridiculously large appetites until Beth had all she could stand. She set the plates on the desktop with a clatter, before serving them both an icy glare. "If you're *that* hungry, you should have bought Mrs. Pickard's lunch!"

Tom and Davy exchanged raised eyebrows. Tom stood. "I'm

going to get some coffee. Can I bring you anything to drink?"

She glanced up, as if surprised he'd ask. "I can get my own, thank you." When Tom gave her an exasperated look, she relented. "All right, some tea please. No sugar."

"I'll have some coffee." Davy piped up.

Tom dropped his gaze to his pint-sized friend. "Listen, squirt, coffee can stunt your growth. Look what it did to me." He glanced to see if his humor had any reaction on Beth, but he could see she was determined to snub him.

He turned to her little brother instead. "Come with me. I'll pour you some juice."

Tom returned just as Beth had everything ready to dish up. Davy followed with his glass filled to the brim, carefully placing one foot in front of the other like a tightrope walker.

The blacksmith lowered his tall body into the front seat, sitting sideways so his back wouldn't be turned to Beth.

"This looks delicious, Miss Patterson."

"Beth's been fussin' over it all day!" For his comment, Davy received yet another scathing glare from his sister. "I helped her though."

Had it not been for the ongoing conversation between Tom and Davy, the meal would have been eaten in complete silence. Tom had given up on trying to engage Beth in conversation.

While she daintily picked away at her food, Tom cleaned his plate and had seconds. Finished and thoroughly satisfied, he leaned back in the desk. "That was worth every penny. Thank you."

"I don't suppose you saved any room for dessert?"

"Let me guess! Vanilla cookies!"

Beth felt her ears color heat as if the extract dabbed behind them was burning through. "No, it's rhubarb pie."

"Huh, could have sworn I smelled vanilla." Tom held out his plate. "But that's okay. I like rhubarb."

She cut him a generous portion and hoped he would bloat on it.

"I've got room for pie, too, please." Davy thrust his plate across the desktop and the rim caught the handle of Tom's coffee cup, spilling freshly brewed coffee over the desktop and onto Tom's lap.

Stifling an oath, he jumped to his feet and held the steaming front of his pants away from his body. Davy, horrified by what he had done, ran from the school, while everyone looked on with concern.

Beth, accustomed to many spills, automatically grabbed her napkin to soak up the liquid, then remembering where the coffee had spilled, thrust the napkin into Tom's hand. He cleaned himself up as best he could and then looked around behind him.

"Where'd Davy go?"

"He ran out."

"I guess I'd better go get him."

Beth followed on his heels. In the cloakroom, he stopped short and turned around. She slammed straight into his chest.

"Miss Patterson, I am quite capable of finding the boy. Go finish your meal. There's no need for you to come."

"Well, I happen to think there is a need, the mood you're in."

"I beg your pardon?"

"You're agitated."

"Because my trousers are soaked."

"I don't want you taking your anger out on Davy."

Tom quietly closed the door between the classroom and the cloakroom. He deliberately kept his voice quiet and in control, but his clenched jaw revealed his mounting frustration. "Miss Patterson, what is your problem?"

"You're the one with the problem."

"Really. And what is that?"

"Your temper. I've seen it, and it's not pretty."

"When have you seen my temper?"

"With Bill. I don't want Davy to be subjected to your rage."

"Rage, huh? Yeah, I guess I raged a little. Bill doesn't exactly bring out the best in me." Tom raked his finger through his dark hair. "But you can't honestly believe I would harm Davy. He's a good kid. Some days, he chatters nonstop about you. He's got you up on a pedestal, but in all honesty, I don't know why."

Beth tried to step around him, but his arm shot out and blocked her exit. When she attempted to duck under, he grabbed her arm and held her.

"Let me go," she spat, stomping her foot. "I don't have to listen to this." She tried to wrestle her arm free, but he had a firm grip on her.

"Oh, yes you do! You may not like what I'm going to tell you, but it's for your own good, so pay attention." He leaned closer to her so those in the classroom wouldn't overhear. "Grow up. Ever since we sat down to eat, you've been pouty and rude like a spoiled brat. You sat through lunch with your pretty little mouth puckered up tighter than a pig's asshole."

Beth gasped.

He never slowed down. "I was surprised you managed to eat anything at all. Too bad, because the food was good. But your company wasn't worth one thin dime."

Beth began to protest, but he cut her off. "Now, I know you don't like me, and that's fine. I really don't care. But you seem to forget there are parents of children you teach here today and you're not making a favorable impression." He watched her face pale. "So, little Miss Schoolteacher, I suggest you start smiling as if you're having a wonderful time." His lips turned up into a wry grin. "If I can pretend, so can you. Now, I'm going out to find Davy, and you needn't worry about his safety. He isn't the Patterson I feel like turning over my knee." With that, he released her arm and he went in search of Davy.

Beth was stunned, then incensed. In all her nineteen years, she had never had anyone give her a dressing down like that. *How dare he suggest I deserved a spanking!* Beth clenched her fists. *Who does he think he is, talking to me as if I were a child? Well, I'm not a child!* She fumed, stomping her foot. She was the schoolteacher and deserved respect! Imagining he was still standing in front of her, she stuck out her tongue.

Then, as if doused with iced water, Beth put her hands to her flushed cheeks. She *was* acting childish, terribly so.

As much as she disliked the man, she hated even more how she behaved. If she kept this up, she *could* be fired and then where would she and her brothers be?

Straightening her shoulders, Beth returned to the classroom, determined to keep a smile pasted on her lips no matter what.

When Tom returned ten minutes later, dressed in dry clothes and with Davy perched happily on his shoulders, Beth had a fresh cup of coffee waiting for him and a slice of pie cut for Davy. She even managed to smile at him, difficult as it was.

Tom lifted Davy over his head and plunked him in his chair. "Okay, squirt, let's dig into that rhubarb pie, shall we?"

She interrupted. "Before you do, Mr. Carver . . . Tom . . . It's all right if I call you Tom?" She hoped that by calling him by his first name, he'd seem less intimidating.

He nodded.

"I've been thinking about what you said. And you're right." Oh, how those words scratched her throat. "I have exhibited very poor manners, and frankly, I'm embarrassed by my actions. I owe you an apology. From now on you will see a far more pleasant and mature side of me."

Tom smiled. "Apology accepted. Now, would you please join us in a piece of pie . . . or are you too full after eating so much crow?"

She wanted desperately to throw the pie plate at him.

*

While the women cleared the dishes and made yet another pot of coffee, the men rearranged the desks and brought up a couple of tables and a few chairs from the basement. Soon folks began playing crokinole and cribbage while others played whist. Some were happy just to sit and visit.

Though the afternoon had turned out differently than intended, Tom planned to spend the evening with Abigail, but before he could ask her for a game of crib, she was sitting with three other women, playing whist.

Earl called across the room. "Wanna join us, Tom? We're playing partner crib."

"You bet."

Three quarters of an hour later, Abigail tapped on Tom's shoulder. "I just wanted to say goodnight."

"You're leaving already? It's early yet."

"I know," she answered quietly, "but I'm not feeling well. I think I'd better go home."

Immediately Tom became concerned. "I'll get our coats."

*

On his way to the smithy the next morning, Tom stopped by Abigail's to see if she felt better. Smoke rose from her chimney, indicating she'd at least been up to stoke the fire.

When she answered the door, she looked haggard and worn, and large dark circles shadowed beneath her eyes. "Tom," she stated flatly.

"I knew I should have stayed last night to take care of you. Looks to me like you should still be in bed."

"I'm all right. I just didn't get much sleep last night."

"Can I come in? Make you some tea or something?"

She hesitated, then without a word, stepped back. Immediately Tom saw the trunks sitting just inside the parlor. "What's this?"

"I've decided I'm going to Auntie Bets after all. She's getting older and could use the help. Besides, it's time I made a change." She turned her back to him and knelt beside an open trunk, tenderly wrapping her treasures in tea towels before placing them inside. "It just isn't going to work out for us."

Tom was stunned. She was leaving town? What had precipitated her sudden decision? Suddenly it dawned on him. "Does this have anything to do with my getting Beth Patterson's lunch yesterday, 'cause that was an accident. There is nothing going on between Beth and me, I swear."

She closed the trunk lid. "Oh, Tom, I know that. You're too honorable a man to cheat on me, but I also know you've been pulling away. We haven't made love in weeks."

"But." *But what?* he thought. *You were planning on ending the relationship. So she did it instead. That shouldn't matter to you, should it?* Tom sank into a chair, leaned forward and rested his elbows on his knees. He stared at the floor between his boots while a heavy blanket of guilt shrouded him. "I'm sorry. I should have given you more."

She touched his shoulder gently and he lifted his head to look at her. "You can't give what isn't in you to give." Her eyes were shiny with tears.

"I do love you, Abby."

"I know, but there are many kinds of love."

Tom nodded. She hadn't said it in so many words but she meant that his wasn't the marrying type of love. And she was right.

"Tom, we've had some wonderful times together, but now it's time to move on. And I'm okay with that." She opened another truck and continued packing knickknacks. "I'm going to auction off my furniture in the spring. It would cost too much to ship it back East, and besides, Auntie wouldn't have room to store it. Until then, things can just stay here. I'll write Mr. Lanson when I get to Toronto. He can make the arrangements for the auction and the sale of the house."

She explained all the details, but Tom barely heard, his mind too numb to take it all in. "When are you leaving?" he asked.

"I'm catching this afternoon's train. It's better this way. Postponing it will only make it worse."

He started to speak, but she stopped him. "Don't. Don't say

anything. My mind's made up." Her voice quivered and a solitary tear trickled down her cheek. "Just go. Please."

He nodded and slowly rose. His heart ached with sadness and shame, with a heaping load of self-loathing mixed in. He closed the door silently behind him.

Though not one to drink, he headed straight to the Star Saloon and rattled the locked door until Sam Churning opened it. "Tom, you know we don't open till noon."

He ignored Sam's protest and pushed past him. When he leaned on the bar, Sam sighed and relocked the door. "It's a tad early in the day to start drinking, ain't it?" he admonished as he rounded the tall counter.

Tom stared at him with dull blue eyes. "I didn't come for a lecture. I need a whisky."

The bartender shrugged his shoulders. "Sure thing." He set a glass on the bar and filled it to the brim with the amber liquid.

"On second thought, leave the bottle." Tom downed his drink with one gulp. He shuddered, refilled the glass, and emptied it just as quickly. Bottle in one hand and his glass in the other, he headed for a table in the back corner.

Sam stacked chairs on the tables and swept up last night's debris. Tom spent more time staring unseeingly at the bottle than drinking its contents. By noon, when Sam unlocked the door and flipped the sign in the window to open, over half the bottle remained.

The first customer through the door was Lewie Hanks. He dragged out a tall bar stool, perched himself on top of it and then slapped his palm down on the counter to get Sam's attention. Sam ignored him.

"Hey, I wanna drink."

Sam moved down the length of the bar and stopped in front of Lewie. "Sorry, Hanks. Your credit's no good anymore. If you want a drink, I need your money first."

"But I kin pay ya this afternoon when I gets paid."

"You telling me you got a job?"

"Yup." Lewie stretched his arms cross the counter to grab the far edge. "Widow Craig is paying me a buck to haul her trunks to the train station. She's going back East today. Guess that blacksmith of hers knows more about shoeing horses than riding his woman. Boy, give me half a chance, I'd climb on her and show her what a man can do."

In three strides, Tom crossed the room, grabbed Lewie by the collar and yanked him backwards, sending the bar stool rolling across the floor. Angrier than he'd ever been in his life, he spun Hanks about. It was all he could do to keep from smashing his fist into Lewie's ugly face.

"Tom!" he exclaimed with a nervous laugh, his voice cracking. "I didn't see you there."

Tom practically lifted him by his collar. "You worthless piece of horse shit." He ground the words out between his clenched teeth. "If I ever hear you talking like that again, I'll make you regret the day your mother whelped you. Got that?"

Lewie nodded, his little head bouncing on his scrawny shoulders as if it were attached by loose hinges.

He pushed Lewie backwards over the bar, closing in until their faces were two inches apart. "Right about now," he began, his lips forming a menacing curl, "I'd just as soon rearrange your ugly face as look at it. So get the hell out of here while you still can." Then he spun him around by the shoulders and pushed him toward the door.

Lewie fell, then half scrambled and half ran out the door as if the devil was on his tail, but Tom let him go, returning instead to his table. Standing, he poured himself another drink and tossed it back, then threw some coins on the table before leaving. "I'll be back. Save the bottle for me."

He found Abigail in the back bedroom of her house. She seemed startled to see him there.

"I guess you were expecting Hanks," he said, his words beginning to slur.

"Tom, you've been drinking."

"You're damn right. I may have resigned myself to your leaving, but I sure as hell won't let that vermin Hanks see you off. Show me what needs to go."

The minute the train pulled away from the station, Tom returned to the saloon. It was busier now, but a table was vacant and he claimed it. When Sam brought him his whisky bottle and a clean glass, he said, "When this runs out, bring another. I plan on getting stinking drunk."

Throughout the day and night, other customers came and went, but Tom remained at his table. The more he drank the harder he was on himself. *You bastard, if Abigail was good enough for you to bed, she should have been good enough for you to wed. And if you had been a man of any decency, dammit, you would have made her your wife before you made her your lover.* Tom had always thought of himself as an honorable sort of guy. That was until today. Now he realized he wasn't much better than Lewie Hanks. He shoved his glass aside and chugged straight from the bottle. By closing time, he had accomplished his objective. He was too drunk to stand.

After the other patrons were gone, Sam nudged him. "Come on, Tom, it's time to go home. I want to close up."

"Leave me alone," he slurred bitterly, slumping forward in his chair. His forehead thudded into the table and his arms hung limp at his side.

"This is handy," Sam growled. "Now how am I supposed to get you home?" He left Tom passed out at the table, locked up the saloon and headed outside to the back door of Betner's store. Earl, dressed in his long underwear, answered Sam's insistent knocking.

"Are you crazy, Sam? It's two in the morning."

"I know damn well what time it is, but I need your help. Tom's drunk."

"So what? Fife gets liquored up every time his mother-in-law comes for a visit. Toss him out. The cold will soon sober him up."

Earl started to close the door.

"Not Tom Fife. Tom Carver. Widow Craig boarded the twelve-fifty-five with her bags, and he's been drinking ever since."

"Damn." Earl stepped aside. "Come in while I get dressed and then we'll haul him back here."

Chapter 7

Whichever woke him first, the bright glaring light beating on his eyelids or the irritating clicking noise echoing painfully in his head, Tom wished they would both go away and leave him to his misery. Eventually the sunbeam took sympathy and slipped away from his pillow, but the clicking continued until he could bear it no longer. He opened an eyelid a slit, and across the room silhouetted against the window, he could see Mary sitting in a chair. Realizing the vexatious clicking was made by her knitting needles, he groaned and then slowly closed his eyelid. Even that amount of movement caused his head to pound. His mouth was foul tasting, as if he'd swallowed swamp mud. He ran his tongue across his lips. "Mary," he whispered painfully, "for God's sake, must you make so much noise?"

Mary set her knitting aside and came to lean over him, tenderly placing her palm on his forehead. He winced. Her hand felt like a fifty-pound anvil. "You poor wretched soul," she said. "Can I get you anything? Do anything?"

When her words finished reverberating in his head, he answered, "Just shoot me." Through half-opened eyelids he saw Mary smile, and he added hoarsely, "It's not funny. My head . . . it's going to explode."

Mary stood back and crossed her arms under her generous bosom. "Well, what do you expect?" she admonished gently. "Shame on you, Tommy Carver. You won't get much sympathy from me."

"I don't expect any," he whispered.

"Do you think you can sit up?" she asked. "I've got some coffee brewing downstairs and Sam gave me something to mix in it. Said it would make you feel better. Come on, sit up. Here, take my hand."

Mary took his forearm and gently pulled him forward, propping a pillow behind him. He moaned in misery.

"There," she crooned, easing him back, "you just rest easy for a minute while I get your brew."

It hadn't seemed she'd been gone at all when he felt the rim of a cup pressed against his lips. He sipped and pulled away from its bitterness, but Mary wasn't one to brook resistance, especially when she believed she was doing something for his own good. She firmly held his head and kept tipping the cup. It was either drown or swallow, but as he drank the vile tasting mixture, he wondered if drowning wouldn't be preferable. Once he'd managed to down well over half, she placed the cup in his hands, and allowed him to lean back on the pillow. It took a few minutes, but eventually the potion started to work, and the pounding in his head lessened somewhat. He sipped at the remaining bitter concoction.

Seemingly satisfied that he was on the way to recovery, physically, in any case, Mary returned to her rocker, but instead of picking up her knitting, she studied him.

"I guess you're waiting for an explanation," he said.

"I have an idea, but I am curious what brought this all about."

"Abigail's gone. Gone back East."

She nodded. "I'm sorry to hear that."

There was an uncomfortable silence between them. Mary was waiting for more, but how could he discuss Abby's leaving? He threaded his fingers back through his tousled hair. "This is something I'll need to sort out myself."

"You won't find the answers at the bottom of a bottle."

"I know. But it numbed the pain . . . for a while anyway . . . and that's all I wanted."

Mary came forward, sat on the edge of the bed, and squeezed his hand. "You didn't have to go it alone. You could have come to me or Earl."

"The way I feel right now, I wish I had."

She took the empty cup from him and placed it on the dresser. Then she reached under the bed, pulled out the chamber pot and set it beside him. "I hate to tell you this, but Sam warned that about half an hour after you drink that stuff, everything will come up. I'd say you're starting to look a touch green, so I think it's best if I leave." She headed for the door, then stopped and turned. "I'll check on you later." She pulled the door closed behind her.

An hour later, Tom weakly pulled back from the chamber pot, certain that if he vomited once more he'd turn inside out. Fortunately, once the spasms quit, he felt better and soon he drifted off to sleep where reality would not intrude.

*

"Sleepy head dog," Davy whined. Hands deep in his pockets, he sauntered over to Tom. "Boy, that Jack, he's so-oo sleepy today."

Tom, absorbed in his work, paid little heed to the boy. Leaning against the horse's flank, he lifted up a hoof and held it between his knees as he fitted a shoe. "Remember, Jack's old," he answered absently.

"I know, but I want to play with him and he won't wake up. He's even too tired to twitch his ear when I blow on it."

"Yeah well, like I said, sometimes . . . " A cold shiver slowly crept along his spine. He gently lowered the horse's hoof and set aside his hammer. Jack was in his customary place behind the forge. Tom squatted down on his haunches beside him and gently lifted his paw. It was cold and lifeless, and when he placed his hand on the dog's chest, there was no heartbeat.

"Oh, Davy." How was he going to break the news to the boy?

But Davy must have read his expression already and had his own suspicions. His voice trembled when he asked, "Is he . . . d . . . dead?"

In a voice nearly as shaky, Tom replied, "I'm afraid so, son." He rose slowly, feeling exhausted, as if the life had been sucked from him too.

The boy shook his head in denial and then threw himself across the dog. "No! You c . . . can't be d . . . dead. You're just sleeping. Wake up, Jack!" Then in a rage, he started pulling on the dog's neck, and shouting, "Get up, you lazy old dog."

Tom felt like there was a chain wrapped around his chest and each time Davy tugged on Jack, the chain twisted tighter and tighter. He reached down and pulled him away. "He's gone, Davy. He can't hear you anymore. Jack's dead. He died in his sleep."

Davy wrapped his arms around Tom's leg and wept pitifully. "But I miss him already."

Tom bent down and lifted the distraught boy up into his arms and held him close, wishing he could ease his sorrow. "I know, son," he whispered soothingly. "I know. I miss him, too, but Jack was old—really old—and he was hurting a lot, I think more than we knew. Maybe it's better he's gone."

Davy pushed back, as if horror stricken his friend would suggest such an atrocity. "No! It's not better. How can you say that?" Needing to lash out against the pain and anguish, he pummeled Tom's chest with his fists, and kicked at his thighs.

Startled more than hurt, Tom set him down. A solid blow to his stomach doubled him over.

"It's not better that Jack's dead. And if you think it is, then you're mean and I hate you and I never want to see you again!" Sobbing, the lad ran from the smithy.

Barely able to catch his wind, Tom straightened up and called feebly, "Davy, come back," but he either didn't hear him or chose not to heed the order. Tom debated going after him, but he knew there was little he could do or say to soothe the boy's sorrow. He'd check on him later.

He led the horse back into his stall, and put his tools away as he'd done so many times before. He could finish shoeing the horse later, but right now, there was a task ahead of him he had to do. Teary-eyed, he scooped up his lifeless dog and whispered for one last time, "Come on, Jack. Time to go home."

To avoid meeting anyone, he left by the back way and down the alley. When he reached the barn, he gently laid his dog on some loose straw in the bed of the wagon. Without his usual greeting for his horses, he solemnly hitched up Benjamin to the wagon, grabbed a shovel and stopped at the house to retrieve Jack's mat.

Some time ago, Tom had decided when Jack died, he'd be buried up on the hill behind the house. Both Tom's parents and sisters were buried there, their side-by-side graves enclosed by a small picket fence. Jack's grave would be outside the fence. Now that the old boy was free from pain, it only seemed fitting his soul be free to run forever.

With it being late in the fall, it took some digging to get through the first layer of frost, but Tom took no notice. Nor did he feel the biting northeastern wind on his hands and face. He dug with grim determination until the hole was sufficiently deep, then spread Jack's mat on the bottom. Lovingly, he placed the dog down, carefully rearranging his limbs.

For the longest time, he stood there, unable to bring himself to refill the grave. Finally, he tucked the mat around Jack, covering his muzzle and eyes, and then he started shoveling. He let his tears flow freely and without shame. As if the heavens commiserated with him, rain began. Before the final shovelful of dirt was patted down, the rain had changed to hard pellet-like snow.

*

It was seven-thirty that night when Beth set aside the paper she was marking and answered the knock at the door, knowing instinctively before she even opened it that it would be Tom. He stood there with his sheepskin coat pulled up around his ears, and his hat pulled low.

"I've come to see if the Davy's all right," he stated. Snow sifted off the roof and gathered in the brim of his hat.

Beth stood firm. "I don't know what happened at the smithy today, but he's very upset and doesn't want to see you." She had heard about the break-up between him and Abigail and how he'd become so drunk he had passed out. Having seen the ugly consequences of alcohol when they lived with their aunt and uncle, she questioned whether he was an appropriate adult for her little brother to befriend. She could only hope his drinking spree was an isolated incidence. "I think it's best if you leave." She tried to close the door, but he thrust his boot through the threshold, holding it open.

"Please, Beth, I just need to talk to him for a minute."

Considering the state her brother was in, she had no intentions of allowing the man inside, but unless she heard him out, she might never know what was troubling Davy.

"Just a minute." She yanked her coat from the peg on the back of the door, draped it over her shoulders and joined Tom outside on the stoop, clutching her coat tightly in front of her. She stayed under the eave's shelter.

"What happened?" she demanded. "Davy came home crying and won't stop. He wouldn't even come out of his room for supper. He keeps saying he hates you."

A pained expression flashed across Tom's face. "Jack, my old dog—."

Beth could tell he was having trouble speaking, for he closed his eyes and raised his head as if asking for divine help. The swirling snow hit his face while he expelled a deep frosty breath.

He looked at her and said flatly, "Jack died today, and Davy found him."

"Oh dear." No wonder her brother was so upset. He loved that old dog.

Tom bowed his head, vividly remembering Davy's heart-wrenching denial. "I swear it broke my heart to see the little guy crying so hard, so like a fool, I tried to make things better. I told him maybe it was for the best, what with Jack being so old and arthritic. I never thought he'd think I meant I was glad Jack died." He reached out and touched Beth's arm. "Please, I can't leave things the way they are."

She nodded and opened the door. "I'm sorry, I didn't realize. Come in. I'll see if I can get him to come out of his room."

Tom waited just inside, hat in hand while she went to speak to Davy. He could hear their muffled voices behind the closed bedroom door and then presently she returned alone. She shook her head. "I'm sorry. He just needs some time."

He bowed his head and stared at the floor. "I wish I could go back and redo this afternoon, handle things differently." He turned his hat in his big hands. "I should have prepared him some. It might have made it easier."

"I'm sure he knew it was bound to happen soon. He just didn't want to admit it, he loved Jack so. But now that I understand the situation, maybe I'll be able to get somewhere with him." She regretted judging Tom so harshly. He was well respected about the town and she'd seen no one else denigrate him because of his drunken state. And he couldn't be all bad if he was concerned about the feelings of a little boy. Suddenly she felt obliged to add, "I'm sure he didn't mean what he said."

"I know." Tom settled his hat back upon his head. He nodded at the stack of papers on the table, "I can see you've got work to do, so I won't keep you any longer. Goodnight."

"Goodnight. And I'm really sorry about Jack. I know he meant a lot to you too."

*

Tom tossed another log in the stove and closed the cast iron door, its clang resounding about the kitchen. It was his second evening without Jack. Resuming his place at the table, he lifted the glass globe off one lantern and set about trimming the wick, a mundane job, but at least one that occupied a few minutes of his time. The hours between supper and bedtime were long and lonesome. He missed talking to Jack and hearing his tail thump against the hardwood floor in reply.

Finished the wicks, he carried one lantern to the parlor and set it on the mantel. He tried reading, but he couldn't concentrate. At loose ends, he decided to go to the barn where horses and the musty smell of hay always soothed him. He shrugged into his coat and opened the door.

Beth was standing there, hand raised to knock.

"Oh, hi," he said, taken aback.

Without any preliminary small talk, she said, "Tom, I need your help." Her voice was on the verge of breaking.

"What's wrong?"

"It's Davy."

"Is he hurt?"

"No, he's not hurt, but I'm worried about him. He's barely eaten since Jack died and he just wants to stay in his room. Honestly, I don't know what to do. I was hoping you'd talk to him."

Tom's jaw tightened. "Do you think it would do any good?"

"Maybe. It's not only Jack he's upset about. I think he feels bad about the things he said to you."

"He shouldn't."

"Would you talk to him then?"

"I'll try."

It was a solemn, five-minute walk from Tom's place to Beth's. They spoke little and only then about Davy.

The moment they arrived, Bill grabbed his coat and took off like a scalded cat, giving some excuse that Tom didn't believe. He hoped he'd at least get a better reception from the younger brother, but he wasn't holding his breath. He rapped lightly on the bedroom door, and pushed it open.

The room was dim. He crossed to Davy's bed. The boy was on his side facing the wall, curled up into a tight little ball.

Tom sat on the edge of the bed, not at all certain what to say to him, or if he'd even listen. He reached out and gently shook him awake.

Davy uncurled and rolled onto his back. "Tom?" his voiced croaked.

"Hi, there. Your sister tells me you've been off your feed. She's worried about you." He could understand why. Davy looked thin and pale.

"I'm not hungry."

"I know. I haven't had much of an appetite myself." He stroked Davy's matted hair. "Still feeling bad about Jack, huh?" When the lad nodded, he continued. "Yeah, me too. It's lonesome without him. I catch myself glancing behind the forge a thousand times a day, but he's not there. Makes me feel like crying."

Davy's eyes opened wider. Tom figured he had never heard a grown man admit to such a thing. Bill had likely told him only sissies cried.

He held the boy's hand. "And now you don't come over any more." He let the words spill out, hoping beyond all hope they were the right ones. "It's almost like I lost my two best friends at once, Jack *and* you. I miss you."

Davy's bottom lip quivered and then a flood of emotions broke through and he sputtered, "I miss you, too. And I d . . . didn't mean it. I don't hate you." And then with a cry that almost tore the man's heart from his chest, he begged, "Please, don't hate me."

"Ah, Davy, I could never hate you. Not ever." His voice choked with emotion. "I was kinda hoping that maybe we could be buddies again. Would you like that?"

In answer, Davy jumped onto his knees and wrapped his arms in a strangle hold around Tom's neck, hugging him fiercely. It was the best kind of hug, the kind that squeezed the heart. In return, Tom held him tight against his chest.

"Now, how about something to eat?" he asked softly when the boy eventually released his neck.

"Can you stay and eat with me?"

He was caught off guard by the request. "Ah, I don't know . . ."

"There's plenty," Beth said quietly from the doorway. "You'd be more than welcome."

"Well, thanks, but I'd better not." Bill already hated him. No point in aggravating the situation by forcing him out of his own home. "I've already eaten." He carried Davy to a chair in the kitchen. "I sure hope you can come to the smithy tomorrow. I'm getting behind without your help."

"You are?"

"Darn tootin'! Don't know how I managed without you." He named all the tasks awaiting the lad's return.

When Beth set about warming some food, Tom turned to leave. "I'd better get going. I got things I have to do at home." *Like sit alone and listen to the clock ticking.*

She accompanied him to the door. "I can't thank you enough."

"I'm glad I could help."

They stood there on the front step, Tom reluctant to leave the company of those who understood his grief. Finally, he stepped back. "I guess I'd better go. You're going to catch a cold standing out here." He sauntered away a few yards, stopped and then said in a loud clear voice, "I'm leaving now, Bill."

Beth watched the blacksmith's receding form and she couldn't help being impressed. He had spoken honestly and openly with Davy about his own grief, when most men would have denied having such feelings. Considering all the trouble she and her brothers had been to the man, he really didn't owe them the time of day. His kindness gave her something to think about.

*

The snow stayed, and more followed as the weather became increasingly colder. Beth started going to the school half an hour earlier each morning to fire up the stove.

The heat in the classroom was never evenly distributed. Students sitting nearest the heater virtually cooked and students furthest away shivered. Often Beth would swing a towel around and around like a windmill to circulate the heat about the room. But despite all the trouble that the cold weather caused, Beth still enjoyed the winter season. She marveled at the beauty of the large feathery snowflakes as they veiled the trees and ground. She loved the sound of her school bell as it pealed loud and clear across the schoolyard, calling the children in from their frosty playtime.

It was the third week in November when Beth decided it was time to begin preparations for the Christmas concert. She wanted every student to partake in the program.

Of course, there would have to be a reenactment of Christ's birth. That was expected. She mentally assigned her older students the major speaking roles. The youngest children could be the animals who would happily "baa" or "moo" on cue. She wondered if Mrs. Young had had her baby yet. Wouldn't a real baby in the manger be wonderful!

From the bookshelf she withdrew a book, *Plays, Poetry, and Prose for Children*. No doubt parents with children in the older grades had watched most of the plays in the book, but she hoped something would inspire her to write something original. A few of her students were exceptional poets. She'd pick the best poems and have the authors recite them.

Ideas were coming so quickly, she went to her desk and jotted notes to remember them all. After vowing she was a great teacher, Beth was adamant that this concert be the talk of the town for years to come.

When Beth announced her ideas to the children that morning, they were so excited they couldn't sit still. She had to remind them that no Christmas preparations would happen unless they got all their work done and it wasn't long before they all buckled down to their assignments.

Inga's mother kindly donated the use of her piano, so Beth felt obliged to allow Inga, who *said* she had taken lessons, to be the pianist. But upon hearing her play, Beth had her doubts. She prayed the girl would improve with extra practice.

For the next month, every available moment was devoted to memorizing poems and lines, perfecting piano solos and duets, practicing Christmas carols and rehearsing the pageant. Notes were sent home with the children as to what props and costumes were needed, and Beth marveled daily at how the ingenuous mothers could fashion something out of nothing.

The concert was scheduled for the Friday before Christmas Day. As a reward for her students' diligence, Beth suspended afternoon classes on the Wednesday and Thursday preceding the big event. The time was spent making Christmas decorations. The youngest children crafted paper chains and strung popcorn and cranberries on thread; the older boys, with stronger, more calloused hands, used tin snips to cut stars from flattened cans; and the older girls' nimble fingers fashioned angels out of lacy remnants. Each child decorated a large envelope to hold samples of his best penmanship and poetry.

The evening before the concert, several men in the community, including Tom, built a stage at the front of the classroom to enable all to see the program.

When the big day arrived, the little schoolhouse was charged with excitement and the students spent the entire day putting up their decorations. Yards of paper chains draped back and forth across the room and angels hung in all the windows. Around the top of the blackboards, winter scenes were stenciled with chalk, while a large "Merry Christmas" was attractively written across the side blackboard. The piano, decorated with spruce boughs and ribbons, was pulled away from the wall and a blanket hung between it and the front blackboard, creating a backstage. The older boys were assigned the task of pushing desks into the back corner, and bringing in extra benches from the shed outside. The small, but stately Christmas tree, cut by one of the fathers, stood proudly on a table in the front corner. Soon it was decorated with the tin stars and popcorn strings.

Beth dismissed the children early in the afternoon so they could rush home, do their chores and have a quick bite to eat. They were to return at six-thirty sharp, half an hour before the concert was to begin. She sent Davy home ahead of her, which allowed her time to secretly place the treat bags under the tree. Everything was double checked, pictures straightened, bits of paper picked up, benches lined up evenly, heater stoked. With a final glance to verify all was perfect, Beth went home to prepare some supper for Bill, knowing that both she and Davy would be too excited to eat.

Chapter 8

Beth and Davy headed for the school, while Bill went to pick up Annaleese, who he'd been seeing regularly since the box social. Even in the brief time since Beth had last stoked the fire, the temperature in the school had dropped considerably. She threw a large bucketful of coal in the heater before preparing the coffee. By six-thirty, the students had arrived and they crowded "backstage" to don their costumes while their parents took their seats.

It seemed as though the entire community had turned out for the evening. The benches quickly filled. Men propped themselves against the walls and soon the schoolhouse reverberated with the din of neighborly conversation and laughter. A few women fanned themselves with the hand-printed programs, which caused Beth to worry that she had added too much coal.

Behind the curtain, the girls giggled nervously, and the boys pushed and shoved, while last minute butterflies stampeded in everyone stomachs. Beth's included.

"Did you see my parents, Miss Patterson?"

"Are my grandparents, here?"

"Mr. Percy from the *Tannerville Chronicle* is here."

"My angel wings keep slipping."

"I forget my lines."

Words rained down on Beth. "You will all do just fine," she reassured.

At seven sharp, she turned to her students and pressed a finger to her lips. Immediately they silenced. The moment they practiced so arduously for had arrived.

"I want you to know I'm proud of each and every one of you. You've worked hard, very hard, and I know this will be a concert to top all concerts. Everyone ready?" Heads nodded.

Beth stepped out from behind the curtain and pounded on middle "C" to draw everyone's attention. When the friendly conversations ceased and the room was hushed, the children filed onto the stage to form three tidy rows, positioning themselves evenly.

"Good evening ladies and gentlemen, boys and girls," Beth began. "Please rise to sing our national anthem." As everyone stood, Inga took her place at the piano, and soon the small schoolhouse expanded with pride as voices rose in unison, drowning out the wrong notes from the piano.

Following the anthem, the stage cleared. Beth squeezed in along the sidewall to watch the proceedings. This came as quite a surprise to most since it was customary for the teacher to remain backstage to ensure things went smoothly. But Beth thought it would be more impressive if the children ran the entire show by themselves. She had great faith in her students, but still she caught herself holding her breath.

Presently the youngest student, little Peter Brown, dressed in his Sunday best and his hair plastered down with grease, strolled out from behind the blanket and stood upon the mark that had been chalked on the stage. With his high-pitched voice he recited:

"Please don't judge me by my size,
Although I'm mighty small.
I have a most important task
To bid a welcome to you all."

He bowed solemnly, chanced a shy wave at his beaming parents and grandparents, aunts and uncles, and then exited backstage while the audience clapped exuberantly.

Following the welcome was a piano duet and after that a poem recitation. As efficiently as clockwork, one student followed another, and halfway through the hour-long program, Beth began to breathe easier.

Tom's aunt, Mary Betner, maneuvered her way over to Beth and squeezed her hand. "My dear," she whispered, "this is the best concert I've ever attended. You should be very proud."

Beth's eyes gleamed. "Thank you, Mary. I am. The children have worked very hard."

"Don't sell yourself short. I used to be a teacher. I know how much work is involved." Mary leaned closer. "Tell me, I'm dying to know. Who did you get to be Santa?"

Mary's question hit Beth like a hard-packed snowball in the stomach. "Santa?" she whispered weakly. "I don't understand. I thought the men decided among themselves."

Mary stared wide-eyed at Beth. "Didn't you see the Santa suit in the cellar?"

The truth was Beth had never ventured into the cellar. There had simply been no need and, besides, the place was too dark and creepy to encourage exploration.

"Listen dear," Mary advised, "you'd better find someone quick, or there's going to be some very disappointed children."

Beth desperately wanted to sit down and bawl. A Christmas concert with no Santa! What could be worse! But she had no time for self-pity. She had to find a willing Santa and fast! She scoured the room for a likely volunteer.

Bill, maybe he'd do it, but then she thought, who was she kidding? He'd never agree.

Lars Anderstom? She could just imagine it. *Have ew been a gewd little boy?* His accent would immediately reveal his identity and negate any beliefs of Santa's existence.

"How about Earl, would he do it?" she asked Mary.

"*My* Earl? Not a chance. He did it one year and he said never again. He does the auction at the box social and figures that's plenty."

Beth spotted Tom. Now, he might do it. After all, he was fond of Davy. And he was on the school board. One didn't take on a position like that if he didn't care for the welfare of children. There was only one way to find out and that was to ask him, and if he refused, then she was prepared to beg. The concert's success and, more importantly, her job, were at stake. She wouldn't let pride stand in her way.

Resolutely she edged between the bench seats, apologizing to those she disturbed. Finally she reached Tom.

"Tom, I need to speak with you," she whispered.

Tom frowned. "Now?" he whispered back. "Can't it wait until the concert is over?"

"No, I'm sorry it can't. Please." Conscious of the disapproving looks cast upon her, she quietly slipped to the back of the room to wait.

She watched Tom excuse himself. As soon as he drew closer, Beth pulled him into the cloakroom and closed the door behind them.

"What's the matter?"

Beth wrung her hands, not certain which would be the best way to approach this. Finally, she just blurted it out. "Tom, I need you to be Santa."

"What?"

"I never realized it was up to me to find someone. I thought—well, never mind, it doesn't matter now what I thought. Oh Tom, please just say you'll do it. Otherwise the children will be devastated and the concert will be ruined and it will all be my fault." She reached out and grasped his forearms. Realizing she was squeezing them a bit too much, she released her grip, and clasped her hands nervously between her breasts.

"But I don't know anything about kids."

"You're good with Davy."

"You think so?" Tom smiled. Suddenly, he shook his head. "I can't be Santa. What if Davy recognizes me?"

Beth shook her head. "He won't. He's so wound up, he wouldn't even recognize *me* if I were Santa."

"Good. Then you do it," he said, taking a step toward the door.

Beth grabbed his arm again. "Please." Her bottom lip began to tremble. "I'm begging you."

"Oh, all right, I'll do it. Where's the suit?"

"In the cellar, but I'm too afraid to go down there to get it." She handed him a wall lantern.

*

Tom lifted the trap door in the floor and grimaced. He could understand why she didn't want to go down there herself; the place had always given him the willies. Lantern in hand, he proceeded down the stairs into the dank smelling cellar. Above his head, the schoolroom's floor reverberated from activity and dust from the floor joists sifted down onto his shoulders. He looked around, and sure enough, he found a large box marked "Santa Suit." He set the lantern down and carried the box awkwardly up to the cloakroom, and then went back to retrieve the lantern. When he returned, Beth was shaking the creases out of the suit.

She held the pants for him. "Hurry, we haven't much time." While he stepped into them, draping the loose suspenders over his shoulders, she delved into the box and came out with a silky white wig and beard. She slipped the beard over his head, unmindful of the stinging snap she gave his chin with the elastic, then slapped the wig on his head and topped it off with the red stocking cap.

"I'll need a pillow or something," Tom said, holding the red pant's expansive girth away from his body.

"Here," She grabbed a couple of coats off the stack on the table and stuffed them down inside.

Tom grinned lasciviously from ear to ear behind the beard. *Who'd have thought the prim little schoolteacher would be shoving her hand where she definitely had no business shoving it.* When he felt himself becoming aroused, Tom grabbed the coats from her. "I'll do it. Get the jacket."

She held it while he shoved his arms into the sleeves, and then came around front of him and buttoned it over his lumpy girth. As if he were a helpless child, Tom held his arms out as she wrapped the wide black Santa belt around his waist and cinched it tight to hold the "belly" from slipping down a pant leg. She stood back to scrutinize the Santa before her.

"How do I look?"

"Passable, but your suit's all creased."

"Well, what do you expect?" he retorted. "I've come all the way from the North Pole in a sleigh." His eyes twinkled behind the beard, like the jolly old man himself.

Beth laughed in relief, hugged him around the neck and kissed his bearded cheek in gratitude. Then embarrassed, almost mortified—her cheeks flaming nearly as deep red as the flannel suit—she shoved the empty box under the table.

"The class is going to recite 'A Visit from Saint Nick.' Come in anytime near the end." She slipped back into the classroom and Tom hoped no one would speculate about the schoolteacher's heightened color.

He stood listening at the door for his cue, unable to ignore the sweet familiar scent of her hair lingering in his silky beard nor the memory of her arms around him. He'd been as surprised as she was by the impulsive hug and kiss. He wished he hadn't been wearing the beard. Then he would have felt her lips upon . . . Stop it! He was beginning to be aroused again. *Wouldn't that make a great entrance? Santa walking in with an erection.* He forced himself to think of the children and what he should do when he got inside.

" . . . and laying his finger aside of his nose." Oh hell, that was his cue. Taking a deep breath and nearly choking on a bit of beard fluff, he opened the door.

No one, other than Santa, could get away with interrupting a group recitation. With a hearty "Ho, Ho, Ho, Merry Christmas," Tom ran down the center aisle to the front of the classroom, ringing a large circle of sleigh bells and causing quite a commotion. Babies began to cry in fright, but the toddlers and older children crowded around him, while the oldest ones, wise to the Santa sham, stood back lest someone think they still believed in such nonsense.

Tom was rather surprised to find he was enjoying himself. Under the guise of Santa, he felt completely at ease with the children.

"All right, boys and girls," his voice boomed above the din, "who'd like to help me hand out these presents I see here under the tree?" After a plethora of "me, me, me's," he realized he couldn't very well choose one student over another without playing favorites, something the *true* Santa would never do. "I've got an idea," he said. "Your teacher can be my helper. What's her name?"

A chorus of children chimed, "Miss Patterson."

Beth was shaking her head in refusal even before Santa motioned her to come forward. "All right, Miss Patterson, come give me a hand." When he saw her hesitate, he hooked his thumbs into his belt and ordered, "Hurry up now. I can't keep those reindeer waiting all night."

Beth was pushed to the front while Santa plunked his bulky body down upon the piano stool, playfully spinning around and around. When he stopped, Beth was standing before him, arms akimbo, green eyes sparkling. "No spinning on the piano stool, please."

"Right. Sorry, Miss Patterson."

The children giggled, delighted to see Santa reprimanded by their teacher.

Beth handed Tom the first treat bag. "This one is for Peter Brown, Santa."

"Ho, Ho, Ho. Peter Brown, come on up here and sit on my knee for a bit. We need to talk." The boy climbed up on Tom's knee and Tom proceeded to question him. "So Peter, have you been a good boy this year?"

"Uh huh."

"Helping with the chores?"

"Uh huh."

"Do you want anything special for Christmas?"

"Uh huh," he answered again, leaning in so close to inspect Santa's beard that Tom had to set him upright.

"And what would that be. Speak nice and loud, 'cause Santa can't hear too well."

"I want a baby brother."

Tom chuckled while Peter's parents shrank in their seats.

"A baby brother. Well, only God gives out babies. But I'll bring you something else. How would that be?"

"Okay, I guess." He slid off Santa's knee and took his treat bag to show his parents.

*

If ever Beth wanted to say a prayer of gratitude, it was now. Tom was a spectacular Santa. He hugged and ho ho ho'ed, handed out candy bags, and entertained parent and child alike. When he finally raced out the school, everyone applauded enthusiastically. As far as she was concerned, his actions tonight canceled any offensive or embarrassing comment that he had previously made to her.

While the children opened their treat bags to find candies and oranges and little toys, the women set out the lunch. There wasn't a mother there who didn't congratulate Beth on the best Christmas concert Whistle Creek had ever had. Beth merely smiled her thanks, humbled by the fact it had very nearly been the worst Christmas concert in the history of Whistle Creek.

Tom returned a few minutes later, the back of his shirt damp, and the dark hair at the nape of his neck curled with perspiration. He stopped at the copper boiler for a coffee, proceeded to the lunch table, and piled a serviette high with goodies. As he made his way to sit with Mary and Earl, he received several hearty back slaps and secretive congratulations on a job well done. He barely seated himself before Davy came over to show him what he'd received from Santa.

Across the room, Beth watched Tom and Davy, their heads close together, taking turns peering through a miniature kaleidoscope. Beth smiled. Tom was a good role model for Davy. At that very moment, Tom glanced at her and returned her smile.

And she felt her heart trip a little.

Chapter 9

Wagons lined up on either side of Whistle Creek's First Methodist Church. It was Christmas Eve and families, bundled in layers of clothing to ward off the cold night air, came in masses to attend the evening service. The yellow glow from the candles and oil lamps inside bid one and all a warm welcome, and soon the small church was filled to capacity.

At the front, fresh evergreen boughs and holly sprigs graced the altar, and Beth had to agree with Davy; she had never seen anything so beautiful.

They sat on the left hand side of the church, squeezed into the pew like peas in an overcrowded pod. Ahead of them, on the opposite side, Bill sat with Annaleese and her family. He spent every spare minute he had with the Hewns. Mr. Hewn worked as a section man for the railway and was often away from home. To ingratiate himself with the family, Bill volunteered to do the chores during his absence. With no boys in the family, his help was most welcome, especially by Mrs. Hewn.

For the third time, Davy pried himself loose from between Beth and the bulky man sitting on the other side to stand and have a gander about. The man smiled tolerantly, though Beth sensed growing annoyance. Still, she decided her little brother was no more restless than any other child on Christmas Eve, so she reprimanded him only slightly. "Davy, you'll have to try to sit still when the service starts."

"I will. I'm just lookin' to see if Tom is here." Suddenly he pointed to the doorway at the back of the church. "Look, there he is. He's with Mr. and Mrs. Betner."

Davy quickly slipped past her and she managed to grab him by the elbow. "Where are you going?" she whispered.

"I'm going to say hi."

"No, you're not." She tightened her grip on his spindly arm. "The service is about to start any minute. You can talk to him afterward. Now sit."

"Jeepers." Clearly miffed, Davy sat down, wiggling his rump into the bench seat. Before long, he rotated again to see if he could see his friend. Beth got him facing forward just as Reverend Harding stepped up to the pulpit with the opening prayer.

When everyone rose to sing the first hymn, she held the hymnal low to accommodate her little brother who was just beginning to read. She needn't have bothered since he was standing on the pew facing backwards, trying to catch Tom's attention. Those nearest were amused by the lad's actions, but Beth wasn't. With a swipe of her arm, she hauled him off the pew to stand beside her.

"Enough!" she whispered vehemently. "Keep it up and you'll get a lump of coal from Santa."

Apparently the ultimate threat worked, because he meekly endured the rest of the service, never once turning about. But Beth, occasionally hearing a strong clear male voice singing above all the others, had to fight temptation not to turn and look herself.

Immediately after the service, the moment there was a clear passage, Davy grabbed Beth's hand and made a bee-line toward Tom who was sandwiched between the Betners. He pushed past Earl and tugged on the hem of Tom's suit jacket. Tom turned and, upon seeing the boy, grinned. "Whoa there, Bud. Don't tear my suit. I've only got the one."

"For heaven's sake, Davy, be careful," Beth admonished.

Tom smiled at her, immediately noting she'd let her hair hang loosely around her face. It suited her. "Good evening, Beth."

"Hello, Tom. Mary, Earl. Merry Christmas." To Tom she added politely, "That was a lovely service."

"Yes, yes it was," he replied just as courteously. "Lots of Christmas carols."

Davy piped up. "I could hear you singing, Tom. You sing real good!"

"Yes, you do." It was out before Beth knew she was even going to say it.

Tom laughed off the compliment. "Must have been someone else." Then speaking to Davy, he added, "Though when I was your age I used to sit on the front stoop and sing at night. Pretty soon, I'd have a whole chorus of coyotes joining in. We got so good, we started singing harmony."

"Ah, go on." Davy knew a yarn when he heard one.

"No. It's true."

Mary gave Tom a good-natured slap. "Such a story and in church no less!" Then drawing Beth aside, she asked, "My dear, Earl and I were wondering if you and the boys would care to join us tomorrow?"

Beth was taken aback. "Oh, Mary, how nice of you to ask, but we wouldn't want to intrude."

"Nonsense! I love cooking for a crowd and now that most of our gang has moved away—well, it just doesn't seem like Christmas unless the house is full. And our turkey is huge this year. Believe me, you'd be doing us a favor." Mary wrapped her arm about Beth's shoulders. "And if the boys want, they can go sledding. Maybe all of us. And then later we could warm up with some hot cocoa."

She was very persuasive and Beth felt herself weakening. "It does sound wonderful, but I imagine Bill will be going to the Hewn's."

"Then you and Davy come."

"May I bring something?"

"It's not necessary."

"I'd honestly like to. I baked Christmas pudding and I didn't realize until it was too late that the recipe said it would feed twelve."

Mary laughed. "Then this is working out perfectly, because I didn't get around to making mine. You bring your pudding and I'll take care of the rest. I plan on having the meal around two. But come early so we can visit while things cook."

The two ladies returned to the men.

"Ready to go, dear?" Earl asked his wife.

"Yes, I think so. I want to get the turkey prepared tonight." She turned to Tom. "Be sure to bring your guitar tomorrow. Maybe you could favor the Pattersons with some of those lovely coyote carols."

Tom and Beth looked wide-eyed at each other and uttered in unison, "You're going to Mary's for Christmas?"

Davy was exuberant about spending the day with Tom. He let out a whoop and a holler, the likes Whistle Creek's First Methodist Church had never heard, and announced, "This is going to be some Christmas!"

Mary smiled. "Yes, hopefully one we will all remember fondly."

*

"Well, that takes care of everything." Mary removed her apron and draped it over a chair. "The potatoes and turnips just have to finish cooking and in a few minutes Earl can carve the turkey. Let's sit and relax a bit." She led Beth into the parlor. "Funny, I thought Tom would have been here by now."

A minute later, Tom burst loudly into the kitchen, stomping the snow off his boots onto a mat. He had a box of chocolates in one hand and his guitar in the other. "Merry Christmas, everyone," he yelled.

There was a scramble between Mary and Davy, but Mary, despite her size, got to him first. She threw her arms around him, chocolates, guitar, and all, and planted a smacking smooch upon his cheek. "Merry Christmas, Tom dear," she said, hugging him close, rocking him like a six-foot tall baby.

Tom grinned helplessly over her shoulder.

Earl came to the rescue. "Woman, at least let the poor man put his things down before you attack him." He divested Tom of his load. "Sure doesn't get that excited when *I* walk through the door."

"That'll be the day when you come home with chocolates," Mary chided.

"Ah, you poor dear. How you suffer." Tom laughed and draped his heavy coat onto a chair and sat down to yank off his boots.

Davy had waited long enough. "Merry Christmas, Tom."

"And to you too, Bud." Tom picked him up, squeezed him, flipped him upside down and carried him around the kitchen, pretending he hadn't noticed he was holding the giggling, squirming boy wrong side up. "Yessiree. Something sure does smell good. Turkey, potatoes—wait a minute! What's that?" He sniffed as if testing the air and then frowned. "I just got a whiff of something rotten." He sniffed until the scent led him to turn and look at the lad's stocking feet. "Well, Davy Patterson, what in the name of holy socks do you think you're doing? Don't you know which way is up yet?" He flipped the delighted red-faced boy around. "There, that smells better."

He grabbed a couple cookies from a tray, giving one to Davy and biting off a chunk of the other before Mary slapped his fingers.

He turned to Beth standing in the doorway to the parlor. "Merry Christmas."

"Thank you. Same to you," she answered, smiling congenially.

Davy practically climbed up Tom's chest to whisper in his ear, and when Tom nodded and set him down, Davy giggled behind his hands.

Beth watched the blacksmith swallow his cookie, brush away the crumbs from his mouth and run his tongue over his teeth as he sauntered toward her. By the time she realized his intentions, it was too late to escape. He grasped her gently by her shoulders and whispered, "Mistletoe. I'd be less than a man if I let this opportunity pass by."

Panic coursed through her as he leaned forward, closer and closer, until his slate blue eyes nearly filled her vision. And then her own eyes closed just as naturally as she breathed and she felt his lips gently press against hers for a few seconds.

Peppermint. He smelled of icy peppermint, though his lips were anything but icy cool. They were soft and warm, and her stomach did a wonderful little flip-flop. *So this is what it's like to be kissed by a man. Rather nice.* Her lips turned up slightly. *I feel so . . . so tingly all over.*

A second kiss brought Beth abruptly from her reverie. Her eyes popped open to find, not Tom's, but Earl's face lifting away from hers. She blushed profusely as chaotic thoughts coursed across her mind. What had Earl thought as she stood there with her eyes closed? Did he presume she was waiting for a Christmas kiss from him also? Across the kitchen, Tom leaned against the dry sink, his arms crossed in front of him, and an amused smirk upon his face.

Though she would have preferred racing out the door to cool her burning cheeks, she held her head high, and thrust her chin out as if daring him to say a word.

"Earl dear, come carve the turkey, would you please?" Mary ushered them both into the parlor and when Beth protested, insisting she should be helping, Mary answered, "Heavens, you've already helped more than any guest should." She pointed to a chair. "Sit. We'll call you when it's ready."

Tom stood until Beth was seated and then he took the armchair across from her. Davy crawled right up on his knee, no invitation extended.

"Davy," she admonished, "there are plenty of chairs."

"I know." Nevertheless, he settled comfortably against Tom's chest.

"Where's Bill?" Tom asked, rearranging Davy so the boy's bony butt didn't dig into his thigh.

"At Annaleese Hewn's," she replied.

"I've seen them together around town." He turned to Davy, who, at the moment, was playing with the strings of his bolo tie. "So, Bud, what did you get from Santa?"

Davy sat forward on his knee. "A spinning top. And it whistles. Don't it, Beth? It's in my coat. Wanna see it?"

"I sure do."

Davy scrambled off his knee and when the boy was out of earshot, Tom said, "I hope you don't mind, but I have a gift for him."

"That wasn't necessary."

He shrugged. "I wanted to. It's my old knife. My pa gave it to me when I was about Davy's age. He's had his eye on it for some time now, and I don't need two."

"But it's from your father. Are you sure?"

"I'm sure." He placed the small wrapped package under the tree and was back in his chair before Davy returned. Soon the two of them were on their hands and knees, chasing the spinning top across the hardwood floor, while Beth lifted her feet whenever it scooted past.

Before long, Mary called them for dinner. "Beth, why don't you sit here and, Tom, you take the seat on her left." She steered Davy by the shoulders to the opposite side. "How would you like to sit beside Earl on the other side? That's a boy."

Tom shook his head and decided if there was one thing his dear aunt lacked, it was subtlety. Mistletoe in every doorway. Special seating arrangement. What a matchmaker! She just couldn't bear to see anyone unattached.

"Shall we bow and join hands for grace?" Mary suggested as she took her seat.

"Who's Grace?" Davy asked.

Beth cringed.

Not to embarrass the boy, Tom patiently explained, "Grace is the prayer we say before we eat to ask God to bless the food."

"You say prayers before you eat?" The look on his face displayed that this was something he'd never before considered. "Gee, I only say prayers at night." He shrugged his shoulders as if he didn't care, so long as he got to eat soon.

Around the table, they all joined hands. Tom's large hand covered Beth's, his fingers curling hers up inside his palm, and he gave her hand a gentle squeeze.

*

"Let's go, Tom." Davy positioned the sled at the top of the hill.

"You go ahead. I'd better wait awhile. I think I overdid it on your sister's Christmas pudding. Here, I'll help you get going." He held the sled while Davy climbed aboard. "Ready?"

At the boy's nod, Tom gave a hefty push. It was a swift ride to the bottom, but a long walk back up. The adults watched as the boy went repeatedly down and up the hill.

"Land sakes, I wish I had that boy's energy," Mary laughed.

"I don't know about anyone else," Tom said, "but I'm ready to give it a go." The next time the sled went down the hill, Tom was on the back with Davy squeezed between his knees.

A short while later they returned and Tom flopped back in the snow, grinning ear to ear. "That was great. You should try it, Beth."

"Yeah, you and Tom go," Davy suggested.

Mary was quick to agree. "Yes, do. That's a wonderful idea."

"But the sled's not long enough for two adults," Beth protested, shaking her head.

"Nonsense. Why it held three of my big strapping boys when they were growing up. There's plenty of room."

"Come on, Beth," Davy coaxed. "Don't be scared."

"I am *not* scared."

Tom grinned as he swept the snow off the sled. "Prove it."

Under duress, she plunked herself down on the sled, rearranging her bulky skirt so it wouldn't drag on the snow or get run over by the runners.

"You'll have to slide forward to make room for me," Tom said.

She wiggled her way forward some and he sat behind her, his bent knees cradling her body in an all too personal way. She felt his arms come around her to hold the rope, hugging her from behind. It was strangely exciting yet disconcerting at the same time.

Tom worked his feet under her skirt and then leaned forward and whispered, "There'd be more room on this sled if you were wearing those britches you had on the first time we met."

That did it! She was getting off, but just as she tried to stand, Earl gave the sled a mighty shove and she fell back into Tom's arms. They were off.

It was a fast, fearsome, heart-pounding ride. Snow from the runners sifted up into her face and the ground passed in a blur of white. Sturdy twigs, poking through the snow, snagged her skirt, pulling until the hem dragged in the snow. The sled veered right. Too late, she saw the jump made by some dare-devil. They hit it going full tilt, sending the sled airborne. Its two passengers flipped and landed like rag dolls tossed upon the snow. Tom, laughing, stood first and brushed the snow off his clothing.

Beth didn't stir.

"Beth?"

She didn't move.

Fear gripped at his heart. He quickly knelt beside her. She was lying face down in a tangled heap of skirts and petticoats. Her hair was torn from its tidy chignon and fanned out upon the snow. "Beth," he repeated, distressed by her stillness, "are you all right?" Ever so gently, he rolled her on to her back.

She blasted him with a handful of loose snow, hitting him in the face. For a fleeting second he was too surprised to respond and she took advantage of his momentary disbelief to scramble to her feet.

"That's for the remark about my britches," she said indignantly, though she had a difficult time remaining that way when he looked so comical with snow caught in his hair and eyebrows and eyelashes. Furling her skirt around her, she turned and trudged up the hill.

Thud! A snowball hit her squarely between the shoulders.

"And that's for scaring the hell out me," he called after her. "I thought you were dead." And then he threw another one at her which whizzed past her head.

She spun about. "And what was that for?"

Tom held up his hands in an innocent shrug, his grin wider than a sickle blade. "No reason. Just because."

Okay, mister, if a snowball fight is what you want, a snowball fight is what you're going to get. She retaliated by grabbing up a handful of snow, forming a hasty snowball and winging it for all she was worth at him. She took refuge behind a cluster of shrubs on the side of the hill.

He raced to the sled, flipped it on its side and took cover. They hurled snowballs back and forth in fast and furious succession, most missing their mark, but a few right on target.

Eventually there was a lull from Tom's front line. *He's stockpiling them to throw all at once.* Beth busied herself doing the same, giggling in nervous anticipation. Cautiously, she peeked around the shrubbery. He was coming toward her, waving his handkerchief above his head like a white flag.

"Truce," he called innocently.

She crouched low behind her cover. *Is that so? Come a little closer and we'll see.* She waited until she estimated he'd be just a few yards away and then she let him have it, two snowballs at a time.

Laughing, Tom charged her, dodging the barrage of snowballs. He dove at her and grabbed her arms with one hand. "Hey, lady, don't you know what a white flag means?" he asked.

"I'm not as gullible as you might think, Tom Carver! Usually when someone raises the white flag of surrender, he doesn't have the other hand loaded with ammunition," she responded, laughing.

He brought his hand from behind his back. "Guilty," he confessed and then tossed the snowballs high in the air so they would come down on her. She ducked them.

Laughing, the couple fell back on the snow, exhausted, and stared at the clear blue sky above them. Then Tom began to chuckle and soon his chuckle turned into a down right good laugh that chugged puffs of white vapor into the air like steam from a locomotive engine.

"What? What's so funny?"

"Oh nothing." He laughed in spite of his reply.

"What? Tell me!"

He could barely get the words out. The more he thought of it the funnier it seemed. "I just remembered the last time I pelted a teacher with a snowball." He broke into another spasm. "He gave me the strap for it." By now, tears were rolling down his face.

Beth raised herself on her elbow and looked at him in disbelief. "And that's funny?"

"No," he answered and then rolled back and forth, arms folded across his gut as he succumbed to another fit of laughter. "It hurt like the dickens."

She stared at him for a minute and then began laughing too. It was ludicrous to laugh about something so serious, but somehow that made it seem all the more hilarious, and they rolled on the snow holding their sides.

Finally, when the humor passed, Tom turned and studied Beth, a smile still playing on his lips. He hadn't had a good belly laugh in a long time. It felt wonderful, and it felt even more wonderful because he had shared it with her. "You know," he said, "I think that's the first time I've ever heard you laugh. I like it."

Beth sat up abruptly.

"And your hair, you should leave it down, like at the Christmas concert. It's real pretty that way."

Pretty! She was unaccustomed to compliments, and especially from him. He was making it increasingly difficult not to like him. It had been so much easier to keep her guard when he had been taunting her. She hastily rolled her damp hair and pinned it back up as best she could and then stood, brushing the snow from the folds of her skirt.

"We'd better get the sled back up the hill before Davy has a fit." She marched on ahead of him, leaving him to drag the sled. And he didn't mind one bit because he got to watch the sway of her skirt as she sallied up the hill. *Not bad, not bad at all.*

Chapter 10

The moment the sun started sinking behind the hill, the temperature dropped drastically and the exhausted group hurried back to the Betner's home.

"Now you all go into the parlor," Mary instructed, taking everyone's coats. "Why don't you get out your guitar, Tom, while I fix us something warm to eat. Earl, would you help me, please?"

It amused Beth the way Mary could take control, firing orders and everyone automatically obeying them. She presumed that years of teaching in a one-room schoolhouse had made Mary that way and it was only a matter of time until she would be the same. She smiled, thinking that, as far as Bill was concerned, she was already too bossy.

After tossing a log into the fireplace, Tom took up his guitar. He tuned it for a minute and then tuned some more, as if reluctant to start playing. "I'm afraid Mary's expectations far exceed my talent," he confessed, but when his fingers gently strummed the guitar and he sang *Silent Night,* Beth was nearly breathless.

"That was beautiful."

"It was written for the guitar," he said simply, taking no credit for his own ability. "Now, what would you like to sing?"

Sing? There was no way under the sun she was going to sing, when he sang like an angel and she like an alley cat.

"Why . . . ," she stammered, " . . . I don't know."

"I know!" Davy piped up. "Can you play *Old Dan Tucker?*"

Tom laughed. "It's not exactly Christmassy, but sure, why not."

"Goodie. You play, and me and Beth will sing."

Tom began to strum.

"Old Dan Tucker was a fine old man. Washed his face in a frying pan . . . " Davy had no qualms about his singing ability when perhaps he should have. He belted out the first verse, got miserably lost in the second, and by the third verse, Beth, whether she wanted to or not, was singing solo. At least Tom had the good manners to ignore the nervous wavering of her slightly off-key voice.

It was a tremendous relief for her when Mary and Earl entered carrying mugs of steaming cocoa and a large tray filled with turkey buns and rich cookies and cakes.

Afterwards, while the adults visited, Davy entertained himself by quietly picking at the guitar strings. If the boy's playing with his guitar bothered him, Tom never said. Soon thereafter, Davy climbed up into his lap, apparently having mastered the instrument.

"Getting tired, Bud?" Tom asked when the boy snuggled his head against his shoulder.

"No," Davy replied groggily.

Beth rose. "I think he's ready for bed. It's been a long day."

"Let me give him my present first, okay?"

Davy's heavy eyelids opened wider and he sat forward. "You got me a present?"

"Nope, just checking to see if you could hear with your eyes closed."

Beth retrieved the gift from under the tree, passed it to Tom who in turn passed it to Davy. "Merry Christmas, Bud."

"Gee thanks." He tore off the paper and when he saw the gift, he was momentarily speechless. Then the words started tumbling out. "Oh boy! Wow! You're giving me your knife?" He turned it over and over. "Wow. Now I can whittle anything I want. Gee thanks, Tom." Davy hugged him, then jumped off his knee and ran to show his sister. "Look, now I have my very own knife."

"I see. Aren't you lucky."

"Come this spring, when the sap is running," Tom said, "I'll teach you how to make a whistle from a willow branch."

Davy showed Earl and Mary his knife, but never let it out of his hands. "This is the best Christmas ever, isn't it, Beth?"

"Yes. We've had a wonderful day. Thank you ever so much for your hospitality, Mary and Earl." She stood. "It's getting late. We should be going."

"I'll go get your coats."

Tom stood and her heart gave a little flutter when he smiled at her. "And as for you, Mr. Carver," she added, thinking she needed to say something to him, "don't think you can throw snowballs at this schoolteacher just any day and get away with it. I may be forced to administer the strap."

Grinning, he stepped forward. Her nose barely came to his shoulder. "Miss Patterson, I don't think I have anything to worry about."

She laughed lightly, enjoying the unfamiliar tingle his close proximity evoked.

Mary returned. "Why don't you walk them home, Tom? By the looks of Davy, he's not going to make it under his own steam."

Beth would have preferred to bid him goodnight in the presence of the Betners, but Mary was right—as excited as the lad was with his gift, Davy could barely keep his eyes open. He whined while they slid his arms into his coat, all the while sleepily insisting that he wasn't tired.

Tom hoisted him up in his arms. Davy hugged Tom's waist with his legs, wrapped his arms around his neck, and nestled his face in the thick sheepskin collar.

They quickly said their goodbyes and thank yous and ventured out into the cold night.

*

Their breath formed small white clouds as they strolled down the main street. Beth smiled at Davy sleeping in Tom's arms and reached across to pull his collar up around his neck.

"He loved the knife. Thank you."

"He did, didn't he?" He was more than pleased with Davy's

reaction. He peered down at the little tyke. As sure as the night air chilled his lungs, this boy warmed his heart.

She opened the door and Tom entered. He waited for her to follow and then kicked the door shut with his heel.

"You get the lantern. I'll carry him to bed," he whispered as he knocked the snow off his boots.

She quickly doffed her coat, then lit the lamp. She followed him into the boys' room. He laid Davy on the bed, and proceeded to remove his coat while she struggled with his boots.

"I'm not going to bother changing him into his night shirt," she whispered. "He's too tired and it's freezing in here."

Tom lifted him up and she pulled back the covers.

"I think he'll need the extra quilt," she said.

He looked around the dimly lit room until he spotted a quilt folded on a chair at the foot of the bed. "This one?" he asked in hushed tones.

"Yes, please."

He handed it to her and then stood back as she draped it over the sleeping lad. As she bent to straighten the cover, coppery strands of hair fell about her face like a golden veil. The soft glow from the lantern cast her features a warm honey color.

"Ah," she whispered, "isn't that sweet? He won't let go of the knife. See?"

"Yes," Tom whispered hoarsely, though he hadn't seen at all. His eyes were fully focused on her delicate profile, her soft full lips, then down her slim silhouette.

She glanced at him and he knew she saw desire in his eyes. She quickly started tucking Davy in, ardently pushing the blankets in around the boy until he was shrouded like an Egyptian mummy.

Tom reached out and touched her arm, halting her administrations. "Beth," he chided softly, a gentle gruffness to his voice, "he has to breathe." He loosened the blankets, eased the pocketknife from Davy's hand and set it beside his pillow where he would easily find it in the morning.

Silently, they exited the room. Her hands shook as she busied herself with the task of getting a fire laid in the stove.

Tom couldn't think of a reason to stay any longer, yet he was loathe to end this wonderful day. He knelt beside the wood box and handed the split firewood to her. "Bill's not home yet?" he asked, then immediately wished he hadn't. *Of course he's not home. Any idiot could see that.*

Beth closed the cast iron door and rose in one fluid motion. She retrieved the whiskbroom hanging behind the stove and bent to sweep up the bark chips and dirt. "I really don't expect him home yet."

"I suppose not. Those two getting kinda serious?"

"Oh, I think they're just good friends. After all, he's only sixteen." She emptied the debris into the top of the stove.

He chuckled. "Don't be so sure. When I was sixteen, I had more on my mind than just being friends with a girl."

Her body grew rigid and he knew he'd overstepped the boundaries of polite conversation.

"Well," she said, shoving the dustpan and broom against his chest, "I am sure you were notorious among the young ladies of Whistle Creek, but Bill is nothing like that. He knows how to treat a lady!"

Yup, he deserved that one. As he hung up the broom he told himself to get home before he said anything else stupid. And with all good intentions of leaving, he *still* kept on talking. "I had a good time today. Did you?"

"Yes. Mary and Earl made us feel so welcome."

Tom relaxed some, relieved she was still speaking to him. "Yeah, they're great. My Mom and Dad and my two sisters died when I was twelve. Mary and Earl took me in. They were real good to me."

He noticed her green eyes seem to lose luster, and remembering she had lost both her parents not that long ago, he felt contrite. "I'm sorry. I didn't mean to spoil this day by reminding you of your recent loss. You know, if you ever need to talk to someone, I'm available."

She shook her head. "Thank you, but I'm fine."

He nodded and took a step toward the door. "I guess I'd better get back. Knowing Mary, she's going to want everything cleaned up before she goes to bed. Earl likely needs some reinforcement."

"I imagine he's up to his armpits in a basin full of dirty dishes."

"Probably." And they both smiled at the image.

"I'm very impressed by Mary. She is so organized. Everything planned to the last detail."

"Yup, right down to the mistletoe and the seating arrangement." Tom grinned. "She fancies herself a matchmaker, you know."

"I'm sure she's very good . . ." Her comment dwindled to nothing. "Between whom?" she asked cautiously. Then her eyes widened with sudden clarity. "You and me? Why that's preposterous! Tom, you have to set her straight. I mean, think of it. It's absurd. We're as opposite as day and night. And besides, I'm only nineteen, and you're—well, I mean—not that someone your age is . . . "

Tom cut her off. "I'm thirty-five. I'm not ready for the glue factory quite yet."

"Oh, no, I didn't mean . . . please . . . "

"Forget it. I know what you're getting at and you're right. Mary is wasting her time. After this thing with Abigail, I'm not ready for another relationship . . . not for a while anyhow." He decided to change the subject. "Are you going to the New Year's Eve skating party? Davy would enjoy it."

"We hadn't planned on going. No skates."

"I'm sure Earl and Mary have extras if you decide to go."

"Are you going?"

He wondered if his answer would influence her decision. "Probably." He found he was holding his breath waiting for her answer.

She took her time deciding, finally saying, "It *would* be an enjoyable way to bring in the New Year. I'll ask the boys tomorrow."

"Good. A word of advice though. If you go, dress warmly. A person can get chilled on the ice."

She smiled, eyeing him sideways. "What, no sarcastic comment about wearing britches? You're slipping, Mr. Carver."

A sliver of a smile crossed his face. "I think that joke is wearing thin, don't you, Miss Patterson?" They stood only a breath apart and he was struck with her beauty. Her lips were lush and a voice inside his head urged, *"kiss her."* He wanted to. All he would have to do is just lean forward and brush his lips against hers. Even at this distance, he could smell the sweet scent of her and he wondered if her full lips would taste as good. He longed to thread his fingers into her copper strands and hold her head as he deepened the kiss. Suddenly Tom halted his wayward thoughts. It was definitely time to leave.

"I best get a move on if I'm going to be any help to Earl."

"I suppose."

"Goodnight, Beth."

"Goodnight."

Beth closed the door and leaned back against it. Her heart beat erratically. For a moment, when he had gazed at her with an intensity that nearly frightened her, she had thought he might kiss her goodnight. She wanted him to, yet at the same time she was relieved he hadn't. A little voice within needled her, saying, *"coward,"* to which she replied silently, *"just cautious."* Too bad being cautious left such a dreadful numbness in her chest.

She slid into the chair at the table, suddenly feeling melancholy. After such a marvelous day, she shouldn't be gloomy at all. But she was and, though she didn't want to admit it, she knew why. While most adults were still out enjoying the company of others, she was home at eight o'clock, sitting all by herself because she had to watch Davy. Normally, she didn't begrudge her responsibilities, but tonight was different. A lump of loneliness obstructed her throat, almost choking her.

She would give anything to have someone she could disclose her secrets to, someone who would listen and understand. Someone who would hold her close and tell her everything would be fine. Someone who would never turn her in for the criminal she was.

The fire in the stove burned down. Beth added more wood and slid her chair closer to the heat. Now toasty warm, she closed her eyes and dreamily allowed herself to imagine that she was like any other young lady on the cusp of womanhood. She pretended she no past and only happiness to fill her days. A languid smile crossed her lips. She was attending a fancy Christmas party. Couples danced. The ladies' gossamer dresses belled out as they twirled about the dance floor. When Beth entered the hall there was a quiet hush and all eyes turned in her direction. So lovely. How beautiful. Royalty. Soft praises drifted about her. The skirt of her shimmering sapphire dress hung like a delicate bluebell from her waist. Underneath, layers and layers of white chiffon clouds whispered as she floated to the center of the room. Women curtsied as she glided past. Men bowed. The crowd moved closer until they surrounded her. The scene shifted and she found herself high in a tree that overlooked the dance floor. The sun peeked through the green leaves dappling her lovely dress with bright shapes of light. She looked down as the dancers twirled. She climbed higher. The branches snagged her beautiful dress.

Do stand back. I may fall.

Fall from grace, fall from grace, the crowd chanted.

Looking for Cally, Miss Patterson?

Did you kill your uncle, Miss Patterson?

Guilty! A faceless being draped a noose around her neck and the branch broke. She dropped.

Beth awoke with a scream caught in her throat.

She was on the floor, sprawled out beside the kitchen chair. Her heart clenched in her chest and she could barely breathe. It was several minutes before she was steady enough to stand. Though it was nothing more than a dream, probably brought on by too many rich foods, she couldn't help thinking how distressing it was to end this glorious day with such an ugly, terrifying nightmare.

The clock on the wall said ten-thirty so she prepared for bed. Despite exhaustion, she couldn't fall asleep. Every time she closed her eyes, she saw the noose dangling in front of her. Was the dream an omen or the guilt of her crime surfacing? She prayed for the strength to carry on. And mercy for her sins. Eventually, she drifted off to sleep.

*

Across the night sky, ice crystals dispersed the light of the roaring bonfire, forming a glowing canopy over those skating on Whistle Pond. Noisy children darted across the ice in wild abandonment, their squeals and laughter carrying clear and crisp upon the night air, their skates chattering loudly across the rough ice surface. Amid the maze of children, adults, some paired arm and arm, skated around the perimeter in unhurried fashion as if they had the entire ice to themselves. Others preferred to watch from the sidelines, enjoying the fire's warmth.

Tom sat on a makeshift bench by the fire and tightened the laces of his skates, all the while keeping his eye on Beth inching her way around the outside of the cleared ice. She was bent forward at the waist and Tom chuckled to himself, thinking she looked as if she were wearing a warped corset. Anticipating a little sporting fun, he quickly finished lacing up, and skated over to her.

She took no notice of him, seemingly intent on staring at the ice directly in front of her, so Tom stooped over too, imitating her posture. "Hi," he said, pretending to scan the ice. "Did you find it yet?"

Beth eyed him peripherally, as if turning her head even the slightest might put her off balance. "Find what?"

"That soft piece of ice you're looking to fall on."

"Believe me, I haven't found any soft ice yet."

"Want some company?"

"If you like."

They skated at a snail's pace, Beth's pace. Tom gently advised, "You'd do a lot better if you tried straightening up a little."

"I've already tried that. It didn't work." She absentmindedly rubbed her backside.

"In that case," Tom said, bowing gallantly and presenting his gloved hand, "please allow me." He never once believed she'd accept his offer, thinking her far too independent, so when she placed her mittened hand in his, Tom lifted an eyebrow in surprise. "Miss Patterson," he said with feigned formality, "does this mean you're starting to like me?"

Beth smiled. "Don't flatter yourself, Mr. Carver. In case you haven't noticed, I'm not much of a skater. I am merely accepting your assistance because it's more desirable than falling, which I'm sure to do before I get back to the fire."

He gently folded her arm securely through his and they slowly skated their way around the frozen pond. "Funny, I never thought I'd hear you admit to such a thing."

"What? That I don't skate well?"

"No." He grinned his most lecherous grin and wiggled an eyebrow at her. "You said I was desirable."

Beth yanked her arm free and surely it was only pure stubbornness keeping her from going right over backwards. "I most certainly did not say that! You twisted my words again!"

Tom tilted his head back and laughed aloud, his guffaws forming puffy vapor clouds against the black pin-dotted sky. "Girl, I have never seen anyone as quick to temper as you. You're always in a huff over something. Can't you take a joke?"

"Of course I can," she snapped, "but why must I be the brunt of all your jokes?"

"Trust me, you're not." he replied. "Except for whenever

you're handy."

"Well, then perhaps it would be better if I made myself less handy." She pushed off, preparing to return to the fire by cutting across the ice, but before she'd managed even one stiff-legged step, a youngster came out from the shadows and ran smack into her, knocking her off balance. She tipped sideways, righted herself, overbalanced and then her feet went out from under her. If it hadn't been for Tom cushioning her fall, she'd have landed flat out. Instead, they both landed hard on the ice with Beth in Tom's lap.

"Sorry!" yelled the boy, skating into the darkness.

"He may be sorry," Tom said, "but I'm sure not. Fancy that. First the schoolteacher tells me I'm desirable and now she's sitting in my lap. Just say the word and we'll find somewhere private to go."

Immediately, Tom cringed, hardly believing he'd said that. He figured there had to be something in the night air, because he would never have suggested anything so provocative to her during the light of day. He fully expected to get a good dressing-down for his indelicate remark.

Once again, she surprised him. She looked angry enough to spit nails, but she gave no reply. Instead, she scrambled to her feet, apparently forgetting completely she was wearing skates. She fell again.

Oh, but this time Tom *was* the sorry one! The most vulnerable part of his anatomy was flattened beneath her palm like a plum beneath a wagon wheel. Tears formed in his eyes. He wanted to swear, certain it would help ease the pain, but when he opened his mouth all that came out was a sickly groan. Finally, he managed through his tight lips, "Sweet mercy, Beth. Move your hand."

Beth saw her hand pressed against Tom's crotch and she drew it back as if she'd touched a red-hot coal. She covered her cheeks in horror. "Oh Tom, I'm so sorry."

Tom fought the urge to cup his injured member with his hands. When Beth tried to stand again, he grabbed her waist, holding her still. "Please . . . wait!" and as if it pained him to raise his voice, he whispered the rest, "Give me a minute and then I'll help you up and take you back to the bonfire."

Gradually he eased his leg out from under Beth and crawled onto all fours before slowly standing, apparently still in great discomfort. He turned to help Beth to her feet just as Davy came skating up, landing unceremoniously in a heap at their feet.

"You gonna skate with me now, Tom?" he asked as he got back up and scraped the snow off his knees.

"Not right now, Davy. Maybe in a bit." Tom formed his grimace into a smile.

"But—"

"Davy," Beth stated firmly, "Tom told you later. Now you leave him be. He's hurt."

"Oh, sorry. You hurt your leg or something?"

Beth's eyes met Tom's, and her cheeks burned. He stared intently at her when he answered, "Yeah, Bud. You could say that." He turned his attention to Davy. "But I'll be skating circles around you in a few minutes." With a crooked grin, he tugged on the ragged pompon on Davy's hat. "You go skate some more. You need the practice. I'm gonna have some cocoa with your sister,"—he looked at Beth and she nodded—"and then I'll come for you."

Tom reached across and took Beth's hand in his and with his free arm supporting the small of her back, they slowly skated without further mishap to the banked edge. They hiked across the granular snow to the fire, filled two mugs with steaming cocoa from the large cast iron pot, and sat on the bench by the fire. The heat on their faces felt good, the cocoa in their stomachs, better. Tom pulled off his gloves so he could warm his palms with the hot mug and the backs of his hands with the fire.

"Do you have the time?" Beth asked.

He thought about asking time for what, but decided not to aggravate her further. Look what it cost him last time he made some smart aleck remark. Tom leaned back and pulled a watch from his pocket, glanced at it and then stuffed it back. "Ten fifteen."

"Good, less than two hours to go."

He noticed her pull her coat tight and hunch her shoulders up. "You cold?" he asked.

"A little. My back."

"Let's turn around then and warm the other side." They did, and the fire's heat penetrated their coats as they watched the skaters gliding by. Several smiled. Tom knew that he, the supposedly heartbroken blacksmith, and she, the prim schoolteacher were the topic of many wagging tongues. He also knew he really didn't care.

Every few minutes Davy would pass, invariably falling in front of them as he tried to show off. Tom chuckled. "He's going to start the year out as a sorry lot of bruises."

Beth smiled. "He's never been allowed to bring in the New Year before. He could barely sit still for supper, he was so excited. He thinks at the stroke of midnight something will happen, something magical. I tried to explain to him it's no different than when one minute changes to another, but he won't believe me." She shook her head. "I'm afraid he's going to be a disappointed little boy because he expects to feel different, like the world changes or something."

Tom looked at her. "I don't know. In a way, I think he's right. Things will be different. When the church bell rings in the New Year, I get this wonderful sense of excitement, you know? I've got an entire year ahead of me . . . perfect, no mistakes, no regrets. Sort of like when you've got a fresh white sheet of paper in front of you and you get to decide what to draw or write on it. It's exciting."

"It's intimidating," Beth countered quietly. She stared thoughtfully at the steam rising from her mug. "I'll be glad when this year is over. It hasn't been easy. I just hope next year is better."

There was a pensive look in her face and Tom quietly reached across and squeezed her wrist. "Hey, you'll be just fine. If there's one thing I know about you, Beth, it's you've got spunk." He released her wrist, stretched his legs out in front of him, crossed his skates, and finished his cocoa. While Beth watched the skaters, Tom allowed his mind to drift to Abigail, wondering what she was doing tonight, if she was alone or out with a friend. There was no despondency when he thought of her now. He'd accepted she was gone and that was that. He harbored no bitterness, no sadness. Nothing. Perhaps it was this emotionless state that told him that Abigail had made the right decision. He hoped she would find happiness. She deserved that and more.

Tom set his empty mug in a box. He leaned over and peered into Beth's cup. "Finished?"

"Yes, thanks."

He rose, took her empty mug and set it aside. "I'm going to go skate with Davy. Want to join us?"

"No, I think maybe I've had enough skating . . . for this year anyhow." She smiled up at him. "But you go ahead. I'll stay here by the fire."

"Okay. I'll be back in a little while to warm up again."

Tom skated off effortlessly and when he circled round the next time, he saw Beth had already exchanged her skates for her boots. She sat cross-armed, her mittened hands tucked under her armpits as if she was settled in for the duration of the year. Tom continued skating.

Five minutes later, he was startled when a youngster skated up to Davy and announced, "Your sister's hurt."

Chapter 11

Tom raced Davy back to the fire and as he ran across the snow, he was relieved to hear Beth say to the throng of concerned people gathered around, "I'm fine, really."

Bill was with her, bent over her foot, but obviously unsure what to do.

"Excuse me, let me through," Tom ordered, his voice calm and even. When Bill saw Tom coming, he backed away.

"Beth, what happened?" Tom asked as he knelt beside her. Concern furrowed his brow.

"I think I sprained my ankle. Nothing serious." Yet when Tom reached down to check, she stopped him. "Don't. Please, don't touch it."

Everyone crowded closer, their attention only adding to her distress. She was so relieved when Tom asked, "Would you like me to take you home?"

"Please." She didn't quite know how he'd manage it without jarring her foot and causing her a great deal of pain, but she couldn't stay here, not with everyone gawking at her as if she was the main attraction in a traveling exhibit.

"It's all right, folks," Tom announced, "I'll see Miss Patterson gets home. Please, enjoy the rest of the evening."

The crowd dispersed and Tom sat down on the bench to remove his skates. Beth told Davy to do the same because it was time to go home.

"Ah gee," he whined. "I wanted to see the New Year come. It's not fair."

Her shoulders slumped. "Davy, I don't feel up to arguing with you."

Tom spoke up. "Wait a minute, Beth. Maybe he should stay." She saw his quick conspiratorial wink. "I mean after all, it's New

Year's Eve. Why should he have to miss out on all the fun, the noise, and the kissing? Bill's here to look—"

"Kissing!" Davy spat, as if the word were poisonous. "You mean they do *that* at New Year's too?"

"Why sure. Especially people who like each other. Bill will probably kiss Annaleese, and I saw a little girl eyeing you up. It would be a crying shame if she missed a chance to kiss you."

Right then and there, Davy plunked down in a snow bank and took off his skates. "Uh uh! That's yucky! No girl's gonna kiss me. Not ever!" By the time Tom had his boots on, so had Davy.

Tom commandeered Davy's scarf and gently, but firmly wrapped it around Beth's boot, immobilizing her ankle. "There, that should help." He leaned closer, speaking low so only she could hear. "Looks like you're going to be in my arms again. I could get to liking this. Come on, grab around my neck."

She was in too much discomfort to protest. He shifted her in his arms, carrying her as if she weighed no more than a small sack of seed wheat. He started for town. Davy tagged along behind, the three pairs of skates slung over his shoulder clattering with every step. They hadn't walked more than a minute, when Tom asked, "So what happened? When I left, you were sitting safely by the fire."

Beth hesitated to tell him, but knew he would worm it out of her somehow. "I went for a walk and tripped over some dead fall."

"A walk? Why in the Sam Hill were you going for a walk? Once you get away from the fire, it's darker than the inside of a black cow."

"I could see well enough. At least I thought I could."

"So you just decided to go for a walk. What were you looking for? It's a tad late for berry picking."

Beth rolled her eyes. Was he really that dense? "If you must know, I was answering the call of nature."

"Oh," Tom stated flatly. "I should have thought of that. Sorry."

*

"Get the door, would you, Davy?" Once inside, Tom carefully set Beth in a chair by the stove.

Beth leaned back and sighed in relief. "Thank you for all your help. I really appreciate it, but I don't want to keep you. I've got Davy here. We can manage now."

"Nope, I'm not leaving until your foot is tended to properly." He took a vacant chair, slipped off his boots, set them on the mat by the door. He took off his coat, helped her with hers and hung them both side by side on hooks above the mat. "Davy, I want you to take a pail and fill it with snow."

Eager to help, Davy grabbed a bucket and headed outside while Tom unwound the scarf and began working with the tight laces of her boot. "Where do you keep your scissors?"

"Whatever for?"

"To cut off your boot."

"You'll do no such thing! These are the only boots I own and I can't afford another pair. Just undo the laces and pull it off."

Tom sat back on his haunches and studied her, as if questioning her rationale.

"Beth, let me cut it off."

She shook her head.

"It'll hurt like hell if I don't cut the sides open. Dammit, I'll buy you a new pair."

"There is no need to swear, Tom. Now, these are a perfectly good pair of boots and I don't want to ruin one. If you don't want to pull the boot off, then I will."

Tom sighed in exasperation. "Fine! Lord Almighty, but you are one stubborn woman." When she opened her mouth to protest his language again, he raised his hands in surrender. "Right, no more swearing." He unlaced the boot fully and pulled it as wide apart as he could, being careful to not twist her ankle any more than necessary. His jaw tensed as he firmly grasped Beth's calf and gave the boot a slow, steady pull.

Beth sucked in her breath and bit her lip as the burning pain shot through her ankle. Tom immediately stopped, but she gritted her teeth and ordered, "Pull it off! Now! Before Davy gets back."

"I'd rather yard out my own tooth, you know."

"Just do it!"

Grimacing, he started pulling again. When the boot was finally free, he tossed it into the corner.

Beth discretely wiped a tear away. "Thank you. I'm not sure I could have done it myself."

Tom propped his back against the table leg, drew a knee up and draped his arms across it. "Yeah, well you're not welcome. I should have said to hell with your precious boot and cut it off."

"If it makes you feel any better, halfway through I almost changed my mind."

"Then why didn't you?" he demanded grimly.

"Maybe because I've got too much spunk?"

Tom glanced up to see her smiling. "I knew I'd regret telling you that."

Davy burst through the door with the pail heaped high with snow. "Is this what you want, Tom?"

"Perfect. Bring it here and I'll need that wash basin too," he said pointing. "And a towel." He dumped half the snow into the basin. "Okay, let's take a look at your ankle."

Beth lifted the hem of her skirt and presented her once dainty ankle, which was now twice its normal size.

"Better take off your stocking," Tom instructed.

"I beg your pardon?" Shocked, she dropped the hem and sat up ramrod straight.

"I said take off your stocking so I can check your ankle."

"I will not!"

Tom heaved a tired sigh. "Beth, be reasonable. I've seen a naked ankle before."

"I'm sure that is true, but it wasn't mine. It wouldn't be proper."

"Listen." His patience was rapidly depleting, "I don't give a flyin' fig about what's proper and what's not. I did what you wanted and saved your precious boot. Now it's your turn to do what I want. Take the damn stocking off . . . or I'll do it for you!"

Beth thumped her hands on the arm of the chair. "How dare you. Why I've never—"

"I'll tell you how I dare!" Tom interrupted, all patience spent. He lunged toward her as if to reach up under her skirt and unfasten the garters himself.

Incensed by his behavior, Beth slapped his hands away. "Don't you dare! I'll do it. Turn your back. You too, Davy."

She needn't have bothered telling Davy. He had spun around the minute Tom attempted to reach up under his sister's skirt.

Too angry to be embarrassed, Beth unfastened the garters, rolled down the cotton stocking and carefully slipped it off her foot, but when she took one look at her swollen ankle, her anger was replaced with dismay. "Oh my," she muttered.

Tom glanced over his shoulder and followed her gaze to her foot. He turned to have a closer look. Her swollen foot was an ugly yellow-purple. "This is a serious sprain, Beth. You really should have Doc Fisher take a look at it."

Davy turned to inspect. "Wow, it looks like a turnip." He would have touched it, but Tom stopped him. Wrapping her foot gently in a towel, he lowered it into the basin of snow and gently packed the remaining snow around her ankle.

Davy watched the entire process with great interest. "How come you're making Beth put her foot in the snow?"

"It will help decrease the swelling."

"Oh." Davy ingested that information. "Would it have helped if you put snow on your leg?"

"My leg?" Tom repeated, intent on his job and not catching Davy's meaning.

"Yeah, you hurt your leg tonight. Don't you remember?"

For the first time ever, Beth saw Tom color and having caught him so unexpectedly vulnerable, she felt prompted to lean forward, and brazenly taunt, "Yes, Tom, remember your *leg*?"

She felt so smug, so pleased with herself. Certainly it was shameless goading, and totally out of character for her, but after all the embarrassing things he had said to her, she felt justified.

Tom thoughtfully nodded as if mentally chalking up a point for her. Then he looked at her brother and smiled. "Well, Davy, when you get older you'll realize sometimes it feels good to have your leg swell."

"Huh?" Davy uttered, perplexed.

Beth could feel heat rising from her neck up face while Tom peered at her innocently. She had a mind to empty the basin of snow over his self-righteous head, and then crown him with it.

Fortunately, Davy missed the gist of the entire conversation, and was busy poking little holes in the snow with his finger. Suddenly, he stopped and jumped to his feet, racing to open the door. "Listen! I can hear the bells. It's midnight!" He stood outside, gazing up to the heavens, waiting for the magic to begin.

Tom crept up behind him, grabbed the boy by the waist, tossed him high into the air, caught him and gave him a tight squeeze and a quick kiss before releasing him. "Happy New Year, Bud."

"You too, Tom," the boy replied, and then ran excitedly to his sister, stopping short before he bumped her foot. "It's the New Year!"

Beth pulled him onto her lap and hugged him close, but Davy, always embarrassed by such affection, soon wiggled loose like a slippery fish held too tight.

He raced back to Tom and grabbed his hand. "Come on. You have to give Beth her New Year's kiss."

"You're right. I do!" Tom grinned licentiously and Beth truly knew what it felt like to be an animal with its foot caught in a trap. Her heart pounded wildly, and her throat tightened as Tom allowed Davy to lead him near. He towered above her and she tremulously looked up the long length of him until her eyes met his. She felt dizzy with anticipation. Tom lowered himself to squat beside her. His smile softened. He encased her trembling hands in his.

"Beth," he whispered, his voice so strangely hoarse it sent lovely shivers dancing up her spine. "This is a New Year. My clean sheet of paper, no past, no regrets, only the future to do with as I choose." With the slightest of smiles, he whispered, "I choose this." He leaned forward and gently brushed her lips with his, testing her response.

His kiss was as light as a butterfly's wing upon her lips, and she waited breathlessly for its return. It did, alighting again, this time staying, becoming more ardent, yet never commanding, never threatening. Beth felt weak, liquid. Her lips parted slightly and Tom's breath joined hers in a sweet sigh. And the butterfly she felt upon her lips now fluttered in her heart. She felt his lips slowly pull away from hers.

"You see, there is magic," Tom whispered before leaning back on his haunches, and Beth thought, *yes, magic*. She was unaware a third face had been leaning in just as closely to witness their kiss.

"Yee-uck!" Davy exclaimed, drawing back and breaking the spell. "Boy, am I glad I don't have a girlfriend!"

Involuntarily, Beth's hands flew to her cheeks. "I am not Tom's girlfriend! I am merely his friend," she said. *When had he changed from a threat to a friend?* She couldn't decide whether his rise in status excited her or frightened her.

"But you're a girl," Davy interrupted her puzzled thoughts, "and you're Tom's friend so how come you're not his girlfriend?"

She knew Davy wasn't trying to be difficult. He honestly didn't understand the word's nuance.

Tom was no help. "Yeah, Beth," he taunted, feigning confusion. "How come?"

"Well," she began, casting Tom a scathing glare, "there's a big difference between a girl friend and a *girlfriend*. Take Penelope Pickard. She's a girl and she's your friend, isn't she?"

Davy nodded. "But she's not my girlfriend, right?"

"That's right!" she answered, pleased her brother was so astute. Her pleasure was short lived.

" 'Cause I don't want to kiss her, but Tom, he wanted to kiss you, so that makes you his girlfriend, right?"

"No! Not right." She took a deep breath. "First of all, Tom didn't want to kiss me."

"Oh, but I did," Tom verified.

"But only because it was New Year's."

"No, not just because of that." He pulled out a chair from the table, sat with arms crossed, and leaned back until the two front chair legs lifted inches from the floor. He was obviously set to enjoy himself.

Had he been closer, Beth would have employed her one good foot to kick the chair right out from under him. To calm herself she smoothed down the folds in her skirt. There had to be some analogy to make this clear, but for the life of her, she couldn't think of one. Finally in exasperation, she said, "I guess you'll just have to take my word for it. I am not Tom's girlfriend. Now, go get ready for bed. It's late."

Davy appeared to be about as perplexed as a dog with two tails. Tom rocked forward, setting his chair back on all fours. He grabbed Davy and pulled him to stand between his knees. "Bud, I know it's hard to understand, but grown-ups kiss on special occasions, just because they want to wish each other good wishes. Now, if they kiss when it's not Christmas or New Year's or some other special occasion—"

"Like birthdays?"

Tom nodded. "Like birthdays. When they kiss for no special reason other than they just want to kiss, well, then they're likely boyfriend and girlfriend." He gave the boy a gentle swat on the rump. "Now, off to bed."

When the bedroom door closed, Beth turned on him, more than a little exasperated. "You could have volunteered that explanation earlier."

Tom shrugged. "It was more fun watching you squirm."

Beth reached down into the basin and threw snow at him.

Tom laughed, brushing the bits of snow off his chest before they melted. He got to his feet, stepping back before she threw more. "Do you have another towel? Your ankle should be bound before I leave."

"There's another in the cupboard."

While Tom tended her foot, Beth mused. If Tom waiting on her hand and foot was what the New Year was going to bring, Beth had to admit that she rather liked it. And she also had to admit that she rather liked Tom. But never to the point of being his girlfriend. Just his girl friend.

Chapter 12

It was only three days into the New Year and Tom already had regrets. First, he regretted ever having kissed Beth. Second, he regretted not having done a more thorough job when he had the chance. Tom was no beginner when it came to kissing, so it didn't make sense that such an innocent, chaste kiss should haunt him. Yet even the mere memory of it sent his blood sluicing through his veins. One thing for sure, if the opportunity ever presented itself again, he would make damn sure he kissed Beth longer and deeper . . . before someone else beat him to it.

He stood another log on end on the chopping block and split it with one downward stroke of the ax. Cutting firewood usually soothed Tom. Today he figured he could cut enough wood for two winters and still be confused. What was it about that kiss?

He wondered if it had affected Beth in the same way. She seemed to enjoy the kiss, but she had certainly become flustered when Davy suggested they were more than just friends. Why, she reacted as if the concept was totally out of the question. Obviously the age difference bothered her more than it did him. So, he was sixteen years older than her. So what?

So what? Tom's conscience spoke harshly to him. *I'll tell you what. By the time you knew how to ride horses and cuss, all Beth knew how to do was eat, sleep and spit up. She probably was learning to eat solids when you first kissed a girl. And playing with her little friends the first time you . . .*

Disheartened, Tom stopped his thoughts. Beth was right. Nineteen was too young for thirty-five. Thirty-five! Why, in horse years he *was* ready for the glue factory! Except he didn't feel old. And for darn sure, his body wasn't acting old. Every time he thought about kissing Beth good and proper, he got rigid.

In frustration, Tom swung the ax down hard. It missed the piece of wood altogether and glanced off the chopping block. *Pay attention, or you'll be minus a foot.* But concentration eluded him, so he set the ax inside the woodshed and stacked the wood.

As he worked, it came to him what he really needed was a night upstairs in Tannerville's Regal Hotel to eliminate his physical problem, at least temporarily. He looked at his watch. It was too late today, but maybe tomorrow, Saturday. Leave early in the afternoon and ride out to Tannerville, spend a pleasurable night rolling about in a cozy bed with a willing woman, one with huge smothering breasts and peroxide-bleached hair and make-up as thick as plaster. One wearing enough perfume to make his eyes water. One who would make him question if he'd be able to walk the next morning. Maybe then he could get the schoolteacher and the kiss they shared right out of his head.

But Saturday afternoon came and went, and the evening found Tom sitting at home staring at the flames in his fireplace. They danced green like the green in Beth's eyes, and the embers flared gold and copper, the color of her hair. *Confound it,* Tom chafed. What did he have to do to get her out of his mind?

He rose, went to the stove, and lifted the coffeepot. Warm enough. He poured himself a cup, then returned to watch the flames. Lately Tom felt as though he was rattling about in his big empty house like a marble in a hatbox. Maybe he should get a new dog, a puppy. Wouldn't Davy love that!

Tom smiled anticipating Davy's reaction. He hoped that someday he could have a couple of kids who were as great as Davy. Of course, he'd have to get himself a wife first.

Piece of cake. Not that he was bragging, but Tom knew he was a much sought after bachelor. Now, with Abby gone, he could have his pick of single women. If he wanted, he could be married within a week. *Okay, maybe that was bragging.*

Tom leaned back in his chair. Methodically, he considered the single women available in the area. Beth came first to mind. *Forget her. She thinks you're old, remember?* Besides, he wanted a wife, not someone he'd have to raise. *Think.* Nan Fuller, *how about her?* She was pleasant enough, but Tom didn't know if he could get around those protruding buckteeth. How did one go about kissing someone when one lip was stretched out over the other one like an overhang on a roof? *Nope, better try another.* Okay, what about Beryl Mason. *Talks incessantly.* Miranda Parsons? *Are you nuts? Too many times around the track.* Tom assessed the other single women, but decided that they were either lacking or downright unappealing. He'd swear to a life of celibacy before he'd marry any of them, and right now celibacy wasn't sitting comfortably with Tom.

The fire snapped and a large ember glowed brightly, reminding him once again of Beth's hair. *Okay, aside from her thinking that you are as old as Methuselah, how about Beth Patterson?* Now that would be one fiery marriage! He sipped his coffee, rather amused at the thought of them together. With her temper, she'd likely snap his head off as soon as the nuptials were spoken. Tom chuckled, remembering how indignant she got when he tackled her in his barn, as if *he* were the one at fault. *She had nice breasts though. Two perfect handfuls.*

Tom forced the charming memory from his head. *Concentrate!* One thing in Beth's favor, she was a damn good cook, if the box social was any indication. Too bad her attitude was so distasteful. He had to laugh. Fate had tricked them both that day. Had it only been a couple of months ago? It seemed so much longer.

He put another log in the fireplace, adjusted the damper slightly and returned to his chair. His thoughts of Beth resumed. She had been pleasant Christmas Day. Of course, that could have been for Mary and Earl's benefit. Regardless, he had enjoyed her company and when he escorted her and Davy home, she'd been amiable, at least until he made that moronic comment about his adolescent yearnings. Even he knew he was out of line with that remark.

Yup, put him and Beth in the same vicinity and trouble would soon arrive. Their turbulent relationship, if he could call their time together a relationship, reminded Tom of soda and vinegar mixed, lots of froth and fizzle. Still, he couldn't deny that their little skirmishes were exhilarating. There was something about her that brought out the devil in him.

As he drank his barely tepid coffee, he thought about her station in life. A single schoolteacher usually had eager beaus knocking at her door, but oddly enough Tom hadn't seen any men, other than Lars Anderstom, even mildly interested in Beth. He supposed Bill and Davy were the reason. Marry Beth and get two brothers in the package. Not many bachelors wanted a ready-made family.

But that didn't really bother Tom. He already had a tender spot for Davy and he could learn to tolerate Bill. And he was already falling in love with Beth.

Tom nearly choked on his coffee. *Falling in love?*

Before Christmas day, he hadn't even thought of Beth as anything more than a pain-in-the-butt, more-trouble-than-she-was-worth schoolteacher. But when she went flying off the sled and was lying there still as death in the snow, his heart constricted. Thinking back, those frightening few seconds might have been the very turning point at which he started to feel more than just mild interest in Beth Patterson. As they lobbed snowballs at each other, he saw a different side of her. She was joyous and carefree. Could one, enjoyable day—Christmas Day—have turned his heart around? Maybe, maybe not. But coupled with New Year's Eve and that kiss, Tom knew he was falling in love with Beth.

Maybe marriage to Beth Patterson was a possibility. At least they would never get bored with each other if the past few months were any indication.

Only one problem, Romeo. Beth isn't interested in an old fart like you. Chew on that for a while! He closed his eyes and smiled regardless. Lots of married couples overcame gaping age differences. There was no reason they couldn't too. He'd just have to make her forget his age by distracting her with other things. Things like his charm and his kisses for starters.

*

Beth was grateful that Earl had given her the wooden crutch as she made her way across the yard to the school. Davy stomped ahead, breaking trail in the deep snow for her.

"Look," he said, pointing ahead.

Smoke poured out the school chimney and she wondered if Bill had stopped on his way to the livery to light the fire for her. When she entered the school, she certainly didn't expect to find Tom poking firewood into the heater.

"What are you doing?" she asked.

Tom glanced over his shoulder. "Baking bread. What do you think I'm doing? I'm getting the fire going. And good morning, by the way," he added cheerfully. "Hi, Davy." He gave the boy a light shoulder punch as he passed by. Davy presented a long face, clearly demonstrating he wasn't at all pleased the holidays were over.

"But starting the fire is my job," Beth objected, removing her coat and scarf.

Tom stood, closed the heater door, and then adjusted the grate openings and the damper. "I know, but with your bad ankle, I thought you could use the help. How's it doing, anyway?"

Beth hobbled up the aisle, the crutch bearing most of her weight. "Better, thank you."

"Good." He strode over to the small cupboard behind her desk, retrieved the bottles of ink, frozen solid, and placed them around the heater's edge to thaw. "You'll have to keep an eye on these."

"I haven't forgotten yet."

"I thought you might need some help putting away the decorations, but I see you've already done that."

"The day after the concert."

"I was kinda hoping maybe there was some mistletoe left hanging somewhere, but I don't see any."

Beth smiled slightly. "Sorry, but I never put any up."

"I guess it might look like the schoolteacher was desperate for a beau." There was a glint in his eye and a wide grin on his face.

Suddenly Beth's emotions were all in a tizzy. Her heart began to patter erratically. Oh, but he had a wonderful smile and she couldn't help recalling how delightful his lips felt on hers. She never knew his kiss would be so delicious and he was only her friend. Just imagine what it would be like with someone she loved. She was jolted out of her musings when she realized she had her eyes closed and her lips pursed. She gave a sideways glance at Tom, praying he hadn't seen her.

Fortunately, Tom was speaking to Davy. "Hey, Bud, want to help with the water? I've got a surprise to tell you."

"You do? What?"

Tom nodded his head toward the door. "I'll tell you while we get the water."

Beth used the moment alone to collect herself. *Quit acting like a foolish school girl.* She took a few deep breaths and deliberately reminded herself, good kisser or not, Tom Carver was a threat. She couldn't let her guard down. For all she knew he might be using the pretense of starting the morning fire so he could garner more information about her past. If he were to discover the truth—she forced herself to concentrate on school preparations.

Minutes later Davy returned bouncing wildly. "Beth, guess what! In the spring, Tom's going to get a puppy and I can help train him. Isn't that great?"

"Hmm." Was it? She couldn't help worry Tom would use the time together to pump Davy for information.

Tom set the pails of water on the backbench, hanging the ladle from the lip of one. "I thought it was time I got another dog for company."

Beth nodded. Maybe she was being unnecessarily suspicious. Maybe Tom *was* getting a puppy because he was lonely. And maybe he included Davy in his plans, not to interrogate him, but merely because he had a soft spot for her brother. No matter his motive, Beth knew without a doubt that Tom cared deeply for Davy. It was probably the only thing she and Tom had in common. She wondered, in light of his fondness for Davy, if Tom would turn her over to the authorities if he discovered the truth.

She dared not risk finding out.

"Is there anything else you need before I go?" Tom asked.

It surprised her she almost wished there was, but she could easily manage the rest of the morning preparations. She shook her head. "Thank you for starting the fire and hauling the water."

"My pleasure," he said, walking to the door. On his way out, he mentioned casually over his shoulder, "I'll come by tomorrow morning."

"If you like," she answered indifferently. She didn't want him to think she needed his help. Still, it was awfully convenient having someone take care of the more arduous morning chores.

As she transcribed the lessons onto the blackboard, she couldn't help but smile. It was rather nice to have someone pamper her a little, even if it was because she had a sprained ankle. Hard to believe that night was over a week ago when everything was still so clear in her memory. His hands had been so gentle when he had tended her foot, his lips so tender when he kissed her. She remembered how their breath had joined in a single sigh and—

Boom! The loud report from a shotgun nearly deafened Beth. She dropped to her knees fearing a second shot might come through a window. She heard a high-pitched whistle and then, boom! Splatters of blue dappled her dress and the floor about her.

Oh no! The ink! She jumped up and, using the hem of her skirt to protect her fingers, quickly rescued the remaining bottles of ink from the stovetop. She looked about the room with dismay. Blue ink on the floor. Blue ink on the desks. Blue ink on her dress. *Why? Why? Why couldn't she get though one day without a major mishap?*

*

Tom came by the next morning, did the chores and left without one word or smart aleck remark about the ink splotches on the floor. Beth was pleasantly surprised. The students however were more than happy to poke fun at their teacher and Beth good-naturedly let them.

Tom returned the next morning and the next until Beth presumed he would do it regularly, or at least until her ankle completely healed. She began to look forward to seeing him each morning, enjoying his company far more than she ever thought possible. Still, she remained guarded.

The Thursday morning of the third week, Davy was outside making fox and goose tracks in the fresh snow, leaving Tom alone with Beth in the school. Beth stood on tiptoe before a makeshift bookcase, rearranging books.

"What are you doing?" Tom asked as he shut the door to the stove. It clanged into place.

"I'm just making room for the new readers." She resumed her task of transferring the rarely used books to the top shelf. Her hand froze in mid-air, then slowly came down to her side as she became nervously aware of Tom's presence behind her.

"Here, let me." He stepped closer until his legs brushed the back of her skirt. "What other books do you want moved?"

Books? "Uh, just this one." There were more, but his intimate proximity made her jittery and anxious.

Tom popped the book onto the shelf and straightened them all, pulling them even with the front edge of the bookcase. All the while, his chest brushed against her hair, causing irrational thoughts to bounce inside her head. When he finished, his hands dropped to her shoulders, and his thumbs lightly rubbed the tight base of her neck.

"You're tense, Beth. Do I make you nervous?"

Yes, very. "No," she replied rather shakily. "Why should you?"

"Well, because I'm a man and you're a woman and we're all alone." His thumbs ran up the soft hairs of her neck, stopping at the base of her chignon. One by one, he pulled out the hair pins, freeing her hair.

"Tom, what are you doing? Don't," she whispered breathlessly, wondering why she couldn't speak louder, wondering even more why she didn't reach up to stop him. Instead, she closed her eyes, savoring the tingly feeling as his fingers drew through her tresses.

"Leave it long today, Beth, for me." His voice was gravelly as if he, too, were having difficulty speaking.

"But I look older with it up," she protested weakly.

Tom gently turned her by the shoulders to face him, and she couldn't draw her eyes away from the half smile playing on his lips. "Now, why would you want to look older? For the children? In case you didn't know, kids think their teachers are old no matter their age. And you can't be trying to fool me because I already know. You're nineteen. Far too young for an old man like me." As he spoke, his hand caressed her nape, lowering his face to hers until his peppermint breath blew cool upon her blazing cheeks.

His mouth covered hers, gently at first until a quiet moan escaped between her lips. *Hmm, magic again,* she thought and she raised her head, seeking more. And more he gave. Each time his lips touched hers, he lingered longer. He ran his tongue along the seam of her lips. He gently nipped at her upper lip, her lower lip. His big hands gently cupped the sides of her head, tilting it this way and that as he covered her mouth with his. Soon his kisses intensified.

Beth's heart slammed against her chest, and her breathing became labored. Her knees felt rubbery and she leaned against Tom for support. This kiss was so urgent, so demanding. *So exquisite.*

"Beth," Tom whispered against her lips, "I should have done this earlier," and he resumed his ardent kisses.

At that same moment, the Waterbury heater clanged, abruptly returning Beth to her schoolteacher self. What was she doing? She worked her hands up between their bodies, and pushed on his chest.

"Tom, stop. This isn't right." She was almost breathless.

"Why isn't it?" he asked, kissing her cheeks, her eyelids, her forehead, distracting her so much she wondered herself why it wasn't. "We're only kissing, Beth. How can it be wrong to kiss someone you like. And you like me." He pulled back and gazed into her eyes. "I know you do."

"But what if we get caught? I could lose my job."

"We're not going to get caught. I'm a school trustee. It makes sense I should be helping with the chores. Now kiss me," he commanded gently. "Don't be frightened of me."

It wasn't Tom who frightened her. And it wasn't necessarily being caught. It was her body's intense reaction to what Tom had referred to as *only kissing*. He made her want more and that worried her. "Davy could come in," she whispered. Even to her, it sounded such a feeble excuse.

"No, he's busy throwing snowballs. I can see him from here."

"But the other children will be arriving soon and I still have the copy work to print on the board."

Tom smiled devilishly. "All right, Miss Patterson, I'll make you a deal. Kiss me once more and then I'll leave. I promise."

She eyed him suspiciously. "Just one kiss? That's all?"

"If that's all you'll give me, then yes, one kiss."

She shouldn't, yet a sense of earthy excitement flooded through her body and told her she should. *One kiss. What could be the harm in that? And* he promised he'd leave immediately after she kissed him. Heaven knows how long he might wait if she didn't, and then her copy work would never get done. The children relied on her, and so her mind twisted the situation around until she felt it was her duty as the teacher to kiss him.

Tom stood motionless. She tentatively placed her hands on his shoulders, pulled him forward slightly and stood on tip-toe. Their eyes met and his burned with such intensity Beth felt compelled to close hers. She pressed her mouth against his, copying how he had kissed her. She wasn't ready to trace her tongue along his lips, although just the thought of it made her feel weak in the knees again.

A few seconds later, she pulled back, half expecting him to pressure her for more, somewhat let down when he didn't. She held onto his arm for a minute, feeling lightheaded and giddy from lack of oxygen. The next time she would have to remember to breathe. *Imagine, already thinking about the next time.*

Tom transferred a kiss upon his fingertip to her lips, and whispered, "I'll go now, and leave you to your work."

As if she could concentrate on anything after that! When Tom closed the door behind him, Beth put a hand to her breast to calm her racing heart. *My heavens!*

*

It was a glorious late January morning, the sky clear blue and the air crisp. As Beth marched to the school, her breath formed beads of ice on her scarf and her cheeks felt frosted, but she didn't mind. She was in a cheerful mood. For one thing, she no longer needed her crutches. For another, smoke puffed straight up from the schoolhouse chimney, which meant Tom was there.

Beth hurried. She looked forward to her few minutes alone with him each morning, to their conversation of course, but more so, to their oh-so-wonderful kisses. She smiled, remembering how Tom had lured her into that first kiss. That night she convinced herself it must never happen again, at least not at the school. It was certainly acceptable for a schoolteacher to be courted, but societal rules required a chaperone be present. And to kiss a beau while alone in the school? Scandalous! She had all intentions of setting Tom straight, but the following day when she arrived at the schoolhouse, he was on his way out the door. He pulled her into the cloakroom, planted a quick one on her lips, and was gone before she had time to react. The next day, the moment he entered the schoolhouse, she voiced her concerns and he chuckled, reminding her kissing was hardly scandalous. Odd, how when she was all alone with her thoughts she could see clearly what they were doing wasn't proper, but when Tom was with her, he made their kisses seem innocuous. And since Beth never really wanted to forego his kiss, she allowed herself to believe him.

Sometimes Davy wanted to hang around in the school, rather than go outside to play. Tom solved that problem by explaining to Davy that if he was going to be inside, he could help with the morning chores. Davy always chose playing outside over sweeping floors or some other menial chore. And should he or some other student want to come inside early, the sound of their heavy winter boots clomping up the steps gave Tom and Beth ample warning.

Beth and Davy trudged through the deep snow, Beth dreamily lost in her thoughts of Tom. There was something thrilling about their stolen morning kiss—

Oomph! Beth nearly fell over Davy as he stopped in his tracks just outside the schoolhouse. He turned to Beth and stated, "It's too cold. I want to come inside this morning."

"Fine. You can sweep the floors then."

"Okay," he replied.

Beth's spirits fell lower than the mercury in their thermometer. She followed Davy into the school.

Tom seemed in a good mood. "Good morning, Bud."

"It's cold out," Davy announced.

"Cold enough to freeze pigeon droppings in mid-air." Tom grinned and Beth forced a smile.

"Davy decided he'd rather sweep floors than stay outside this morning," she explained, hoping Tom might come up with some other subterfuge to get Davy outside, hiding her frustration when he sided with Davy.

"Can't say as I blame him one iota. Well, grab the broom and get with it, Bud. I've got something to fix in the cloakroom. I want your opinion, Beth, if you can spare the time."

She followed him silently, the day having lost some of its luster now there would be no morning kiss.

Tom closed the door behind them. "Do you see what's wrong?" he asked as he shrugged into his heavy coat.

Beth gave the room a careful check. "No."

"It's these."

Puzzled, she looked at Tom. He was pointing to his lips. "They're not covered."

Her heart leapt and her face brightened. "I should correct that, shouldn't I?"

"Hmm," he agreed.

She stepped closer and he took her in his arms and pulled her against his body.

"That feels better already," he murmured as his lips warmed hers.

Hmm. Yes. She longed to linger in his arms where she felt safe, where her haunting past could not intrude and the frightening future was held at bay, even for just those few minutes. But soon the heavy clomping of boots heralded the arrival of children and her reality returned with all its responsibilities and trepidations.

Chapter 13

The ominous white cloud bank that formed early afternoon worried Beth. Prairie winters were unpredictable. Wind could churn a gentle fall of feathery snowflakes into a blinding blizzard with little warning and sadly more than one child had perished on the way home in such a storm. Beth swore never to let that happen to any of her pupils.

She kept a wary eye on the fast advancing cloud, and before the first flake of snow fell, she decided to send the children home. Fortunately, more than half her students lived right in Whistle Creek, and the remainder lived within a two-mile radius.

"Quickly," Beth urged as they dressed in their winter clothes. "Peter, put on your hat or your ears will freeze. And don't dawdle today," Beth sternly warned.

"I go past his place. He can ride double with me on Star," Martha offered.

"Thank you," Beth said in relief as the two headed out the door, following a mass of other children to the barn.

Inga and her older brother Nels lived the furthest away. "I'll hitch up the horses," Nels said.

"Hurry. I think you'll be able to stay ahead of the storm." But the first pellets of snow were already falling. Beth hastened the remaining students into their coats and boots. With every passing moment the snowfall increased, as did the wind—and her anxiety.

Beth opened the door. The old maple in the schoolyard was no longer visible. The drifting snow formed a curtain of white.

"It's too dangerous," she told her students. "You'll have to stay here until the storm passes."

While the children took off their coats, Beth put hers on. She wound a scarf around her head and another around her face.

"Where are you going?" Davy asked with a worried look.

"I've got to stop the others from leaving. Norman, you're in charge. Keep the stove going and don't let anyone leave under any circumstance." Norman nodded gravely.

Outside, the fierce wind nearly blew Beth off the school steps. Visibility was next to impossible. Ahead of her loomed a whirling whiteness. Running one hand along the school's edge, Beth maneuvered herself to the east side where she was sheltered somewhat from the storm. Snow swirled off the roof, already forming sharp-edged drifts, and several times she stumbled. At the back corner of the school, she stopped and shouted, but the howling wind swallowed her calls to the barn. Though it was no more than thirty feet directly behind the schoolhouse, Beth couldn't see it. It was as if the barn was gone.

When she stepped beyond the shelter of the schoolhouse, the angry storm whipped at her scarves. She secured one with a fat knot, and pulled the second scratchy scarf over her nose and cheeks. Leaning into the storm, she staggered blindly in the barn's direction, one step in front of the other. She counted her steps, small and halting against the forceful wind. If she took more than forty, she would know she had missed the barn completely. Though her forehead ached from the cold, and the wind buffeted her, she hunkered down and kept moving forward.

As she stumbled along freezing tears formed. She blinked, her eyelashes coated with ice. She had taken only twenty-six steps and she was physically exhausted. Still she pushed onward against the wall of wind and snow. Finally she had reached forty-one steps. *Dear Lord, how could I have missed the barn? Surely I must be near it.*

She swung her arms about her and took three more heavy steps. Her right hand hit something. It was either the barn or one of the outhouses. She felt the walls. The slabs were horizontal. She had made it to the barn!

With renewed hope, Beth hugged the wall as she made her way around to the east door. She pulled on the heavy latch, but the door wouldn't open. A drift held it shut. She kicked it away, her weakened ankle aching under the strain. When she tried the door once more, someone pushed from the inside.

Beth nearly collapsed inside the barn. "Oh thank God, you're still here."

The walls creaked so loudly Beth could barely hear Penelope's reply. "Martha and Peter left five minutes ago."

"They left?"

"Martha said her horse was smart and would find its way home."

Beth's heart felt frozen. Martha, who always was ready to help, and sweet little Peter. *Please don't judge me by my size, although I'm mighty small.* Now they were out in this blizzard.

"Miss Patterson. I'm cold."

Beth knew she must focus on the remaining children's safety. "We have to get back to the school or we'll freeze."

Including herself, they totaled eight. If they all held hands . . . Beth did a rapid calculation. Even forming one long line, they wouldn't span the distance between the barn and the school.

"Quickly, gather all the reins and rope you can find, anything to tie ourselves together so we don't lose each other on our way back to the schoolhouse."

"But what about the horses? They'll freeze."

"They'll be fine. Horses are better suited to the cold than we are. Now start looking."

"I found some old ropes," Jonah exclaimed shortly, "and here's our reins."

"Wonderful!" Beth took the frayed ropes and the reins, and began tying the students' wrists together, leaving at least a foot long span in between. The smaller children were spaced between the older students.

"Jonah, you will be at the back and I will lead. If we all stretch our arms out straight . . . " she demonstrated " . . . we should reach the school without Jonah letting go of the barn."

Penelope, second in line, looked terrified. "It's okay," Beth assured. "We can't get lost because we're tied together." She yelled so the others could hear her, "Now, when I reach the school, I will shake Penelope's arm, like this." She gave the girl's arm two firm pumps. "Then Penelope will shake Ricky's arm and Ricky will shake the next one and so on down the line. Understand?"

The children nodded.

"Jonah, don't let go until you feel Dorothy's handshake."

He nodded his head solemnly. "I will be the anchor."

"Exactly," Beth said. *That stodgy old inspector should see my students now. Jonah might forget his times table, but when it came to matters of great importance, he was dependable!*

Gordon, Penelope's youngest sibling, began to cry.

"Don't cry, Gordie," his sister consoled. "It's just like playing crack-the-whip, only a lot slower."

Bless her heart. Beth wanted to kiss her for acting so brave.

"Okay, let's go." It was far easier walking with the wind, than against it. Penelope stumbled over a drift and the leather rein yanked on Beth's wrist. Beth waited a moment then continued, again counting her steps. This time she was at thirty-seven when she felt the school wall. She moved to the leeward side, then stopped and gave Penelope's arm two hard shakes.

Beth felt Penelope shake Ricky's arm, but from there she was uncertain how their crude means of communication fared. She waited a half minute, giving ample time for the handshake to pass down the line, then began moving again.

As she opened the school door, she was met by the other students. One by one, the trailing line of students came through the doorway, shaking off snow as they entered. Each child was met by a rousing cheer from his classmates. When all were safe inside, Beth closed the door.

While students helped each other free themselves from their bonds and coats, they all spoke at once. The sounds of laughter and chatter filled the schoolhouse, and for a moment even the wind outside couldn't compete.

It was Norman who asked, "Where's Martha and Peter?"

Slowly the room became reverently silent as, one by one, the students realized two were not among them. Quietly Beth told them, "They left before I got there." Taking a long hard breath, she steeled herself against thoughts too horrible to consider. "Let's dry our clothes by the stove."

*

Tom could stand it no longer. If he didn't get to the school and see how Beth and her students were faring, he'd go insane with worry. Somewhere in the smithy was an old roll of binder twine; he remembered coming across it not that long ago. He searched for a good five minutes before finding it under a shelf in the back. He inspected it. "Dammit," he muttered. Mice had gnawed at it. But beneath several outside layers, the core of the roll seemed intact.

He pulled on his heavy sheepskin coat, his hat with the large ear flaps, and finally his gloves with the sheepskin lining and backs. He was already wearing winter boots. The hard-packed smithy floor was cold in the winter. With the binder twine under one arm and a knife to cut it in his coat pocket, he figured he was as ready as he'd ever be.

With the buildings on main street practically bumped up against each other, Tom had little problem navigating from the smithy to the bank on the corner. Tom secured the free end of twine to the hitching rail out front of North's Bank. Trusting his good sense of direction, he headed out.

*

Beth heard the clomping of boots in the schoolhouse. Someone had arrived! *Please be Martha and Peter.* "Tom!" she exclaimed when saw him in the cloakroom. She gave him a hearty hug and a kiss on his icy cheek. "I can't believe you made it here."

"I had to see if you were doing okay."

"We're managing." She took Tom's ice-crusted coat from him, shook it, and hung it on an empty peg.

Tom saw the other coats hung around the cloakroom. "Thank God you kept the children."

Beth looked at him and he immediately knew that something was very wrong. He closed the door between the cloakroom and the classroom.

Tears flowed freely down Beth's cheeks as she explained about Martha and Peter.

Tom reached for his coat. "It's not your fault. This damn storm hit so fast it caught everyone unaware. I better go looking for them."

"You can't go out again."

"Beth, I can't stay here, not when there's a possibility they might still be out there. Don't worry, I'll be fine. Just keep the others calm." Before she could protest further, he was out the door.

Beth fought back tears.

Ricky started crying for his mother and Beth remembered Tom's order to keep the children calm. Drawing deep from her reserve of strength, Beth returned to the classroom. She comforted the little ones, telling them what an adventure this was going to be, staying overnight at the school. The boys were told to pull the desks in close to the stove while the girls were to gather leftovers from lunch pails.

Three apples, some cookies, half a sandwich, some raw carrots, and a large piece of chocolate cake—it wasn't a feast, but at least something to nibble on, should they get hungry. They boiled melted snow to drink and the older students offered their meager share of food to the younger ones.

It was a good hour before Beth heard the heavy clomping of feet. She and the children had been singing to help pass the time and occupy their thoughts, but the footsteps brought a silence filled with dread. They waited to see who came through the cloakroom door.

It was Tom, but only Tom.

Beth hurried to him. He was shaking, barely able to hold himself upright from fatigue. She took the heavy coat from him, and led him to the stove. His face was red with white splotchy patches on them, indicating frostbite. Beth brought him a cup of hot water to drink, and allowed him a few minutes to absorb the warmth before asking, "Did you find them?"

Too cold yet to speak, he could only shake his head. A minute later, he forced words through his chattering teeth. "I never made it t . . . to the Brown's place, but they might . . . t have. Don't jump t . . . to conclusions."

Beth nodded bravely. As he warmed, Tom explained the white-out conditions and how he thought he would have been near Peter's place when he ran into the maple tree. All that time he'd been wandering around the schoolyard. It was by pure chance he was able to find his way back to the school. Until the blizzard ended, they would just have to wait to find out about Peter and Martha.

The walls of the schoolhouse almost wheezed with the strong gusts of wind. The windowpanes rattled in their casings. Snow sifted down from the rafters and the room became chilled despite the roaring fire in the stove. The morale in the classroom dropped as quickly as the temperature. Beth peered into the heater and added the last few chunks of coal. The oil lamps were lit and hung near the center of the room to add a small measure of heat. The light cast long shadows along the outside walls, and as children are wont to do, they soon made their own fun, seeing who could form the oddest shaped shadow. They were too occupied to notice Tom putting on his coat and heading for the door.

"Where are you going?" Beth whispered anxiously, following him into the cloakroom.

"We need more coal," he answered. "I'll use the twine as a safety line. You get back inside where it's warm."

Tom brought in several buckets of coal, enough to keep them toasty warm through the night. When the younger pupils began yawning, he and the older boys skidded desks together to form makeshift beds. Many were asleep before the coal oil lamps burned out shortly after nine o'clock. They slept fitfully. Jonah and Nels sat together, propped against a desk, and talked. Inga and Penelope tried to stay awake, but soon were sound asleep on the floor beside the stove. Beth covered them with an extra coat left after the Christmas concert.

"They're all such good kids," she said, returning to sit beside Tom.

"And you're a good teacher."

Beth made no reply. *A good teacher would have kept all her children safe.*

"Are you chilly?" he asked.

"A little."

"I'll stoke the fire again."

Other than to get up and tend the stove or to comfort a child's sleepy whimper, they sat long into the night, leaning back against her desk, talking about the children and their families and how each was somehow related to another in the community. They deliberately avoided speaking of the missing children's families.

Around two or three in the morning the storm began to abate and Beth felt herself nodding off. Tom put his arm around her, pulled her head against his chest and ordered gently, "Get some sleep. I'll stay awake."

She couldn't remember if she even protested. Sleep came immediately, but an hour later, she woke. Something was strange. She realized the strangeness was silence. The storm was over almost as quickly as it had begun.

Well before dawn, fathers began arriving to retrieve their children. Each time Beth heard the crunch and stomps of snowy boots in the cloakroom, she prayed it was neither Peter's nor Martha's father.

Six children remained to be picked up when Mr. Simpson entered, his face ashen. "I passed the Pickard children. They told me Martha isn't here."

"She didn't arrive home?" Beth's voice broke. She felt for the nearest desk and sank into it.

Tom swung on his coat. "Peter Brown was with her. We'll get some men and go looking for them."

As soon as the door closed, Beth slumped over her desk, dropped her head onto her folded arms and quietly wept. Her students did their best to console her, but nothing helped. Martha and Peter were her sole responsibility and she had failed them.

*

When the sun rose that morning, Whistle Creek had been transformed into a world iced with swirls of snow. Drifts wrapped graceful sculptures around trees and posts. Barbwires, taut as fiddle strings, stretched between fence posts. After the last student was picked up, Beth and Davy trudged home through the drifted snow. The wonder and beauty were unseen by Beth, replaced by haunting visions of two small forms frozen in death's icy grasp.

With a sense of hopelessness, Beth started a fire in the cook stove, reaching up to adjust the damper to draw properly. Heat slowly chased the chilliness into the corners of the room.

Bill came home just before dinner and complained immediately because nothing had been prepared. Beth made a broth soup, while Bill and Davy swapped their storm experiences over a game of checkers.

Whenever they laughed, Beth wanted to scream. *Don't you care? Peter and Martha are probably dead.* Finally, she fled to her room, slammed the door behind her and fell onto her bed. She covered her head with her pillow to block out everything except her sorrow.

Her door crashed open and Beth yelled at her brothers from

under the pillow, "Get out. I want to be alone."

"Beth." It was Tom. "Beth, we found them. They're fine . . . cold, but fine."

Beth pushed the pillow aside, and stared at Tom's bulky form in the doorway. "They're alive?" she asked incredulously, sorting between her nightmarish imaginings and the incredible truth.

"We found them in a hay stack, wormed in deep like a couple of fleas on a hairy dog. That old horse stayed with them the whole time. Had an inch of ice on his back, but stayed right there. That's how we found them. Doc Fisher is taking a look at them right now, but the main thing is they're safe."

Beth sat up, swinging her legs over the side of her bed. Trembling fingers covered her lips as a small cry escaped.

Tom crossed to the bed and gathered her in his arms. Though his coat was covered with snow and ice, she held him close and wept with relief. He supported her for several minutes. No words were necessary to explain their feelings of thankfulness.

A loud cough pulled them apart. "You've had plenty of time to say your piece, so I think you should leave now," Bill said. His wide stance almost filled the doorway as Tom's had only moments before. Davy's head poked around Bill's leg.

Beth straightened from Tom's embrace. "Bill! That's no way to talk to Tom. He knew how worried I was and he came to tell me they're safe."

"Well, now you know, so there's no point in his stayin'."

Tom stood. "He's right. I should be going. I'll see you later." He stooped and dropped a kiss on her forehead, which surprised Beth because they had been so careful to keep their burgeoning relationship a secret.

At the sight of them kissing, Bill nearly growled, while Davy jumped up and down with delight. "Tom and Beth, sitting in a tree. K. I. S. S. I. N . . . " His song was cut short as Bill dragged him out the doorway.

"Shut up, Davy! You don't know nothin'," Bill spat.

Beth began to rise, but Tom gently pressed her back. He pulled up the quilt at the bottom of her bed and covered her. "You rest, I'll let myself out."

After Tom departed, Beth curled up under the quilt and listened to Bill and Davy arguing. "He is not!" Bill yelled.

"Is too! He kissed Beth for no special reason. That means he's her boyfriend."

"Does not!" Bill countered.

While the two quarreled, Beth found herself siding completely with Davy.

Chapter 14

With the Valentine's dance a few days away, Ernie Brown was doing a rip-roaring business in his barbershop. Three long-haired, unshaven men sat along a bench, while other men leaned against the wall visiting with one another as they waited their turn in the chair.

"Get your wife a card yet?" one asked.

"Oh, jees no! I'd better remember to head over to Betner's after my cut."

"The best cards are almost gone," another said. "I was there yesterday."

"I gotta get one! I forgot last year and Flora wouldn't speak to me for three days."

"Now there's an idea!" said Ernie. All the men chuckled.

It was Mr. Pickard who held out his hands for silence. "I don't give my wife a Valentine's card," he announced proudly.

"And you don't get in trouble?"

"Nope, 'cause I give her a book of sonnets instead. Been doing that for quite a few years now."

"Sonnets. Shee-it! What's that?" asked Flora's hubby.

"Poetry," said Pickard.

"Yeah right! There once was a farmer named Tucker," one fellow started and the rest broke out in wide-mouthed grins.

"No, no! Don't you fools know anything? Women want romance. My Emmy, she loves romantic poetry. She thinks I'm *sen-see-tive* when I give her that stuff. Puts her in the romantic mood, if you catch my drift." Pickard nudged the fellow beside him.

"Why, Pickard, you sly rascal!" Ernie pointed the shears at him. "Considering you have more kids than anyone else in the community, I'd say there's method in your madness."

"Better believe it," Pickard replied smugly.

Lewie Hanks happened to be in the barbershop, not for a haircut, though he needed one badly, but more for the company. He was lonely and listening to the men usually brightened his spirits, but today, with all their talk about sweethearts and love, he felt lonelier yet. He should try to get himself a sweetheart.

As if the heavens were listening, he spotted Miranda Parsons strolling along the boardwalk across the street. She was single, and as far as Lewie was concerned, she was fair game. Like a rock from a slingshot, Lewie flew out the door, dashed across the street and came to a sliding stop on the icy boardwalk in front of her.

"Hey, Miss Miranda. You look purdy today."

"What do you want?" she asked, her nose pointed upward in disgust. "I told you at the box social I never want to see you again."

"Heck, thought maybe you might have changed your mind."

"I haven't!" She pushed past him to walk away, but Lewie kept up.

"Gonna be Valentine's Day soon. Got yourself a sweetheart yet, 'cause I'm available."

Miranda halted and nearly snorted. "You? Listen, if the only two men left on earth were you and a bald headed old boar with green teeth, I'd gladly choose him. Now leave me be!" She marched away.

Lewie turned and stomped off in the other direction. He kicked a frozen horse apple across the street. Then he remembered something, which in itself is a revelation for Lewie Hanks. He remembered Pickard's strategy. *Poetry.* Maybe Miranda wanted a poem or two. Suddenly Lewie knew what to do—he'd send Miranda some love poems. Problem was, he was darn sure he couldn't write one on his own. Why he could only think of one word that rhymed with 'Tucker' and Lewie wasn't sure it sounded romantic enough.

Maybe he could get hold of a book of sonnets from the school and copy out a few short ones. That's what he would do! He'd better rush though. He was mighty slow at printing and he only had a couple days.

*

Valentine's Day was so cold Beth allowed her students to stay inside during the noon hour if they so chose. A group of girls circled round the stove, intently staring at its flat top. Occasionally they erupted into giggles.

Curious, Beth went to investigate. In the middle of the stovetop, two apple seeds bounced around like water droplets on a hot griddle.

"Whatever are you doing, girls?"

Inga answered for the group. "One apple seed is a boy and the other is a girl and if they bump into each other it means they are going to get married and have lots of children."

"I see," Beth said smiling. It didn't take a teacher's certificate to know the girls had named one seed Tom and they were taking turns being the other seed. Ever since the storm, all the girls were hopelessly enamored with him and his charming ways.

She stared at the two seeds on the hot stovetop, and for a lark imagined she was the second seed. The seeds jumped about, popped toward each other, collided and then bounced quickly apart again. The girls giggled uncontrollably while Beth blushed candy-apple red.

"Such nonsense," she managed, though barely able to conceal her smile as she returned to her desk. Not that she would ever marry Tom. Heavens no! She couldn't risk it. And children? She had Bill and Davy to take care of. They were plenty.

*

That afternoon, Tom shut the shop down early so he could see if Beth needed help decorating for this evening's Valentine's dance.

All in all, he thought things were progressing well between them. Tonight he hoped to advance their relationship. He had it all worked out. After the dance, he'd walk her home and this time when he kissed her goodnight, he would show her there was more to kissing than pressing two sets of lips together and some labored breathing. He intended to use his tongue, just a gentle probe until she got the feel for it, and then, if she seemed receptive and venturesome, he'd tease her tongue until she invaded his mouth with hers. The mere thought of it aroused him.

That arousal was quickly squelched when he stepped off the boardwalk at North's bank and saw Lewie Hanks leave the schoolyard. Tom bristled. *What the hell was Hanks doing at the school?* Something in his gut told him it couldn't be good. Worried that the reprobate may have harmed Beth, Tom ran to the school and took the three steps going into the schoolhouse in one leap.

*

Beth hummed as she cleaned the day's lessons off the board. She turned and smiled warmly when Tom burst through the door.

"Oh, hello. I didn't expect you so early. What a fun day! The children spent all afternoon cutting hearts out of crepe paper." She pointed around the room at all the decorations. "Doesn't it look pretty?"

"I just saw Hanks leave. What did he want?"

Beth set the brush on the ledge and dusted off her hands. "He was returning a book."

"A book? What kind of book? I didn't even know he could read."

"Yes, I have to admit I was taken aback, too. He borrowed a book of sonnets. Imagine that, would you!"

Tom snorted.

"Oh, Tom, you should have seen how embarrassed he was when I asked him if he enjoyed poetry."

"That guy is crazy. I don't want him around you."

In such a happy mood, Beth paid little heed to Tom's warning. "Well, as I said, he was just returning a book."

"What makes him think he can borrow books from the school?"

"Tom, you know people ask to borrow books from the school all the time."

"Not people like Hanks. He's sick in the head. He's dangerous," Tom growled.

"Well, I never *felt* threatened. Besides he was here for less than a minute. What could possibly happen in that short of time?"

"Beth, you're so damn naïve!" he scoffed.

Beth felt her temper flare. "I am *not* naïve!"

"A man like Hanks? You here all alone? There's no telling what he might have done."

"But he didn't and I really can't—"

"If he ever comes around here again, I want you to leave immediately. You hear me?"

Beth was furious. *How dare he order me about as if I were his property. He has no right telling me what to do!* She walked right up to him and said, "Now, you listen to me, Tom Carver." She poked his chest with her finger. "I'm a grown woman and I make my own decisions about who I do or do not see." Another poke. "And what Mr. Hanks chooses to do has nothing to do with me." Poke. "If it bothers you that he comes over here, then tell him!" Poke. "Not me!" Poke.

"Don't worry, I will!" he growled.

"Fine!"

"Fine!"

Tom slammed the door behind him with such finality Beth thought her heart might stop.

She held her breath. Surely Tom would come back through the door with a big grin on his face saying it was all an elaborate joke. But he didn't and now her lovely afternoon of making hearts and dreaming romantic thoughts was ruined . . . and it was all Tom's fault.

Tears threatened and she blinked them back. She pulled open her desk drawer and picked up a lacy, red paper heart. "Do you want to know what else we did today, Tom Carver?" she said with no one but the four walls to listen. "We made Valentines. This is the one I made for you." She held up the dainty heart in both hands and carefully tore it in two. Then she burst into tears, for it felt as if Tom had done the very same to her own heart.

*

Tom started in on himself before he'd made it to the bottom step. *You jackass! What's the matter with you, talking to her like that? She did nothing wrong and you lit into her as if it was her fault that Hanks was at the school. She was happy before you arrived and now she's mad as a hornet. You need to apologize. You need to turn around, march up those steps and beg for her forgiveness.*

His foot was on the first step when he heard someone call his name. He spotted Davy running across the school toward him. *Oh, hell, not Davy. Not now.* Tom blew out his frustration in a resigned sigh. *Well, maybe with any luck, this won't take long.* Tom stepped down and waited.

Davy was winded when he arrived and it took a moment for him to catch his breath. "Tom, I gotta ask you a question."

"Okay, shoot."

"Do people kiss at a Valentine's Dance?" The boy had a worried, almost distasteful look on his face.

"Why do you want to know?"

"Penelope has been following me around all day and if I go to the dance, she's gonna want to kiss me, sure as shootin'."

Tom smiled ruefully. "Well, Bud, sorry to tell you, but some people do kiss at the Valentine's dance." Though he knew it wouldn't be him and Beth.

"Then that's it! I'm gonna ask Beth right now if I can go to Gordie's house for the night."

Before Tom could convince Davy to hold off for a moment, the boy was inside the schoolhouse and Tom's opportunity to apologize was gone. *So much for luck.*

Scowling, he returned to the smithy, telling himself he'd come back in a half hour to apologize. But when he unlocked the wide doors of the shop, there was a farmer waiting to have his horses' hooves tended to. By the time Tom finished, it was too late. He'd have to apologize at the dance.

*

The fiddler at the front of the classroom was sawing out a lively polka and the dance was in full swing when Tom arrived. He sidled along the back wall, greeting folks as he went, but more intent on scanning the room for Beth. He felt hollow in the pit of his stomach knowing it would be his fault if she decided not to come.

His spirits lifted when he spotted her sitting on the far side, sandwiched between two women, both of whom were talking nonstop around her. *Maybe you could get back in her good graces if you just sauntered over there and rescued her.*

Her eyes darkened when he headed in her direction. *Then again, maybe not.* He could practically see steam rising about her. *Damn!* She was still seething from the afternoon's spat. He watched as she quickly extricated herself from the two women and made a hasty retreat, skirting around to the other side of the room.

He tried a different approach, and she moved again. Each time he attempted to come close to her, she eluded him like quicksilver until he eventually gave up his pursuit. No point in appearing desperate. He poured a cup of coffee and sat beside the coffeepot. He faced the agonizing fact he might have lost Beth for good and that thought seared his gut worse than the strong brew.

Mr. Pickard asked Beth to dance, and while they twirled around the room, Tom watched in grim silence. In fact, he spent the better part of the evening guzzling coffee, watching Beth in the arms of other men, and wishing he'd kept his big mouth shut this afternoon.

It seemed to Tom that the one making the most progress on the dance floor was Beth's brother, Bill. Annaleese Hewn was obviously head over heels in love with the chump. The sight of them enjoying the evening stuck in Tom's gizzard, making him feel even worse.

"You're not dancing tonight?" Mary asked.

He glanced sideways, noticing for the first time his aunt had sat down beside him.

"I would," he said, "but the one I want to dance with seems to have an aversion to me."

Mary didn't need to ask to whom he was referring. "I thought things were coming along fine between you and Beth. What happened?"

Tom ran his forefinger around the rim of his cup. "I did something I shouldn't have."

Mary frowned. "Tom Carver," she scolded, her voice low, but stern, "that girl is young. Don't you be taking liberties with her."

"Calm down, Mary, it's not what you think."

"Then you better explain just what I should be thinking."

He was almost embarrassed to tell her. "This afternoon I saw Lewie Hanks leaving the school and I kinda got testy. Said a few things that maybe I shouldn't have."

"To Lewie?"

"No, Beth." He raised his hand. "Please, don't say it. I know it was stupid, but it just came out."

Mary quietly snorted with indignation. "Men! They're all a bunch of fools. Poor Beth."

Now he felt even worse. He stared down at his freshly polished boots, thinking he wasn't much better than the muck he had scraped off them earlier. "Yeah, well, now she won't let me get within ten feet of her to apologize."

"So you're going to sit all evening and mope. Land's sakes, I've never known you to be a quitter." Mary brushed down the folds in her skirt as if she were brushing crumbs off her lap. "Do you remember that horse you used to have when you were a kid? The one that was tricky to catch?"

"Sally?"

"Yes, Sally's the one. Remember how you spent hours trying to catch her and when you finally gave up and went for another horse she'd come right up to you?"

A sly grin slowly spread across Tom's face. "Are you suggesting I try to make Beth envious?"

"I am saying no such thing. But it's obvious she likes to dance, and most of the men here can't find a beat even if they were handed a stick and a drum. It's a crying shame she's out there getting her toes stomped on when she could be dancing with you." Mary stared her nephew straight in the eye. "Of course with you sitting all night like you're part of that chair, how would she know what she's missing?"

In all the years Tom could remember, Mary's advice had never been wrong. Maybe he should dance. It was either that or go home, and since going home offered no hope of reconciliation, Tom asked Mary to dance.

He liked dancing and he'd been told many times he danced well. If that was true, he had Mary to thank. When Mary's boys and Tom were gangly teenagers, she insisted they learn to dance or at least to master the basic dance steps. So for three Saturdays in a row, the rug in the Betner parlor was rolled back and six clumsy boys paired up and stumbled through waltzes, polkas, and two steps. At the time, Tom thought it was a big waste of time. He was thankful now that Mary had been persistent.

He danced several sets, but Beth paid him no heed. So much for ignoring her and hoping she'd approach him. He decided on another tactic. When he was dancing with Mrs. Brown, Tom maneuvered his unsuspecting partner around the floor until they were adjacent to Beth and her partner. Then he stepped sideways. "Oops, sorry," he said when he bumped Beth's shoulder, "an accident." He grinned and shrugged apologetically.

Beth gave him a glare, cold enough to have frostbitten him, but Tom merely smiled and danced away, feeling rather pleased. At least now he had her attention.

Whenever Beth danced with a new partner, Tom deliberately bumped into them, each time saying the same thing, "Oops, sorry. Accident."

*

Accident? My left foot. Beth knew exactly what Tom was doing. There was no way on God's green earth she would dance with him, though she found dancing with Lars Anderstom an ordeal.

"Ew are rather tense, I tink," said Lars. "Are ew not happy vith my dancing, Miss Patterson?"

Beth blushed. "Oh . . . no . . . you dance fine . . . really. It's not that. It's my shoes," she lied, "I'm afraid they're too small." *More likely your feet are too swollen from him stepping on them.*

"Den perhaps ew vish to sit for a vile?"

And have Tom descend upon me like a fly on raw meat? "No, I would rather keep dancing. It's been so long since I've been to a dance, and we're doing so well together."

Lars beamed at Beth. "Yah, I tink so, too."

*

Tom stole a glance at the banjo clock at the front of the classroom. It was nearing midnight, and soon the women would be bringing out the lunch and the dance would be over. The only one he had yet to dance with was Beth. He decided Mary's plan had failed. Beth was no more receptive to the idea now than she had been earlier. Frustrated, he headed for the cloakroom to get his coat. The fiddler announced it was time for the Sunset Reel, and everyone clapped. Tom paused, debating if he should give Beth one more try. It was a long shot, but what had he to lose? With long determined strides, he approached her.

*

Beth saw Tom closing in from one direction, Lars from another. Deciding her feet had taken enough abuse for one night, and she'd rather dance with a rattlesnake than with Tom, she turned to Earl standing nearby and announced, "I've been looking forward to a dance with you all evening, Earl." She dragged him by the arm onto the dance floor.

"Well, if that don't beat all!" Mary said when Tom joined her. "Beth got Earl up to dance, something I haven't been able to do in years."

"Given the right incentive, she can be very persuasive." Tom held out his arm. "Shall we?"

She smiled. "Let's."

For the Sunset Reel, the men stood in one line with their lady partners opposite them in a second line. Tom and Mary took their respective places just as Bert Parker began to call to the music, "Lead couple bow and do-see-do, down the line and away you go."

The end couple nearest Bert was the lead couple and they followed the caller's instructions. With a series of turn-throughs with those in the line, alternating with partner-swings in the middle, they worked their way down to the column's other end.

"Make an arch, make a steeple, couples turn to thread the needle."

The lead couple joined hands to form an arch while the couple at the opposite end folded to skip between the two rows. They in turn were followed by the next couple and so on until all had ducked under the arch and circled around the outside to form a new column.

"Clap your hands, clap your knees, give your partner a great big squeeze."

That completed a series of moves ending with a new lead couple. Soon it was Mary and Tom's turn to lead the reel, and they worked their way between the two lines. When Tom turned with Beth, he executed a quick trade, leaving Mary in Beth's place and taking Beth with him down the line.

*

It all happened so fast, Beth was momentarily confused. By the time she realized what had transpired, it was too late. Like it or not, she was Tom's partner. And she did not like it at all! When they held hands to form the arch, she glared at him.

Tom returned a smug smile.

Ooh, he thinks he's so clever.

The dance continued, and when it was time to give their partners a great big squeeze, Tom hugged Beth tightly and whispered, "We need to talk," before releasing her.

Beth had no time to reply for immediately another lead couple was dancing between them, but she had a caustic rebuttal prepared for the next time they sashayed down the column and under the arch. Only Tom beat her to it by whispering, "I'm sorry, Beth. Forgive me." And then they were separated again.

Beth found it infuriating to be subjected to this one-sided, disjointed conversation. On their last time through the column, Tom grasped firmly onto her hand and led her directly out to the cloakroom. He shooed a couple of boys back into the classroom, and closed the door.

"What are you doing?" she demanded when they were alone. "We can't just walk out in the middle of a dance."

Tom shrugged. "They won't miss us. Besides, if you weren't so stubborn, I wouldn't have to be so devious." He grinned, displaying no remorse.

"This is ludicrous. What will people think, you dragging me out here like this?"

"They'll probably think I couldn't wait to give you your Valentine's kiss."

Beth's heart lurched at the thought of Tom kissing her again, which made her just as vexed with herself as with him. "Not on your—" she began, but Tom raised his finger to his lips.

"Shhh. Careful. If they hear you, they'll think we're having a lover's quarrel."

Lovers! Never! She grabbed her coat from the heap on the table, shoved past him, and bolted outside.

It was snowing, big flakes falling like bits of torn paper. Tom followed her. She heard his muffled shout of surprise as he slipped on the steps and went down. She ignored him, yanking on her coat as she stormed across the schoolyard.

"Beth, wait!" Tom ran after her.

She glanced over her shoulder and yelled, "Leave me alone." She quickened her pace, holding her coat shut against the cold and the snow, hurrying to outdistance him.

"Slow down, or you'll hurt your ankle again."

"Don't tell me what to do, Tom Carver!"

She got to her house and slammed the door, only to hear Tom throw his shoulder against it. Beth, no match for his strength, jumped back and the door crashed open. Tom burst through, then kicked the door shut behind him.

Chapter 15

It was pitch dark inside the small house. The only sound was their angry breathing. Finally Tom said, "Well, are you going to light the lantern or not? We need to talk."

From the darkness, Beth snapped, "We have nothing to talk about!"

Cursing silently, Tom felt along the wall until he located the lantern, fumbled with the matches in the adjacent tin box, and lit the lamp. At least now he could see her, though she was on the far side of the room with her back to him.

Anger and frustration surged through him and he reminded himself that he could make things worse if he didn't watch what he said. He dragged in a deep breath and started again, far more quietly. "Beth, please. Let me explain."

She harrumphed in response.

He hadn't expected her to make it easy for him. But maybe if he explained why he had behaved like an idiot she might consider forgiving him. "Lewie and I have some bad history between us and I let my opinion of him cloud my better judgment." She offered no response. "I know that doesn't excuse my behavior," he continued, "but I truly am sorry."

If only she would turn to face him, but she didn't, not even when she said, "You practically blamed me. Like it was *my* fault he wanted to borrow a book. You acted as if you were jealous."

"Maybe I was. I don't know."

"But jealous of Lewie? That's ridiculous."

"I know, but love can make you do ridiculous things. You must know by now that I love you." His words hung suspended in the room, as if waiting for a response that never came. "I'd do anything to take back what I said and did, but I can't. The best I can do is promise it won't happen again."

Slowly, Beth's head turned. "You love me?" she asked, looking incredulous.

"With all my heart."

She shook her head. "But why? I've been nothing but trouble since the day we met."

Tom smiled. "True, we have had our difficulties, but we've also had some wonderful moments. Good times or bad, Beth, I love being with you."

"You love me," she whispered again. "Other than my parents and Davy, no one has ever said they loved me."

Her admission nearly crushed Tom's heart. "Ah, Beth. Come here." He opened his arms.

She went into them willingly.

His arms, the size of stovepipes, came around her and her soft body slumped against him. Oh, that he could hold her in his arms forever. He wanted to provide and protect her. He wanted to love her and make love to her. He wanted to spend a lifetime making her happy.

His finger gently lifted her chin and he kissed her lips tenderly until he felt them part with a sigh. His tongue traced between them, lightly coaxing her to allow him further entry. She opened her mouth wider in invitation. His tongue probed fully inside and she moaned. He pulled her hard against him.

Their kiss lengthened and deepened. Their breathing escalated to hungry gasps. Their hearts thrummed in unison.

Tom's lips pulled away. "Ah, Beth," he whispered, "there's more between us than either of us dare to admit." Then he closed his mouth over hers again.

They lost themselves in each other. Their heads twisted this way, then that. Their impassioned kisses crushed and bruised their lips against their teeth. It was nothing either of them had ever experienced before, hot and urgent and needy. But even as a raging fire burns down to embers, eventually their passion abated to soft kisses.

Tom led her to a chair, then sat and pulled her onto his lap. She nestled her head against the crook of his neck and released a contented sigh.

"What are you thinking?" he whispered.

She didn't answer right away. After a moment he heard her whisper, "I like it when you kiss me."

Tom chuckled lightly. "Me too." He hugged her closer.

Everything seemed so serene, so silent. Then as quietly as the snow falling outside, Tom whispered against the top of her head, "I love you, Beth. Please don't ever doubt that. You have captured my heart as no woman ever has. You would make me the happiest man on earth if you would marry me."

*

Beth's heart dropped. Though her entire being wanted to say yes, she knew the desperate reality of her situation made marriage impossible. She pulled away from his embrace and turned in his lap to face him. "Tom, we barely know each other. You don't know me."

"What more is there to know?"

"A lot."

"Then tell me," he urged.

Dismally she rose and crossed to the window. Staring out at the flakes, she shook her head. "I can't. I'm sorry." She discreetly brushed away a tear.

Tom came to stand behind her and placed his hands lightly on her shoulders. "I'm sorry. I told myself to be patient, but my feelings are so strong, I can't help myself. Beth, I need you in my life and I think you need me too. You have feelings for me. I've felt it in your kisses." She bowed her head. "Maybe you don't love me yet, but I'm positive you will. I've never been so sure of anything in my life. I'll be a good and faithful husband to you."

Yes, you would, she thought. Tom was an honest man, a man

of his word. A decent man like him would only hate her for what she had done.

"Is it because of the boys?" he asked.

Bewildered, she looked at him.

"You know I'll take care of them. They can stay with us. The house is big enough or we can add on if need be." He stroked her hair. "Just promise me you'll at least consider my proposal. Please?"

She nodded slowly, only to appease him. "I'll consider it," she said, but in her heart she knew marriage to Tom was impossible. He knew nothing of her except the lies she'd told him, and she cared enough not to hurt him further by building a marriage on a foundation of deceit.

*

Later, in their houses at the opposite ends of Whistle Creek, Tom and Beth both lay awake, trying to make sense of their emotions and what had happened that night. Their thoughts ran parallel, yet separate.

Damn, why did I blurt out marriage?

Why did he have to ask me?

I should have known she'd say no.

If only I could have answered yes.

I was so wound up in my own feelings, I never considered hers.

There are more than my own feelings to consider. There's Bill and Davy's.

I frightened her, moving too fast.

I am so afraid to lose him.

But I can't help it. I love her.

God help me, but I think I love him.

She will learn to love me, given time.

In time, he would grow to hate me.

Someday we will have a future together.

There can never be a future for us.
And we shall share more than kisses.
How will I manage without his kisses?

*

Days after his proposal, Beth's emotions still wavered back and forth. She had fallen in love with Tom. She hadn't wanted to, but it had happened. And she believed him when he said he loved her. But the problem wasn't that he loved her. The problem was did he love her enough? She wrestled with that thought. If she married him and he found out later about her unlawful past, would he forgive her or would he end the marriage? Or worse yet, would he continue the marriage, despising her and every moment they were together?

Beth set her pencil on the kitchen table. She might as well give up on next week's lesson planning, since concentration was as elusive as the answer to her dilemma. Could she dare marry Tom? Had she no brothers, Beth might have gambled her future on his love. But when she considered Davy and Bill, the risk was too much. They needed to maintain a low profile. As Tom's wife, she would receive far too much attention and she would have to consider everything she said—to Tom and to the townsfolk. One slip-up and the entire sham would be exposed.

As much as her heart ached at the thought, she knew she would have to turn down Tom's proposal. And if she couldn't share her life with him, it would be easier if she never saw him again. No, she bemoaned, not easier, but wiser. She knew each time she saw him about town, her heart would clench.

It seemed her past would ruin every future aspect of her life. A single tear slid from the corner of her eye. With great effort, she stifled any further tears that threatened to come. Crying would not help her situation, no matter how good it might feel.

She considered her options and decided the smartest thing to do would be to leave Whistle Creek. She loathed the thought of uprooting Bill and Davy, especially when they were both doing so well here. It suddenly struck her that maybe she didn't have to take her brothers with her. What would happen if they stayed behind and only she left? Bill would manage, but what about Davy? How could she possibly contemplate leaving him behind? He was so young and had already lost too many of his immediate family. No matter how she looked at her predicament, she couldn't come to a single resolution that didn't break her heart.

She rose from the table. "I'm going to lie down, Davy. I have a headache. Wake me when Bill gets home from work."

Davy was sprawled out on the floor, playing with sticks he'd recently whittled into what he thought resembled farm animals. "Okay." He barely looked up from his play.

It wasn't long after Beth's head sank into her pillow, she drifted off to sleep. Sadly, it was anything but peaceful. A gruesome shadow surfaced from her fugitive past and it reached out a long fleshless finger to point at her. *You*, it wailed. *You did this to me.* The shadow moved closer, congealing into darkness, moving forward, suffocating Beth with its nearness. Death's face loomed before her now, skin hanging in decay. She knew this death by name. Uncle Mead. His lips peeled back, revealing stained teeth imbedded in a gray jaw. It opened and a long black vapor escaped. Choking, Beth struck out at the ghost of her uncle. *Leave us alone. You're dead. Leave us alone.* Beth's arms flailed.

A crashing sound brought her bolt upright in bed and rescued her from her nightmare. Yet when she took a breath, she still couldn't get air. Suddenly the fogginess of her mind cleared completely. *Fire!* She flew from her bed and into the kitchen.

There was no fire, but soot and smoke rolled across the floor, and more billowed up from the open end of the stovepipe. A wooden orange crate leaned against a chair that had tipped on its side. Beyond the chair and crate lay another smoke-spewing length of pipe. Davy stood there, shaking his head. Then he started coughing.

Before they were overcome by smoke, Beth grabbed his arm and hauled him outside.

"What happened?" she demanded.

Two white eyeballs stared out forlornly from Davy's black sooty face. "Nothing."

"You call this nothing? I try to rest for ten minutes and look what happens. What did you do?"

"I didn't think the stove was drawing right so I tried to adjust the damper."

"The stove was drawing fine."

"But I was cold so I added more wood."

Beth felt herself getting angrier by the minute. "How much wood?"

Davy stared at his feet. "Till it was full."

Beth gave her brother a well-deserved shake. "You could have caused a chimney fire!"

"But I was watching it, Beth, and when the fire got too big I threw in a bucket of water. That's when I needed to adjust the damper."

Beth was exasperated. "You were supposed to be playing with your animals, not fiddling with the stove. Now there's an awful mess to clean up." Shivering, she crossed her arms in front of her and watched the soot settle, turning the snow outside the door black. "How did you think you could turn the damper? I can barely reach it."

"I stood on a chair . . . with an orange crate on top," he added sheepishly. "I guess it was too tippy."

"Obviously! You're lucky you weren't burnt." *Lucky the whole place didn't burn.*

Bill arrived and, after assessing the situation, cupped his hand over his nose and mouth, raced inside and quickly reconnected the stovepipe. On his way back outside, he grabbed Beth and Davy's coats.

"What a mess."

"It's my fault," Davy confessed, near tears.

Beth shrugged into her coat. "Never mind that now. We'd better get it cleaned up."

"There's no point doin' it tonight," Bill said. "It's still too smoky to breathe in there. We'll clean it tomorrow."

"And just where do you suggest we stay then?" Beth snapped.

"Hey, don't get mad at me."

For once Bill was right. Getting angry was futile. Better to transform her rage into something productive. "Let's all think. If Mary and Earl were home, I'm sure we could go there, but she told me at the dance they were going to Tannerville this weekend and wouldn't be home till Tuesday."

"We could go to Tom's," Davy submitted.

"No!" Bill and Beth answered in unison.

"What about staying at Annaleese's home?" Beth asked.

Bill shook his head. "I don't think so. I just left there and Mrs. Hewn isn't feeling well."

"You're right. If she's ill, she certainly doesn't need company."

Davy brightened. "I know, we could sleep at the school again, like we did when it stormed."

Beth tried to envision another night at the school. "Surely there has to be some place more comfortable." The possibilities were slim.

Davy started to whine. "I'm cold. I wanna go to Tom's."

"We are not going to Tom's!"

Half an hour later, for lack of a better solution, the three headed to the Carver place. Bill lagged far behind grumbling the entire way he wouldn't accept charity from that man while Beth reminded herself again and again to guard her emotions. And if he were to press her about his proposal she would have to be direct and make sure he understood in no uncertain terms that she would not marry him. She prayed he would drop the subject. Oh, why couldn't they just remain friends and leave it at that? Falling in love complicated everything.

Tom answered the knock at his door, took one look at Davy's sooty face, and gave a wry grin. "Stove trouble?"

"It was my fault," Davy confessed again, biting his bottom lip to stop it from quivering. "I was fiddling with the stove."

Tom wisely refrained from comment.

"We didn't know where else to go," Beth explained, wishing she could pull her attention away from Tom's lips. "I know it's an imposition, but could we stay the night? The floor and walls of our place are covered with soot."

"Come in. I've got plenty of room." He stepped aside.

Beth and Davy entered and Tom stuck his head out the door, glancing both ways. "Where's Bill?"

"He wouldn't come in. He's in your barn."

"That figures." He hung up their coats. "Make yourself at home. I was just about to make some coffee. Want some?"

Beth pulled out a chair on the far side of the table. "No thanks. But don't let us stop you."

Tom shrugged. "I'll have one later." He turned to Davy. "Looks like you could use a bath, Bud."

"I just had one yesterday."

"You should have thought of that before you fiddled with stove. Here, use this to get off the worst." He handed Davy an old rag before dragging the galvanized washtub, standing on end in the corner, to the center of the kitchen.

When he started pailing water across from the copper boiler on the stove, Beth jumped up. "I can do that."

"It's all right. Sit. I'll take care of it."

Feeling useless and uneasy, she sat again. She guardedly looked around the kitchen, taking in the cook stove and its shiny black top, noting the dry sink with a towel neatly folded on the bar in front. She longed to touch the dishes kept in the glass-windowed cupboard. Everything was in its place. Tom kept a tidy kitchen and this could have been her kitchen if the situation were different. She imagined them having supper around the table. Doing the dishes together. Extinguishing all the lanterns, except the one that would light their way to their bedroom.

The clatter of the pail against the stove brought Beth from her thoughts. "There you go," Tom said, straightening up. "Peel and hop in, Bud, before the water gets too cool." He lifted his coat from a hook. "I'll just go to the barn, see if I can convince Bill to come inside."

Her face felt flushed. "Fine. Yes, that would be nice. Thank you."

As soon as the door closed, Davy started shucking his dirty clothes. His naked body was lily-white except for his still somewhat sooty hands and face. He eased himself into the water.

Wearily, Beth bent over the tub. "Lean back and wet your hair so I can wash it," she instructed, grabbing the lye soap.

Davy did as he was told, stretching out in the tub. As she rubbed the bar over his hair, she idly ran her eyes up and down his skinny length. They paused momentarily to watch his little penis bob like a cork in the water.

Davy opened one eye a crack and stated, "Tom has a big one."

"I beg your pardon!" The bar of soap shot out of her hand and landed, plop, in the water.

"Tom has a big bathtub. I can lay right out."

"Oh . . . yes . . . yes, it's big." Flustered, she hastily finished scrubbing his head, desperately trying to erase the unsettling image that Davy's comment evoked.

"Now sit up and I'll rinse you." She used the dipper sitting on the table and poured water over Davy's head. That done, she washed his back and then handed him the bar of soap. "You can do the rest. Hurry now, but do a good job."

*

Tom found Bill settled back into a stack of loose straw, his hands folded behind his head. "Hi," he said, not at all surprised by Bill's lack of response. "I just thought I'd tell you there's an extra bed upstairs you and Davy can share. 'Course if you'd rather stay out here, well, that's fine by me."

Bill gave no indication of preference so Tom pointed to a wooden box, saying. "I keep a couple of horse blankets in the trunk over there if you get cold," and then he departed. He wasn't going to coddle Bill.

Tom entered the kitchen. "Oh, right," he said when he saw Davy still in the tub. "Sorry. I'll just wait in the parlor until you're finished."

*

A minute later Beth sent Davy, dressed in his long johns, to join him. She gave the rest of dirty clothing a thorough shaking outside, folded them and then set them on the chair in the kitchen. She stared at the long oval tub. How long had it been since she'd enjoyed a bath where she could recline without having her knees tucked up under her chin? She fingered the water again. It was tepid, and surprisingly not too dirty.

She shook her head. *Don't even think it.* She couldn't bathe in the middle of Tom's kitchen. Reason and temptation played a mental tug of war.

It would be totally improper.

Only if someone found out.

Tom could barge through the door any minute.

He couldn't come in if I barred the door first.

It would take too long to bathe.

Not if I hurried.

But the water is getting cold.

All the more reason to hurry.

Temptation won. Beth put her ear to the door leading into the parlor, listening to the muffled voices of Tom and Davy. Quickly, and as quietly as she could, she propped a chair under the doorknob. Then she crossed to the outside door, locked it and pulled the curtain on the window. Feeling secure, she added another bucketful of warm water to the tub, pinned her hair up and stripped.

Oh, the water felt wonderful! And oh, the tub was large! Suddenly a strange gentle tingle ran through her limbs. Here she was in Tom's tub, naked, sitting where Tom had sat many times, naked. She cautioned herself not to think about that. But she couldn't *not* think about that. The conjured image of Tom, naked in the tub, was branded in her mind. Suddenly that gentle tingle was no longer gentle. Her body pulsed deliciously, and in private places that had never pulsed before. She closed her eyes and leaned back against the tub's back, savoring the wonder and pleasure of this peculiar new sensation.

When the chair crashed to the floor, Beth's eyes popped open.

Seeing Beth reclining naked in his bathtub, Tom's eyes opened even wider. "Ooh, la la," he said, rubbing his hands together in delight.

Beth gasped and instinctively pulled her knees to her chin, hugging them close in an attempt to hide from his sight.

"You get out this minute!" she ordered in a harsh whisper.

Tom shook his head slowly. He put his finger to his lips. "Can't go yet," he whispered, pulling the door shut behind him. "Davy wants to play Fish. If I go out there without a deck of cards, he's going to be very, very disappointed. Call me an old softie, but I just don't want to let the boy down." Staring appreciatively at her, he circled around to the sideboard where the cards were kept.

"Don't you have the manners to knock?" she hissed, keeping a wary eye one him while willing her heart to cease its pounding.

He paused. "Knock? This may come as a shock to you, but most people don't knock to enter a kitchen. If they do, then I'm afraid I was remiss in learning that detail."

"Apparently you were also remiss in learning how to behave as a gentleman. If you had any morals you'd leave immediately."

His eyebrows lifted and a smile touched his lips. "Beth, honey, it's my morals keeping me from crawling right in there with you, that and the fact your brother is in the next room. It wouldn't do his innocence any good to find us thrashing about in the water like a pair of otters."

Pulse! Pulse! Pulse! A rhythm throbbed deep within her and in shockingly rapid succession. Desire tap-danced inside her. "How dare you!" she raged, looking to throw something at him.

Tom ducked as the bar of soap skimmed past his ear. Grinning, he raised his hands in submission. "Relax. I'll just get the cards and then the kitchen is all yours. You can stay in there until you look as wrinkled as a peach pit."

Watching her, he backed toward the cupboard and opened the drawer to get a deck of cards. "When I got up this morning I asked myself, Tom, what kind of day do think you'll have? Never in a million years would I have guessed it would be this good."

"You breathe a word of this to anyone and I'll never speak to you again!"

Ignoring her threat, he retrieved the bar of soap from under the wood stove, picked out the imbedded bits of wood and tossed it into the tub, splashing her in the face. At the door he studied the chair, just then realizing its intent.

Chuckling, he turned to face her. "The next time you use a chair to bar a door, make sure you know which way the door swings first." He slid through the door into the parlor.

Chapter 16

Make sure you know which way the door swings first, Beth mimicked as she slapped the soap up one arm, across her breasts and down the other arm. *My morals are keeping me from crawling right in there with you. Morals. Hmph! That man wouldn't know a moral if it came up and formally introduced itself.* Fuming, Beth attacked her legs with the bar of soap.

He's a rogue, a tyrant! Whatever made you even consider marrying him?

Because he turns me inside out with desire. Lord, help me, but I want him.

Much to Beth's relief, Tom barely glanced up when she entered the parlor fifteen minutes later.

"Do you have any sevens?" he asked Davy.

"Go fish. Do you got any fours?"

"Ah, nope. Go fish. Do you have any nines?"

"Shoot!" Davy handed across a card. "Wanna play, Beth?" he asked.

"No, thank you," she answered, feigning indifference, while her body still throbbed traitorously. "I prefer to watch."

"Actually," Tom stood, holding out his cards, "you can finish my hand while I go empty the tub."

Anything to get him out of the room, she took his cards. She had just settled into his chair when he yelled from the kitchen, "I haven't seen water this murky since I gave Jack a bath after he got stuck in Millar's slough. I can't believe one person could be this dirty!"

That degenerate. "Okay, whose turn?" She turned a deaf ear to any further comments coming from the kitchen.

"Mine. Do you got any jacks?"

Nearing the end of their second game, Beth announced, "Right after this, bedtime."

Tom entered just as Davy collected the last pair. "Where am I gonna sleep, Tom?"

"You can sleep in the guest bedroom upstairs."

"What about Beth?"

"She can sleep in my bed."

Cards flipped out of Beth's hands and scattered in as many directions as her flustered thoughts.

Tom grinned. "And I'll sleep on the sofa."

Beth bent to collect the cards and her senses. "I wouldn't think of putting you out of your bed. I'll sleep on the sofa," she said.

"If that's what you want. The sofa's all yours."

*

The guest bedroom was at the top of the stairs on the right. Beth set the lantern on a chair beside the bed, and then pulled back the quilt for Davy. She listened to his long litany of God blesses, even a God bless Tom which she thought probably was wasted on a man so full of the devil.

"Good night, Davy," she whispered, bending to kiss him.

"Beth?"

"Hmm?" She reached for the lamp.

"Did ya ever notice how Tom smells like peppermints?"

Her heart did a little skip. "Yes. Yes, I've noticed."

"I like it. It makes me think of nice things—like candy canes."

She smiled. *And Christmas and mistletoe and kisses.* "Go to sleep, now. Sweet dreams, little man."

Closing the door behind her, she paused at the head of the stairs. Across the landing was another room—Tom's room, for it smelled faintly of peppermints.

She stole a furtive glance down the stairs. *What would it hurt?* She tiptoed into his room, knowing it was improper, but doing so regardless.

Tom's bed was bigger than the one Davy slept in, higher too, and she ran her hand over the patchwork quilt to smooth out the wrinkles he'd missed. Which side did Tom sleep on, or did he sleep in the middle? *Pulse, pulse, pulse.* She quickly removed her hand.

Along the opposite wall stood his bureau. She moved across to it, cautioning herself not to touch anything. Tom's personal belongings were scattered on top: loose change, armbands, cufflinks, horseshoe nails, peppermints, and at the back, a framed photo of Abigail.

Beth stood the lamp on the bureau, and disregarding her own advice, picked up the photo, studied it momentarily and turned it over. There was no inscription on the back, no endearment.

She peered again at the image, studying Abigail's comely face, her full breasts covered by a lacy white blouse dotted with pearl buttons down the front, her tiny waist cinched by the wide waistband of her skirt and her broad hips flaring out the pleats. Not much wonder Tom had been attracted to her.

Compared to Abigail's voluptuous figure, Beth felt as flat as unleavened bread. Tiny breasts, flat tummy, narrow hips. *No wonder he thought I was a boy when he tackled me in his barn.*

"I'm making coffee now," Tom called up the stairs. "Do you want a cup? Or I can brew some tea if you'd rather."

Beth almost dropped the photo and she hastily returned it to the bureau. *Don't come up, don't come up,* she prayed, but the creaking of the stairs told her he was on his way. Other than diving out the second story window, there was no avenue of escape, so she stood silently steadfast, awaiting her humiliation. Certainly this couldn't be any more embarrassing than being caught bathing in his kitchen. Surely not.

"My, my," he drawled as he peered around the doorway, grinning like a cat having just cornered a mouse. "Did you get lost? Or are you just checking out what you'll miss by sleeping on the sofa."

She lifted her head proudly, as if she had every right to be in his room. "Maybe I was checking to see if you had any skeletons in your closet."

"And did you find any?"

"One." She reached for the photo.

Tom's eyes seemed to dull. "Oh," was all he said.

"Did you love her?" Beth asked, her vocal cords tight.

"I thought I did," he answered and she gave him credit for his honesty.

Suddenly, one question burned in Beth's mind and no matter how embarrassed she was to ask, she had to know. She needed to know. "Were you . . . I mean . . . did you . . . "

"Beth, are you sure you want to hear the answer?"

She nodded, though by asking his question, he'd answered hers. Her eyes brimmed.

"Okay, yes, we had been intimate. But after a while it became routine."

"Routine?"

"Beth, you have to understand, we were comfortable together. It just became an unspoken agreement we'd be together on Friday nights. Yes, I made love to her, but I was never really *in love* with her. Does that make any sense?" She didn't answer, so he continued, "Then things began to change and I didn't feel right about her and me and we drew apart. If it makes you feel any better, the last couple of months or so, we weren't intimate."

Seized with a need to get away, Beth pushed the photo against his chest, and tried to go by him. Tom grabbed her arm. "Beth, I am sorry . . . really . . . but I can't change the past." His grip tightened.

"Please let me go. You're hurting me."

"God, Beth, I'm in love with you. I have never loved anyone more than I do you. You have to believe me."

Her brain felt numb, her heart rock heavy. "I don't know what to believe. I need time to think. Please."

Sighing deeply, he released her arm. Beth fled from the room and scurried downstairs, leaving Tom alone to stare at the smiling image of Abigail. Why hadn't he rid himself of the photo? It meant nothing to him now. Shaking his head, he dropped the photo, frame and all, into the wastebasket, and then picked up the lamp.

Before going downstairs, Tom opened the door to Davy's room.

"You still awake?" he asked when the boy rolled over to look at him.

"Uh huh." Davy sat up.

"What's the matter?"

"Nothing. I was just thinking."

"About what?"

"Stuff." He picked at the tufts of yarn used to tie the quilt. "Tom, if you was to marry Beth, would that make you my dad?"

Tom certainly was not expecting that question. "Did your sister say anything to you about marrying me?"

"I was just wondering."

"Well then, if I married Beth we'd be brothers-in-law."

"Oh." Davy's shoulders sagged with definite disappointment.

"But I guess," Tom continued, "being how as I'm so much older than you are, it would seem like I'm your dad."

Davy looked up. "I'd like that a whole bunch."

Tom smiled. "Between you and me and the bedpost, I'd like that a whole bunch too. Now slide back down and try to go to sleep. It's late." He tucked the quilt under the boy's chin. "Goodnight, Bud."

Beth was seated at the kitchen table when Tom came down. He poured her a coffee, slid the cup across the table to her, and then poured himself one. He flipped a chair around, and sat astraddle, draping his arms across the chair back.

She couldn't look at him. The silence between them almost echoed with unasked questions and unsaid explanations.

It was Tom who braved the first words. "I'm sorry, Beth. I guess maybe I should have told you earlier about my relationship with

Abigail, but somehow the timing never seemed right."

When would the timing be right to say such a thing? she wondered dismally. *I love you and by the way I was intimate with Abigail Craig on Friday nights, but don't worry, it was as routine as washing clothes on Mondays or ironing on Tuesdays.*

"You don't owe me any explanations," she said quietly, striving to keep the hurt from her voice.

"I shouldn't have kept something so important from you, especially since I asked you to be my wife."

What did he expect her to say? That she was glad he had told her now? Besides, considering the enormity of her secret, who was she to cast the first stone?

Tom traced the rim of his cup round and round with his index finger. "I just assumed you would have known. Most men my age have been with a woman." Beth turned her head aside. She couldn't bear to hear affirmation of his carnal past.

"Are you angry with me?" he ventured gently.

"Yes," she answered hastily and then dropping her forehead into her hands, said, "no . . . oh Tom, I don't know. I'm so confused." It was difficult to elucidate her emotions when she didn't know herself. Hurt, jealous, fearful, angry. *Dear Lord, I have no right to feel these emotions. His indiscretions are like a speck of dust compared to what I've done.*

Bill burst through the door. "Dammit, Carver, but you've got a passel of mice in your barn. How's a fellow supposed to sleep with them crawling through the straw?"

Tom pointed. "At the top on the right." Tension clipped his words.

Bill grunted.

Beth felt relief at her brother's inopportune timing. She wasn't going to marry Tom, so what difference did Tom's past relationship make. He was not obliged to give her any explanations. Emotionally spent, Beth pushed herself slowly up from the table. "I'd like to retire for the night now."

"Beth, we need to hash this out. At least let me try to explain."
"I'm too tired to think. Please, I just want to go to bed."
He nodded. "I'll go get you some bedding."

*

Long after the house was quiet, when the crackling in the fireplace had ceased and the logs had settled down into powdery coals, Beth was still awake. The steady ticking of the mantle clock counted off the seconds, while its chimes marked the hours of the passing night. Three o'clock.

She wanted so desperately to go to sleep. Her body was tired, her emotions hurt and confused, but her mind was actively mulling over and over all the evening's events. When her thoughts collided with Tom's admission he'd been intimate with Abigail on Friday nights, her heart ached.

Every Friday night. That meant he likely had been with Abigail just before he tackled her in his barn, *and* with Abigail the night he brought Bill home and confronted them in the kitchen. It struck her there had been many more Friday nights between then and when Abigail left.

Beth rolled onto her back, staring at the dark ceiling above her. When Davy had been born, her mother had explained the very basics of procreation, but Beth was left with more questions than answers. Her mother had promised she would explain it all in more depth when Beth was older. Sadly, their parents were killed soon after, and she and her brothers had been sent to live with her father's brother, Mead, and his wife, Tilly. Beth didn't dare broach the subject with them so what she learned initially about sex she got from glimpses of domestic animals mating on the farm. At the time, she thought it rather repulsive. The animals grunted, but displayed none of the affection her mother had spoken of.

Then once, while she was picking Saskatoon berries, Beth had come upon an amorous young couple. They were on the other side of the bushes, kissing and fondling, and totally unaware of her presence. She watched in curious fascination, but when the lovers started removing their clothing and Beth realized their intentions, she looked away.

The amorous couple had presented her with an awful dilemma. Should she go or should she wait? She knew if she went home with an empty pail, she'd receive a beating from her uncle. So she quietly sat on her side of the bushes, with her back to the passionate activity on the other side. Though she could see nothing, she certainly heard plenty. Again there was lots of grunting and moaning, except Beth got the feeling they were enjoying themselves. When the two finally dressed and left, Beth quickly filled her bucket. As she stripped the branches of their berries, she had pondered the perplexing idea of sex being enjoyable. Was that possible?

Now, here she was, nineteen and still as naïve as when she had picked those berries. As she shifted on the sofa in Tom's parlor, she almost wished she *had* watched the young lovers. Then at least she wouldn't be so ignorant. Other women, younger than her, knew what sex was all about. The rate she was going, she would probably end up an old maid, provided she wasn't captured and hanged for murder first. Either way, she would *never* have a chance to experience the act of love making even once, let alone once a week.

Immediately her mind was back to Tom and Abigail.

Beth tried to sort out her feelings about Abigail. She wanted to hate her, but it was difficult to hate someone she barely knew. Still, she recognized she was jealous, jealous that Abigail had known Tom intimately. Without a doubt, their time together had been enjoyable because whatever Tom did, he did well.

He certainly was an adept kisser. The past couple of months, Beth had found Tom's kisses very pleasurable. She warmed just remembering the feel of his lips on hers and his tongue inside her mouth. She could only imagine how much more pleasurable it would be if he were to . . . *Pulse, pulse, pulse. Stop it! You are only making yourself crazy. Tom will never be intimate with you. He wants you as a wife first.*

But Tom and Abigail weren't married. Where were his morals then? Did he leave them on her bedroom floor along with his clothes when he took her to bed?

Pulse, pulse, pulse. Drawing her knees up, Beth tucked her hands between her thighs, sliding them down until the heels of her hands pressed hard against the pelvic bone and temporarily alleviated her throbbing need.

A moment later, Beth flipped the blankets back and sat up, swinging her legs over the edge of the sofa. She threw some wood into the fire, then stood rocking back and forth in an attempt to relieve the tension of her body. She wrapped her arms around herself, holding tight, not because she was chilled, but because she felt as if she might explode otherwise. She squeezed until the delicate lace of her chemise irritated her nipples. Better to feel discomfort rather than this restless urgency that nearly drove her to distraction.

She heard Tom cough upstairs, and she wondered, did he often cough in his sleep or was he awake thinking of her? More likely it was the strong coffee causing his insomnia. Or maybe he simply had a tickle in his throat and would be coming downstairs any minute for a drink of water.

Beth hastily returned to the sofa, pulling the scratchy blankets over her. It wouldn't do for him to see her in her undergarments, though she wondered why she concerned herself with such proprieties now.

Her mind drifted back to the moment when he had caught her bathing in the kitchen. At the time, she had been outraged and thoroughly embarrassed by the situation, but thinking of it now shot sexual excitement through her.

What if Davy *hadn't* been in the next room? Would Tom have held firm to his morals or would he have stripped and stepped into the tub?

And what if he had? A surprising and delightful heat touched her feminine core. Hoping to experience it again, she deliberately thought of Tom touching her naked body. The pleasurable feeling returned. *You're playing with fire,* she warned herself, but Beth ignored her voice of reason. Settling her head back onto her pillow, she closed her eyes and imagined Tom standing in front of her, removing his clothing. She imagined him tugging his shirt free from his pants, then unbuttoning each button one by one, exposing more and more of his chest, which caused her heart to thrum in her own chest. She envisioned lots of dark hair covering hard muscles.

Suddenly that delightful thrumming pulsed through her with shocking intensity. Flushed with heat, she kicked her leg out from under the covers. *Stop it. Now.* But hot desire overwhelmed her common sense. She envisioned more of Tom's body. It made sense that he would be bigger than Davy . . . down there . . . but how much bigger?

Beth felt as if she had a fever. Kicking the blankets off completely, she heaved a great sigh of frustration. Ask her what seventeen times sixteen was and she could rattle off the figure immediately. Ask her to list the names of renowned explorers, recounting the routes they took, and she would answer confidently and correctly. But ask her what a naked man looked like, or ask her exactly what happens between a man and a woman . . . Beth was embarrassingly naive.

Naive, yes, but she possessed a great aching desire to learn.

And the man to teach her all she wanted to know was a mere staircase away.

Chapter 17

Tom lay wide awake on his back, severely castigating himself for having the sensitivity of a cow patty and the brains to match. Now he was likely back to square one again. He should have been straightforward from the beginning about his relationship with Abigail, but who'd have thought his feelings for Beth would have developed so rapidly? Certainly not him.

Ah, Beth. He couldn't stop thinking about her sitting naked in his tub. Even outraged, she was the most beautiful woman he had ever seen. Her skin was flawless and pale, almost white. He'd have given five years of his life if he could have run his hands along her lithe body to see if she felt as silky smooth as she looked. He ached to see more than glimpses of her perfect breasts hidden behind her pulled-up knees.

He groaned. His arousal was full and throbbing.

When he was a kid, he'd heard a rumor about men's testicles turning blue from lack of release. He never really believed it, but he wondered if he might experience some sort of permanent damage from ignoring the very frequent sexual urges he was having of late. Never in his adult life had he been without sex for so long. When he was with Abby, the sex was good. But he wanted more than good sex with Beth. He loved her more profoundly than he ever thought possible. He wanted a far deeper connection with her than just a physical one. He wanted commitment. Marriage. " 'Til death do us part." After their wedding, he'd gladly carry his beautiful wife to their marriage bed, and together they would—

Unless you want to be changing sheets, think of something else, something undesirable. Think of . . . manure. Stinky, lumpy horse manure. Good. Already he could feel the pressure lessening. He forced himself to visualize other disgusting things, anything to erase Beth's lovely image from his mind. A few minutes later, his member was flaccid. *Good, stay that way!*

He thought he heard the sound of footsteps and he stilled his breathing to listen. Definitely, someone was coming up the stairs. Who was prowling around? Silently rising up on one elbow, he lit the lamp beside his bed, turning the wick down low.

A moment later, Beth stepped through his doorway, a blanket draped around her like a cloak.

"What's the matter, Beth?" he asked, surprised to see her. "Are you cold? Give me a moment and I'll get you some more blankets."

She shook her head, quietly closing the door behind her, and suddenly Tom understood her intent. His heart pounded until he thought it would fire right through his rib cage. Lord, help him. He could only take so much.

"Beth," Tom whispered hoarsely, "don't. Don't come any closer. Go back downstairs. You don't know what you're getting into."

"Then teach me." Silently she moved to the side of his bed, letting her blanket slip from her shoulders to fall to the floor. She was clad in drawers and a cotton chemise, and he could see the twin peaks of her small breasts jutting through the lacy material.

Oh hell. Tom clenched his jaw. He longed to reach out and pull her to him, but he dared not give in. He knew she was innocent about such things.

Her voice sounded like satin on glass when she whispered, "I want you to show me how a man and a woman make love."

Suddenly, and not fully understanding why, Tom felt angry. He sat up, bunching the blankets across his midriff and behind him. "Why," he asked, agitation in his voice, "because you're curious about sex? Dammit, girl, go back to the sofa where you belong." Hoping his angry remarks would send her running down the stairs, he slid down in his bed and turned away from her.

He felt her hand grasp his shoulder and her skin felt hot on his.

She firmly pulled him onto his back. "I'm not a girl. I'm a woman, Tom, and I know what I want."

I doubt it! Frustrated, he lifted onto his elbows. "You may think you do, but if I allowed you in my bed, sure as there's a heaven and hell, you'd hate me and yourself in the morning."

"I could never hate you, Tom. No matter what happens. And if you love me as you say you do, then you'll make love to me." Her voice was a raspy whisper.

Tom groaned. *Send her away. She just learned how to kiss, for crissakes.* He strove for patience. "I do love you, and I will gladly make love to you, but not tonight." It took all his strength to suppress his desire for her and, considering his erection, it felt like he was losing the battle.

"Don't you like the way I look?" she asked, her voice nearly breaking. "I know I'm not voluptuous or—"

"Stop," Tom said with a note of sadness. "Beth, you're beautiful, perfect. And God knows I want you. But it would be better for us to be married first."

"You weren't married to Abigail."

It was a simple statement—and true—but it had no bearing on this relationship. "That was different, and you know it," he said gruffly, wishing they could get past his former relationship.

"No, I don't know it. I don't know anything about any of this. Before I met you, I didn't even know what it felt like to be kissed by a man. You showed me how wonderful it can be. But my body yearns for something more and we both know what that is. Please, Tom. Please don't turn me away."

"You think I *want* to turn you away?" He pushed himself up to lean back against the brass head rail. "God, Beth. Saying no is nearly killing me, I desire you so much." He raked his fingers back though his thick dark hair. "I've dreamed of you in my arms every night for weeks now. Every time I kissed you, hell, every time I *looked* at you, I wanted to make love to you. And then tonight . . ."

He closed his eyes and sighed. "You have no idea how much I want you. But still, I want to wait until we marry. Then it will be right and legal."

"But," she started.

Before Tom lost his struggle and caved in to his growing lust, he ordered more firmly than he intended, "Enough! I've given you my answer, now go back downstairs!"

"No!" Beth answered just as firmly. "I am not some child you can order about. I'm nineteen, a grown woman. Many women my age are married and have borne children. They've experienced life while I am watching it go by. I'm like the child who doesn't know the truth about Santa when everyone else does. Well, not anymore." Crossing her arms low in front of her, she grabbed the hemmed edge of her chemise and lifted it up and over her head in one fluid motion, then let the garment drop to the hardwood floor. She stood statue still in front of him.

Oh, she was beautiful, her small breasts proud and firm, her stomach flat, and her hips gently rounded. Except for the rapid rising and falling of her breasts, Tom might never have known her nervousness. *His beautiful Beth.* He could no longer fight against his male urges, his need for her so great, his love for her greater. He could no more turn her away than he could suspend time.

In the past, the women he'd slept with had been experienced and there was a mutual responsibility for their sexual satisfaction. But Beth was so innocent, so naïve. He realized the onus was upon him to ensure her initial sexual experience was pleasurable and gratifying. It was a weighty responsibility, and it frightened him, yet he would never relinquish this honor to another.

He closed his eyes in silent supplication for guidance, wondering if it was right to pray for such a thing, then slid over to make room for her in his bed.

She lifted the covers and quickly slipped in beside Tom. He could feel her limbs trembling.

Go slow, he cautioned himself. "Face me, Beth."

She did and he gazed into her green eyes and saw her vulnerability. He had never felt more protective of anyone in his life and he pulled her into his embrace. "Any moment you want to stop, just say and I'll stop. Understand?"

"Yes," she whispered, and her breath was hot against his chest. He raised her head gently and touched his lips to hers.

And Beth kissed him back. Tentatively, at first, and then as if to show she was a willing participant, she engaged all he had ever taught her about kissing into that kiss. She brazenly opened her mouth, inviting his tongue to parry with hers.

He tasted. He teased. Their tongues touched and rolled, pursuing each other playfully. He probed in and out, savoring her sweetness. And when she finally dared to thrust her tongue inside his mouth and sweep it from side to side, Tom groaned.

Beth immediately began to pull away, but he held her still and whispered hoarsely against her lips, "When I do that, Beth, it's a good thing. It means I like what you're doing." His lips kissed hers lightly. "And if I do things you like, you might make a few sounds, too. And it's all right. Allow yourself to do or say whatever feels good. Don't be afraid or embarrassed." He kissed her again, this time far more passionately, nearly assaulting her lips. She reciprocated boldly. Their breathing became hot and husky and she forgot all about her apprehensions, and he forgot all about sending her from his bed.

*

The sun roused Beth first, and for a moment she was disoriented, waking in an unfamiliar room. When she remembered what brought her too this room, she sprang from the bed. "Tom, wake up! What time is it?"

Tom opened a sleepy eye. His feet hit the floor less than a second later. He snatched up the clock on the night table. "Damn. It's eight-twenty. You better get downstairs before Bill gets up."

The clanging of the stove door downstairs told them it was already too late.

Chapter 18

Beth scrambled into her underclothes and then wrapped the blanket around her. Silently she tip-toed down the stairs, praying Bill hadn't noticed the sofa was vacant. She peered around the edge of the doorway. He was standing before the dry sink, gazing out the window as Beth slipped noiselessly past.

"There's no point in trying to sneak around," she heard him say.

She backed up to the kitchen doorway and tried to seem cheerful, as if nothing was amiss. "Oh, good morning, Bill. You're up early."

"It ain't early. The sun's been up for some time, but I guess it don't get around to *his* window until later."

Beth blanched. How could she have allowed herself to fall asleep in Tom's bed!

"You must think I'm stupid, that I don't know what you two been doing up there."

"Oh, Bill. Please don't pass judgment. We need to talk about this, but I don't have time right now. I'll be late for school if I don't hurry. Please, promise me we can talk about this later."

He shrugged his shoulders, still looking out the window. "Don't see as there's much to talk about. You spent the night with him, plain and simple. What more is there to say?"

Tom came down the stairs, tucking in his shirttail, and Beth threw him a desperate, pleading look. Standing on the step behind her, he placed his hands on her shoulders and gave them a reassuring squeeze through the blanket. "Don't worry." His voice was low and reassuring, "I'll handle Bill." He pointed her toward the parlor. "Go get dressed."

Bill kept his back to Tom when he entered the kitchen and

crossed to the stove. There was coffee from last night. Tom felt the pot and though it was cold, today it would do. He grabbed a mug down from the cupboard and poured himself a cup. "Want some?" he asked, but received no reply.

He dragged out a chair from the table and sat down. Taking a deep breath, he started, "I guess there's no point in denying what happened. You're old enough to figure things out."

Bill grabbed the edge of the dry sink, squeezing until his knuckles turned white. "Yeah, and I'm old enough to know right from wrong and what you two did was flat out wrong."

Tom stared calmly across the mug's rim at Bill's back. "We love each other very much."

Bill snorted derisively.

"This may come as a shock to you," Tom continued, "but life is not always black and white. There's a whole world of gray out there and the older you get the more you'll understand what I mean." He felt like he was talking to a stone wall. "Dammit, Bill, the least you could do is look at me when I'm talking to you."

Bill spun about and leaned over the table until his face was menacingly close to Tom's. "You horny bastard! You were just waiting for your chance to get my sister into the sack with you, weren't you?"

Beth, having finished dressing, entered the kitchen and recoiled at her brother's caustic words. "Stop it, Bill! It wasn't like that at all. You're making it sound cheap and it wasn't."

He glared at her with contempt. "If you believe that, then you're no better than Miranda Parsons, screwing anything wearing pants."

"That is bloody well enough!" Tom yelled, rising from his chair and knocking it over backwards. He slammed his cup down on the table and the coffee sloshed over the rim. "Apologize to your sister!"

Bill shoved the table against Tom. "Go to hell! Both of you! It's what you deserve." He stormed outside, slamming the door so hard it bounced open.

In the aftermath of the verbal explosion, there was complete silence. Tom closed the door.

Beth set his chair upright and held onto the back for support. "Oh, what have we done? He'll never forgive us."

"Beth, he's young. Give him time. He'll come around."

"No," she said, shaking her head, "no, he won't. You don't know how stubborn he can be."

Tom had a pretty good idea. Stubbornness seemed to be a Patterson family trait. "There's nothing we can do about it now, except let him cool off." He came around behind her and wrapped his arms about her waist. Bending low until his stubbled cheek rested against her silky one, he whispered, "I want to know . . . how are you feeling after last night?"

Heat coursed through Beth's body, all the wonderful intimate details of the previous night vivid in her memory. Still, she felt embarrassed to be asked such a personal question in the light of day. "I'm fine," she answered, her voice barely audible.

He kissed her head, and Beth wanted to turn in his arms and hold him and be held, but time wouldn't allow it.

"I'd better finish getting ready." She headed to the parlor, then came up short, remembering her other brother was still upstairs asleep. "What about Davy?"

"Don't worry about him. Just get ready. I'll bring him over later."

That morning, school started ten minutes late, but the children didn't seem to notice, or if they had, they kept quiet. And if any of them wondered about her untidy hair or her sooty dress, they were too polite to ask.

*

Despite Beth's valiant efforts to keep the family together, ultimately it was her actions that drove Bill away. Back at their own place, after the black filth had been scrubbed clean, he went to his room to pack his things.

"Please, don't go," she pleaded, standing in his doorway, watching him drag his clothes from the closet and toss them on the blanket spread out on his bed.

Davy cried. Fat tears rolled down his cheeks, and dropped into his small lap. "Did I make you mad, B . . . Bill?" He swiped at his cheek. "I p . . . promise I won't do it again if you just t . . . tell me what I did."

He paused to look at his little brother. "It ain't nothing you did, Bud," he reassured softly, and then realizing he had used Tom's endearment, abruptly resumed lugging things out of his closet. "I'm just going to the livery. You can come visit me whenever you want. Hey, some night why don't you sleep over?"

"Really?" Davy brightened somewhat and turned his tear-streaked face to Beth, seeking her consent.

Bill seemed to think she had forfeited her right to comment. "Sure," he continued, "I think the room behind the livery is big enough and if it ain't, you can sleep in a feed bunk."

"Wow, just like the baby Jesus in the manger."

"You bet. Now get to bed, squirt, so I can get going." He drew the blanket's four corners together and slung the bag over his shoulder. He stopped in front of Beth, refusing to look directly at her, waiting silently until she moved aside to let him through.

"What will you do for food?" she asked, following him into the kitchen, twisting her hankie into a white knot.

Bill dropped his things at his feet while he dragged on his coat. "I'll figure something out."

"I could send something over with Davy."

"Don't bother." He hoisted his belongings over his back and looked around the room in a final farewell. He gave Davy an affectionate punch on the shoulder. "See you around, kid." And then his eyes met Beth's.

Tears pooled in hers, threatening to spill over. She dabbed at them with her abused hankie.

Bill grabbed her hand and pulled her out to the front stoop, closing the door so Davy couldn't hear what he had to say. His words came out hurried.

"You ain't nothing like Miranda Parsons and if anyone should go to hell, it's me for saying you was."

"Oh, Bill—"

"Wait, I ain't finished yet. I know you never would have done what you did if Tom hadn't tricked you. He's older and smarter about them things and I hold him responsible for what happened."

"No, Bill, you're wrong. He didn't trick me. He loves me and I love him."

"Well, if that's so, why ain't you married?"

She tipped her head back as if beseeching the stars above to help her explain. "You know why. I killed Uncle Mead."

"It was an accident."

"But I pushed him. If I hadn't pushed him—"

"You were protecting Davy."

"That doesn't change anything. Mead is still dead and it's my fault. What do you think it would do to Tom's reputation if folks found out he was married to a murderer?"

"Is it any better he sleeps with her?"

Suddenly they were both silent. They had come to an impasse. Bill shifted his heavy bag. "I gotta go."

"You don't have to. It's not too late to change your mind."

He looked at her, his eyes emotionless. "Yeah, it's too late." He stepped off the stoop, and headed toward the livery. Soon his form was swallowed by the darkness.

*

The next day, when school was dismissed, Davy raced over to the shop to tell Tom about Bill's leaving.

Tom was stunned. The last thing he wanted to do was come between Beth and her brothers. He hung his leather apron on a wooden peg. "Listen, I want you to go to Betner's store for a while. Tell them I sent you. I need to step out for a bit."

"Where're you going?"

"To see your sister."

"Then I'll come with you."

"Nope."

"Then I'll stay here and look after the place until you get back."

"No, Davy. You go to Betner's like I said. I'll come get you later."

Tom gave no more thought as to whether Davy would obey him. It was the furthest thing from his mind as he headed toward the schoolhouse.

He found Beth inside, sitting at her desk. Her head was bowed. Tom stood in the threshold not sure what to say.

"I heard about Bill. Davy just told me."

He made his way up the aisle, watching for her reaction, but there was none. She kept her head down, her finger tracing aimlessly along a crack in the desktop. Tom's hand covered hers.

"It won't hurt Bill to be on his own, you know. Plenty of boys his age do it. They like to be independent."

She shook her head slowly, then pulled her hand away, letting it fall into her lap.

"We can't change what happened, Beth."

"I know." She looked up at him then, her eyes brimming with tears. "But we can prevent it from happening again."

He leaned over the desk until his face was mere inches from hers. "Is that what you want?" he asked softly.

His nearness suspended coherent thought and she fought to concentrate. "What I want is to have Bill back home where he belongs."

Tom straightened. "That's up to him now."

"It's our fault he's gone."

Fault? How it pained him to hear her put it that way, as if Bill had convinced her what they had done had wronged him personally. Tom came around the desk and put his hands on her shoulders. He felt them stiffen and he ached knowing this woman whom he had held so intimately mere hours ago now tensed at his touch. "Beth."

"He's my brother, Tom. I'm prepared to do whatever is necessary to get him home again. I've decided it would be best if we didn't see each other for a while."

So it had come to this. He closed his eyes against the pain. "Ah, Beth. Don't say that."

She blinked and tears dropped to her lap. "I think you'd better go. It's just for a while."

Rage and frustration rose in Tom. "And how long is a while? A week? A month? Beth, we can't put our lives on hold indefinitely." Tom spun her about, chair and all, and when she looked away, he firmly grasped her jaw and forced her to look up at him. When he saw her face, etched with as much anguish as he felt, his voice softened. "It's not right. Either you love me or you don't."

"I do love you," she said quietly.

"Then don't shut me out. Please."

"But I have no choice."

"Yes, you do. There's always a choice."

Another tear slipped over her lashes and ran down to the corner of her mouth. She wiped it away with her palm. "You'd better go," she choked.

Tom's shoulders slumped. "All right. I don't want to argue with you, but with all my being I know this is wrong." He went to the door and paused, as if to try one more protest, then changed his mind and left without another word.

*

If one thought it coincidental that Tom entered Betner's General Store only a few moments after Beth did, he'd be wrong. Tom knew she was there. He had watched her go in a few minutes ahead of him and had followed her on purpose. Though he was acutely aware of Beth standing behind a tall shelf, he strode right past her.

Earl was at the front counter, dividing large sacks of sugar into smaller portions. "Hello, Tom. Haven't seen you all week. Keeping busy?"

"So-so. Things are a little slow this time of year." Tom lifted the lid of a glass jar sitting on the countertop and helped himself to a peppermint. "I'm taking off for a while. I hired Pat Flanagan's two teenage boys from Tannerville to mind the shop for me and look after my horses. Told them they could come to you if they ran into any trouble. Is that all right?"

Earl stopped measuring. "Sure. Where are you going?"

"Toronto."

Mary came out from the back, wiping her hands on her apron. "Did I hear you say Toronto? Whatever for?"

"I got a letter from Abigail yesterday. She's getting married and I'm invited to the wedding."

Mary beamed. "How nice for her. Did she say anything about her intended? It certainly must have been a whirlwind courtship."

Tom shrugged. "All she said was he's a widower with two little girls."

Mary clasped her apron and pulled it to her bosom, holding it like a bouquet. "Oh, I'm so happy for her."

Earl glanced at his wife. "Woman, you're happy when two horses get hitched."

"And you're just as sentimental, Earl. Don't give me that," Mary scolded, all the while smiling.

Their easy display of affection keenly reminded Tom how lonely he'd been this past week and a half. Staying away from Beth had proven far more difficult than he'd expected.

"At first I thought I wouldn't go, but then, with things being slow and everything, I thought, why not. There's nothing holding me back."

"So when are you leaving?" Earl asked.

"Tomorrow noon."

"Can't say as I envy you. It's a long train ride."

"Yeah, well if I get bored with the scenery, I can read. And I've got some thinking to do."

"Don't forget, I'll expect a full account of the wedding when you get back," Mary instructed.

Tom grinned. "I'll make notes."

"Now don't get cheeky, Thomas Carver."

"I wouldn't think of it, Mary dear." He stretched across the counter and gave her a peck on the cheek. "I'll be back in a month, give or take a few days."

"Don't worry. We'll check your place," Earl said and Mary added, "Give our love to Abigail."

As Tom headed for the door, he saw out the corner of his eye that Beth hadn't moved from her hiding spot. He hesitated, debating whether she deserved a personal good-bye, but then he thought against it. She had made the rules; he was just abiding by them. He left the store.

*

With blurry-eyed vision, Beth started putting items from her basket back on the shelves, too upset to purchase anything now. A month. The last week and a half without Tom had almost been unbearable. How would she be able to endure four more? The thought made her miserably ill.

Mary came around the corner. "Oh, thank heaven it's you, Beth. I heard this rustling and I thought we had another mouse."

Beth couldn't reply, certain if she opened her mouth a sob would come forth. She turned her head away, blinking back her tears.

Mary put a concerned hand on her shoulder. "Are you all right, dear? You look a little peakish."

Shaking, Beth sucked in a long unsteady breath. "I'm not feeling very well. I think I'd better go home."

Mary's maternal instincts took over. She put a hand on Beth's forehead. "You don't have a fever. Do you feel sick to your stomach?"

Suddenly a sob burst through Beth's lips. "Oh, I've made such a mess of things."

Mary wrapped a consoling arm about the young woman, recognizing Beth's ailment as a serious case of heartache. "Come in the back, Beth, and let's have a talk. Maybe it'll make you feel better."

Beth shook her head and then sniffled loudly as she dug in her pocket for her hankie. "I don't want to bother you with my problems. I'll be okay in a little while. Really." She flashed a valiant smile. "I'm sorry. I'm not normally a crybaby."

"There's nothing wrong with a good cry once in a while. Tears cleanse the soul."

Beth thought her soul must be sparkling clean by now, for she'd wailed a bucketful every night since she'd broken off with Tom. She had no idea she would miss him this much, miss his kisses, miss his touch. Another small sob escaped her lips.

Mary led Beth to the back of the store, through the archway and down a short hall to the adjoining living quarters. Beth recognized the parlor where she'd sung songs with Tom at Christmas and the memory pulled painfully at her heartstrings. They passed through the parlor into the kitchen, and Mary sat Beth down at the table. The mistletoe of course was gone now, but Beth remembered clearly her first innocent kiss in this room, and then all the other kisses and so much more she and Tom had shared. Flooded with emotions, it was all she could do not to break down completely and sob all over Mary's crocheted tablecloth.

Mary set about making tea, humming to herself. She poured them both a cup and then sat down. "Here, dear, sip this." She reached for a plateful of cookies sitting on the sideboard beside her and set them on the table. "And have a cookie. Food is very calming." She patted her round girth. "It works for me, anyway."

In spite of how dismal she felt, Beth managed a smile and removed her coat. "Thank you."

Mary studied Beth and then stated, "Unless I miss my mark, Tom has something to do with this. Am I right?"

Beth nodded, staring at the tea leaves swirling to the bottom of her cup through tears welling in her eyes. One round tear escaped and dropped into her tea and the tea leaves lifted before settling again. Mary handed Beth a napkin before tears diluted her tea further.

"He never told you he was planning to go to Toronto, did he?"

Beth shook her head.

"Oh dear, I thought that tiff you and he had at the Valentine's dance would have been resolved by now."

The Valentine's dance? That night seemed almost a lifetime ago. So much had happened since then, none of which Beth could possibly share with Mary. She raised her hands to her face, wishing she could just crawl inside herself and die.

Mary patted her shoulder. "There, there. It can't be as bad as that."

"It's worse. I told him I didn't want to see him anymore."

Mary huffed. "Well, if that's true, then pigs fly and flies oink. Look at you. You don't look like a girl who's getting what she wants."

"That's just it. I don't know *what* I want," Beth bemoaned, though in her heart she knew exactly what she wanted. Tom. And now he was leaving, because "he had nothing holding him back." She didn't think she would ever forget those words.

"Then maybe a little time apart is just what you two need to sort things out."

Fresh tears brimmed. "But he's going to see Abigail. What if he finds out he still loves her?"

"Heavens! Do you really think if he still had any amorous feelings for her, he'd want to attend her wedding?"

Beth swallowed a sob, shook her head and then dabbed at her eyes. "I guess not," she conceded and then sat in miserable reticence, sipping her tea and nibbling at a cookie, which contrary to Mary's advice, did nothing to soothe her. Beth still felt ill at heart.

Mary chatted on and on about how the time would fly by.

Beth listened, but didn't believe a word. After some time, she resigned herself to the fact that life in Whistle Creek would carry on without Tom's presence, and so would hers.

Mary took another cookie. "I hear Bill is staying at the livery now."

Beth nodded. "We had a disagreement and he moved out. I was hoping he'd be ready to come home, but apparently not. Mr. Compel has fixed up a bit of space for him and Bill says he likes having his own place."

"Well, don't you go worrying about Bill. What I've heard of that boy, he can take care of himself." Mary gave Beth's arm a squeeze. "And don't you go worrying about Tom either. Knots always have a way of working themselves out if you don't pull too hard. Some just take longer than others."

Beth nodded, rose and donned her coat. "I have to go and pick up Davy. He went to see Bill after school and I don't want him interfering with Bill's work." On impulse, Beth gave Mary a hug. "Thank you. I do feel a little better."

"It's amazing what a little cup of tea can do," Mary said as she saw Beth out.

Chapter 19

If it were possible to be sick from missing someone, Beth was. A good dose of melancholy had hold of her and all weekend long she fought the urge to stay in bed and cry. She had no appetite and cooked merely for Davy's sake, nibbling sparingly at her own food because he insisted. "Remember how sick I felt when I didn't eat after Jack died?" he reminded.

Monday morning she felt even worse, but she forced herself to get up. There was school to teach and moping about in bed on a school day would only get her fired. Besides, pining for Tom wouldn't bring him back any sooner.

Her legs were weak and she felt dizzy when she crawled out of bed, and little wonder, she thought as she wrapped her shawl about her. She'd hardly eaten for two days. *Davy is right. I'd better eat.*

Resolutely, she made a hearty breakfast for the two of them—eggs, thick slabs of bacon, toast with puddles of melted butter. Beth forced down the breakfast, only to race to the outhouse minutes later where it all came up.

When she returned, pale as egg whites, Davy was concerned. "Are you okay?"

Beth mopped her brow with a cool damp cloth. "Not really."

"Were you throwing up? I always throw up when I'm sick."

If Davy said the words "throw up" once more, Beth was certain she would have to make a run for the outhouse again. Feeling wretched, she sank into a chair. "Just go get ready for school."

"Are you going to teach today?" he asked.

"I'm going to try. Once I'm up for a while, I'm sure I'll feel better."

"But what if you throw up at school?"

Her stomach heaved and Beth flew out the door, wondering if

she'd even make it to the outhouse, let alone the school to teach.

Midway through the morning classes, Beth started feeling better. She wondered if she had eaten something tainted, except Davy exhibited no ill effects and they'd eaten the same food. No, she decided, she must have some bug. It would be early to bed for them both. The last thing she needed was Davy to come down sick too.

*

"How many more sleeps until Tom gets back?" Davy asked as he crawled under the covers.

"I'm not certain. He said he'd be gone about a month." Had it been only three days since he'd left for Toronto? It seemed so much longer.

Davy held his hands out before her face, fingers spread. "How many?"

"Okay. Let's see." She sat on the edge of his bed and folded down his fingers as she named the sleeps. "Tonight is Monday night. Then there's Tuesday. Wednesday. Thursday..." When she started through a third set of ten digits, she felt more disheartened than Davy looked.

"Jeepers. That's almost three handfuls. How will I ever be able to wait that long?"

How indeed would either of them?

Beth stayed awake in bed for many hours. Tom's words kept repeating in her head. *Nothing holding me back. Nothing holding me back.* What a fool she had been. Tom was gone and all because of her ridiculous notion they shouldn't see each other for a while. *Nothing holding me back.* Beth pulled the covers up over her head. Was she really nothing to him now? She had no more tears in her, but she had regrets, a heart full.

*

Tom didn't mind the smell of a good cigar, but what was drifting from that roll of tobacco across the aisle was anything but pleasant. It had no sweet lingering aroma, but an acrimonious stench that permeated everything on the train. Tom opened his window slightly to let in some fresh air, shifted to a more comfortable position on the hard leather bench seat, and stared out at the vast emptiness, counting the hours until he'd be home.

It took nearly two weeks going and two weeks coming back. The few days in between while he was in Toronto had passed quickly. He wondered how everyone was at home, how his horses had fared and if the Flanagan boys had had any trouble with the shop. It would feel good to get back to work.

He brought back maple sugar candy for Earl's sweet tooth, and maple syrup and a tin of fancy biscuits for Mary. He brought nothing for Davy or Beth, not because he forgot, only because he didn't know how he would be received when he returned.

He thought of them every moment he was away, and he wished he could show them the beautiful sights of Toronto. Maybe one day he would. It all depended on Beth. For all he knew, she might have decided to accept Lars Anderstom's attention. Mary had always told Tom not to borrow trouble, but try as he might to heed her warning, worry was his seat partner all the way home.

The train had chugged westward through Manitoba and then Saskatchewan. Mile upon endless mile of snow-covered fields passed Tom's window. At times, it was difficult to distinguish between land and sky, and Tom decided nothing could be bleaker than the flat prairies. Spring had arrived by the calendar, but nature didn't know that yet. Occasionally, he saw a desolate farmstead, standing brown and foreign against the banal white landscape. Only a gray plume of smoke rising from its chimney indicated the shack was inhabited.

Eventually the landscape changed. Rolling hills loomed in the distance, and the snow didn't appear as deep. Patches of brown grass and clumps of trees dotted the hillsides while amber colored bushes erupted through the melting snowdrifts along the rails. Tom began to get restless, knowing he was getting closer to home.

Farmyards were more frequent now. Fences marked where one homestead ended and another began. Horses ranged the pastureland, nibbling at the fresh sprouts of spring grasses. Cattle, penned during calving season, rested on the straw mounds, while others licked up the last few wisps of hay fed during the morning chores.

By late afternoon, the train had reached the foothills and it snaked its way through the valley, passing through Tannerville. It crossed the trestle spanning the deep creek bed of Whistle Creek.

Tom peered down. In the fall, only a small creek trickled along there and during winter it was frozen dormant. But in the spring, the run-off from the hills and mountains to the west filled the creek bed. Today, the water was deep, murky with mud, twigs and debris washed along by the swift current.

Far ahead, Tom saw the spire on the Whistle Creek Methodist Church. He was home.

The train rocked from side to side, and Tom widened his stance as he hauled down his belongings from the overhead shelf, ready to disembark even before the conductor announced the next stop was his town, Whistle Creek.

The man with the cigar had fallen asleep again, his hands folded upon his generous belly, which rose and fell in rhythm to his loud snoring. Glad to be rid of him, Tom headed down the aisle, and waited by an exit. When the train eased to a brake-screeching stop, Tom stepped from the train. His legs felt hollow, now that the train's rocking motion was absent.

He looked toward the station, and his heart skipped a joyous beat. Beth and Davy were waiting there. Davy waved exuberantly and broke free from his sister's grasp to run to him, throwing himself into Tom's open arms. "I'm so glad you're back! I missed you so much!"

Tom hugged him close. "I missed you too, Bud. How have you been?"

Davy pulled back. "I lost a tooth. See?" He bared his teeth and poked his tongue through the vacant space. Then he pushed against the adjacent one with his tongue, wiggling it. "And this one's loose, too."

"Well, so it is!"

But Tom wasn't interested in loose teeth. He straightened to look across at Beth, still standing by the station. From the distance, it was impossible to read her face, and he wondered if she still felt the same about him. He allowed Davy to lead him over.

Chapter 20

"Hello, Beth." He kept his voice carefully passive. "It's good to see you."

She nodded. "How was your trip?" she asked when really she wanted to ask, "Did you miss me?"

"Good . . . long," he answered when really he wanted to answer, "Lonesome, terribly lonesome."

There was an awkward pause in the conversation, but Davy quickly filled it. "Beth's been sick," he volunteered.

Tom raised a worried eyebrow.

She waved his concerns away. "Nothing serious."

Suddenly Davy remembered his gift. He pulled a short crude-looking wooden spoon out of his pocket. "I whittled this for you with the knife you gave me."

Tom accepted the gift graciously.

"Only a couple of nicks in his fingers too," Beth said, smiling.

Davy reached out, turning the spoon for Tom's inspection. "It's good, huh! I worked on it every night before bedtime. I had lots of time to make it real good. Beth and I counted the sleeps until you got back." In his excitement, one sentence led to another.

Tom grinned.

"He missed you," Beth said.

Tom looked into her eyes as if trying to see into her soul. "Just Davy?"

She blushed and shook her head. "No. I missed you too."

Tom smiled in relief. He had a thousand things he wanted to say, a thousand things he wanted to ask, but not with Davy around.

"Bill's still living at the livery." Davy answered one of Tom's questions. "He's got it fixed up real good. Got a cot in there and a place for his clothes and everything. I can sleep over sometime if I want. And guess what? I might be able to sleep in a manger . . . "

Davy rattled on, but Tom barely heard past the part about Bill still living at the livery. "So, he won't come home?"

"No. He's happy there."

"What about you? Are you happy?"

"Now that you're back, I am," she answered almost shyly.

"Mary told us you were coming in today," Davy explained.

God bless her soul. Tom had telegraphed just before the train departed Regina, but he never said a word to her about telling Beth when he would arrive. He was grateful she had.

He stuffed his hand down inside his trouser pocket and withdrew a shiny new nickel. He squatted down to Davy's level. "Do you see this? I brought it all the way back from Toronto especially for you. Why don't you go buy some candy with it?"

"Oh boy!"

Finally, they were alone, as alone as two people could get on a Saturday afternoon on the loading platform of the train station at train time. Forgetting his luggage, Tom led Beth further under the wide canopy of the station's roof where the shadows offered privacy, albeit minimal.

"I missed you so much, Beth." He took her hands in his, his thumbs running across her knuckles.

"And I've been miserable while you've been away."

Tom took a quick glance over his shoulder to make sure no one was watching and then kissed her lightly on her trembling lips. "You don't know how much I've missed doing that. This has been the longest few weeks in my life. I thought about you every minute, wondering how you were, what you were doing, whether you would even speak to me when I returned." He pulled her close in a breath-squeezing hug, and whispered, "Ah, Beth, I love you."

"And I love you too," she replied, happy tears flooding her eyes. "I was a fool to insist we stay apart."

He released the hug and smiled. "We belong together, Beth.

When I saw Abigail and her new husband at the altar I realized I want to marry you even more."

Beth's eyes shifted downwards. "Tom, before that can ever happen, I have things I need to tell you. Things—"

"Okay, but not here," Tom interrupted. "Not with everyone in Whistle Creek standing within hearing distance. Let's go somewhere more private."

Beth nodded. "Where? Your place?"

"Or yours. I doesn't matter." He took her arm and they started down the boardwalk when Tom remembered he'd left his luggage sitting on the platform. "I'll be right back. Wait here."

While Beth waited, she looked about for Davy, seeing instead a ghost from her past step down from the train.

Uncle Mead.

Alive.

In Whistle Creek.

Any relief she should had felt knowing he was alive was short-lived. Instead, a dark shadow of fear closed in upon her. What was Uncle Mead doing here?

She watched in horror as Mead grabbed Tom's arm when they met on the platform. When Tom pointed in the direction of the livery, the ground spun and the dark shadow rose up and engulfed her.

*

In Doc Fisher's waiting room, Davy sat on Tom's knee with his face buried against Tom's broad shoulder. "Beth's gonna die," he wailed. "I just know it."

Tom did his best to comfort him. "Shhh. She just fainted, Davy. She'll be fine."

"No, she won't. She's been sick for a long time. Throwing up every morning. I know she's gonna die."

"Don't worry. She—" Tom halted mid-sentence. Had he heard

Davy correctly? "What did you say?"

"She's gonna die."

"No, before that. Did you say she was throwing up every morning?"

Davy nodded and sucked in three jagged breaths. "Bill told her to go see the d . . . doctor, but she kept thinking she was getting b . . . better, but the next morning she'd be sick again."

Tom cradled Davy's head. Could it be? Their very first time? He never once considered the possibility, but after listening to Davy's tearful account of Beth's illness, it seemed very likely Beth was carrying his child. Tom's heart warmed, as if the thought were a heated blanket held against his chest. *A baby. Our baby. I'm going to be a father!* Then he cautioned himself. He didn't know for certain Beth was pregnant. Still, it was definitely possible.

Doc Fisher came from the examining room and closed the door behind him. Davy began to wail even louder, assuming the worst when Beth didn't follow.

Tom stood, Davy's arms and legs wrapped around him like a vine. "How is she?" Tom asked.

"Better."

"Can we go see her?"

Doc nodded in Davy's direction. "Just the boy. I want to have a word with you."

"Did you hear, Davy? You can go in to see her," Tom whispered gently in the boy's ear.

"I can?" He wiped his nose on his sleeve.

"Your sister is fine," the doctor repeated, taking a seat behind his desk. "But she's resting so you can't stay long."

When Davy went through into the examining room, Tom got a glimpse of Beth lying down, a white sterile sheet covering her. She was crying softly. *Crying?* Then the door shut.

Doc entered notes into a ledger, closed it and put the pen into the holder. He propped his elbows on his heavy wooden desk, rested his chin on his laced fingers, and studied Tom. "Please, sit down. There's a few things you need to know."

Doc's serious tone sent ice through Tom's veins. His heart was no longer warm, but squeezed by the cold clutches of dread. He sank into the chair, afraid to hear what Doc had to say. Maybe there wasn't a baby. Maybe Beth was crying because of a serious illness.

Doc began. "Beth's main problem right now is malnutrition. Unable to keep most foods down, she simply collapsed from hunger. Now, I've given her something to help settle her stomach, but I'd like her to stay the night so I can keep watch over her, just in case."

Tom leaned forward, his palms sweaty. "In case what?"

"Well, she took a nasty fall when she fainted. I want to be sure there is no threat to the pregnancy."

She is pregnant! Tom should have been overjoyed, but his happiness was diminished remembering Beth was crying in the other room.

Doc continued, "Beth wouldn't say, but I assume you are the father."

"Yes. The baby is mine."

Doc Fisher leaned back in his chair. "I don't expect there to be any complications. Other than morning sickness, which should pass soon, Beth is healthy."

"I want to see her."

"I'm sorry, Tom, but you'd better not. She's upset right now. Come by tomorrow, and if she's better, then you can see her."

Tom nodded and rose to leave, but Doc motioned him to sit again. He kept his voice quiet so it wouldn't carry into the next room. "Tom, I'm not breaking any confidences when I say I know you and Abigail Craig were intimate. Half the town suspected it, but without a baby to show, they had no tangible proof. But this time is different."

Tom knew where the doctor was heading with this conversation and it made him angry. If Beth hadn't come to him in the night, then this morality lesson would be unnecessary. *No, dammit*, he chastised himself harshly, *I never should have allowed her into my bed. I'm the one responsible for all this!*

"Don't worry, Doc. I'll take care of things. Beth and I will be married soon." He stood. "Now is there anything else you wish to say or am I free to go?" he asked curtly.

Doc rose, meeting Tom eye to eye. "I'm sorry, Tom, but it's my job to look after the welfare of my patient, first and foremost."

Tom extended his hand and smiled sadly. "I know, Doc. I know. And thanks. I appreciate it." He headed for the door and then stopped. "When Davy is through seeing Beth, send him to my place. He can stay with me for the night."

*

"Thought you'd seen the last of me, boy?"

Bill spun about and almost dropped to his knees when he saw his uncle standing hale and hearty in the livery's doorway.

"What are you doing here?" Bill tried to hide the panic in his voice. "Go away and leave us alone."

"Uh uh. I didn't travel no two hundred miles to go home empty handed. I come to take you boys back where you belong. Where's Davy?"

"He ain't here."

"I kin see that! Where is he?"

Bill crossed his arms in front of him to stop them from shaking, but Mead mistook his stance as one of defiance.

"Don't you be insolent, boy. I still have the right to take a belt to you and by cracky I will if you don't tell me where the young'n is."

Emmett Compel came out from the feed room. "What's all the racket about? You're scaring the horses."

Mead puffed out his chest with an air of importance. "Sir, I am Mead Parkerson and this here boy is my nephew. He and his younger brother run away from me 'bout seven, eight months ago and I'm here to get them back."

Emmett seemed unimpressed. "Listen, buster, I don't give a

cow patty if you're the second coming of Christ. You're scaring the horses and if you don't leave immediately, I'll throw you out!"

Mead face bulged with outraged. "Ain't you been listening? I have every right to take this boy with me."

"And I have every right to toss you out on your fat ass in the middle of the street. Now get moving!" Emmett, no small man, bellied up to Mead.

Mead, all fat and no spine, backed down. "Very well," he huffed, "I'm gonna take this up with the authorities." To Bill he warned, "I'll be back for you, never you worry," and stormed out.

"You in trouble, Bill?"

"No," Bill answered, then rethought his answer and asked, "Mind if I quit early? I've got something I need to do."

"Just finish this last bit. Then you can go."

Ten minutes later, Bill hammered on Beth's door, once, twice, and then poked his head inside. "Beth? You home?" He was met by silence.

Bill stood on the stoop. *Where was she?* He needed to warn her. Suddenly he felt sick. What if Mead had come by while he was finishing up at the livery and had already taken Beth and Davy with him?

Bill forced himself to think rationally. Knowing his uncle's penchant for drinking, Mead would likely stop for a pint or two first. There was a good chance he hadn't even been here yet. Beth and Davy were probably just out, maybe visiting Betner's. He headed there next.

It was Mary's suggestion he try Tom's place, saying Tom had just returned on the afternoon train.

Bill's knee-jerk reaction was to think they didn't waste any time getting back together, but as he neared the Carver place, he started hoping she *was* there. Otherwise, he didn't know what to do.

Tom answered Bill's second knock.

"Beth here?" Bill demanded, pushing his way into the kitchen without bothering to say hello.

"No, she's not."

At Tom's reply, Bill's belligerent attitude wilted. "She isn't?"

Tom gritted his teeth. Bill was the last person he felt up to seeing. "I thought you'd have probably heard by now. Beth fainted and she's staying at Doc's overnight for observation," Tom said.

"Fainted? Beth's never fainted before." Bill was white and Tom wondered if he'd soon be picking a second Patterson up from the floor.

"Doc said she'd be fine."

"Where's Davy then?" Bill's eyes darted nervously about the room.

"He's upstairs sleeping. He was fairly upset."

"Upset? What about?"

Bill's question puzzled Tom. "About Beth fainting, of course."

"Oh, right. Do you think Doc will let me see her? I need to talk to her."

"He might. I don't know."

Bill began to back out the door, but Tom put his hand on Bill's shoulder to stop him. "There's something wrong, isn't there? Maybe you'd better tell me." He knew Beth was in no condition to be burdened further. "Come in and sit down." He pulled out a chair at the table and then took one himself.

Bill stared for some time at his hands clasped on the table before he began carefully, "Do you remember when you once said things aren't always black and white?"

How could Tom forget? It was the morning Bill had confronted Beth and him in the kitchen. "I remember."

"Well, I'm thinking this is one of them gray sort of things." He looked solemnly at Tom.

Tom steeled himself for what he was about to hear.

"Me and Davy and Beth are in trouble."

"What kind of trouble? With the law?"

"I don't know. I thought we were. Now, I'm not so sure."

Tom frowned. "Maybe you'd better start at the beginning."

"All right. First of all, our last name ain't Patterson, it's Parkerson. We changed it when we came to Whistle Creek."

"Why?"

"Give me a minute. I'm getting to that part. About four years ago, our parents died in an accident—"

"That can't be. Beth told me they died last summer."

Bill banged his fists against the table. "Will you shut up and listen! It was four years ago. Ma and Pa were picking up feed over at the mill and there was a dust explosion. Anyhow, after the funeral, we were sent to live with Dad's brother and his wife in Duggan, Saskatchewan. I was twelve then, Beth was fifteen, and Davy . . . I guess Davy was only two."

Tom listened silently, troubled and perplexed by what he had heard already.

"Anyway, Uncle Mead and Aunt Tilly were usually drunk. Us kids did all the work, the chores, the cookin', the cleanin'. Everything. They didn't do diddly. Just sat around and drank. 'Course, when they drank they were mean." Bill stopped for a moment. Tom could tell the memories were painful to recall. "I don't know why Uncle Mead suddenly got worse, but he'd go off crazy mad over any stupid thing. We started to be afraid he might kill us in one of his rages, so we decided to get away. Our plan was to leave in the middle of the night when Uncle Mead and Aunt Tilly had passed out. We knew where they had hid some extra money."

Tom had questions, but he held them.

"That very evening Uncle Mead started yellin' and hittin' Davy for leaving marbles on the floor. It was getting pretty bad, so Beth jumped in and pushed him away. Uncle Mead fell and hit his head on the corner of the hearth. He didn't move or nothin'. Just laid there. There was lots of blood like his head was cracked wide open. We was so scared, we grabbed the money and ran."

Tom felt ill. Sweet mercy. Beth had killed her uncle. *And all this time she was afraid to tell anyone, even me.* It pained him that she didn't trust him. "Where was your aunt during all this?" he asked.

"Sleeping it off in the bedroom."

"How did you end up in Whistle Creek?" Tom asked.

"We walked along the train tracks for a couple of days, hiding whenever we heard a train coming. By the third day, we were starving so at the next town we stopped to eat. We decided it would be safe to take the train from there. Just before we bought our tickets, Beth saw your ad at the train station. Right away she wrote up a fake résumé. She mailed it off and then we waited."

"Now I see why you changed your name."

"Yeah. We didn't want anyone to find us. Every day Beth would go to the post office to see if there was a reply. We almost gave up hope and then finally the letter came. I don't know what we would have done if you hadn't hired her."

And what would they have done if he hadn't convinced the other trustees to let them stay, Tom thought. "Where were you while you waited?"

"We hid in a barn close to town. Belonged to an old farmer and his wife. We raided their garden at night."

Tom thought for a moment before speaking. "Seems to me, you should talk to the authorities. Mead was killed in self-defense."

"No, no. Uncle Mead wasn't dead after all. Today he showed up at the livery."

Tom heaved a heavy sigh of relief. He got up and went to the stove and poured himself a coffee. He raised a cup at Bill, but Bill declined. When Tom returned to the table he said, "If it's the hidden money he's after, I'll reimburse him."

"I wish it was only that. He wants to take me and Davy back, 'cause he still has legal custody. If I had to, I could go. I could probably handle it again," he stated bravely, though his voice broke, indicating otherwise, "but Davy, I don't know. What do you think we should do?"

"First of all, don't worry. You won't be going back, either of you—not if I have anything to say about it."

"You're gonna help us?"

Tom nodded, forming a plan. "I'd better talk to Aaron Lanson.

Maybe he can give us some legal advice. Got any idea where your uncle might be?"

"Probably in the saloon."

Tom went for his coat. "All right. We'll go there first."

Bill shook his head. "I don't want to talk to him."

"You won't have to. Just point him out to me. Then you can come back and stay the night here. Someone needs to stay with Davy."

A few minutes later, standing in the doorway of the crowded saloon, Bill pointed across the smoky haze. "There he is, the guy with the cigar."

Tom recognized him immediately. He gritted his teeth in anger, remembering how the foul-smelling man from the train had accosted him on the street and asked directions to the livery. "Okay, I'll handle it from here."

"Whatcha gonna do?"

"Don't know yet. What I'd like to do is illegal." He squeezed Bill's shoulder. "Go back to my place. I'll get this mess straightened out somehow."

Chapter 21

Mead Parkerson sat alone at a table.

"Mind if I join you?" Tom asked, fighting off his repulsion. A rotting, three-day-old carcass smelled better than what Mead had poking out the side of his mouth.

Mead obliged by pushing out the opposite chair with his foot. "Beginning to think folks around here were downright unfriendly." He drew deeply on his cigar and exhaled the putrid smoke in Tom's face, then set the cigar across the ashtray and studied Tom. He brightened. "Hey! I remember you from the train."

Tom turned and gestured for Sam to bring him a pint. "What brings you to our town?" he asked.

"Family business." Mead took a swig of his ale, winced, and then belched. "I'm waiting to see the lawyer. Hear tell he comes in every evening at eight to play pool."

Tom glanced at the clock hanging behind the bar. Seven-thirty. Somehow he would have to prevent Mead from talking with Lanson.

Mead slugged back more of his ale, belched again loudly, and then rubbed his belly. "Don't know what I ate at that joint 'cross the street, but it sure as hell ain't sitting right. Feels like my stomach's on fire or somethin'."

With any luck it was tainted food and it will kill you. "Marcia is Mexican. She cooks spicy."

"That's why I got me a glass of elixir right here."

While Mead guzzled his ale, Tom came up with an idea, inspired by the word elixir. "Say, if you've got an upset stomach, Sam can fix you something to take care of it."

"Who's Sam?"

"The bartender."

Mead loosened his belt buckle and undid the top button of his trousers. "I'd surely like to give it a try. I feel like I'm gonna explode."

"I'll ask him to make you one."

"Why, that's might friendly of you."

"Think nothing of it." Tom approached the bar.

"Evening, Tom," Sam said, drying a glass and setting it under the bar.

"Sam," Tom returned. "See the guy I'm sitting with?"

"Yeah, who in blazes is he anyway? He and his damn cigar are costing me money."

"His name is Mead Parkerson. Listen, do me a favor? Remember that special coffee you made for me that time I got so drunk?"

"Yeah, I know the one." Sam draped the towel over his shoulder and braced his palms on the bar. "What about it?"

"Think you could do something to make it a bit more palatable?"

"It's not supposed to be a social drink."

"Oh, I know, but could you?"

Sam nodded. "I could make horse piss taste good if I wanted."

Tom's lips turned up into a lecherous grin. "I'll make you a deal. You mix him that drink, I'll get rid of the cigar."

Sam peered across Tom's shoulder at the smoke curling up from the ashtray. "Deal." He drew a big mug out from under the counter. "I'll bring it over in a minute. On the house."

Tom returned to the table just as Mead lifted one side of his rump to pass gas. "Hope he hurries with that drink," Mead whined.

So did Tom. He found it impossible to believe this disgusting boor could be related to Beth.

The drink arrived and whatever Sam did to it, he must have improved the taste immensely for Mead downed it like he was guzzling cherry cordial. "Hey." He patted his belly, "I think it's starting to work already."

Tom smiled to himself. *Give it a minute.* "You got relatives here in Whistle Creek?" he asked, fishing for details.

"A niece and two nephews. They's my brother's kids. When he and his wife died, my wife and I took them in, but them ungrateful brats run away. It was just by chance, I learned the girl is teaching out here and the oldest boy is working at the livery. I come to get the boys back to help do the farm chores. The place can't run itself." Mead frowned, and wiggled in his chair.

"Who's taking care of things while you're gone?"

"The wife."

"What about your niece?" Tom asked. "Aren't you taking her back too?"

"Nah, don't want her. She was always a troublemaker. Defiant sort." Mead's eyes grew big, sweat beaded on his forehead and his face turned the color of moldy hay.

"You feeling all right?" Tom asked, hiding his satisfied grin behind the rim of his beer glass.

Mead grimaced. "Shit. Feels like someone's tying my innards in a knot. I think maybe I should—" Unable to finish what he was going to say, Mead bolted for the door, practically bowling Aaron Lanson over on his way out.

Tom snubbed out that damnable cigar and exchanged a thumbs-up with Sam.

Aaron Lanson was chalking a cue when Tom approached him. "I was wondering if I could bother you for a few minutes. I need some advice."

"Certainly." He nodded toward a table. "Let's have a seat. What's on your mind?"

As Tom proceeded to explain the situation, Lanson leaned forward in his chair and listened, occasionally interjecting a question or uttering an, "I see."

At the end, Tom asked, "Will you help us?"

It was a few minutes before Lanson said, "I have to say, this case is intriguing, but I'd like to talk to Bill for more details first before I make any decisions."

"Of course. He's at my place right now. Would you mind?"

"Not at all." Both men pushed away from the table and made their way to Tom's place.

*

Tom stared at the black ceiling long into the night, his mind mulling over all he'd heard the last few hours and, in light of his new understanding, he felt like shooting Parkerson right between the eyes. The man was cruel and if he *had* died at Beth's hands, it would have served him right. Tom vowed to do everything in his power to see that Mead wouldn't lay a hand on those boys or Beth again.

He thought of the baby growing inside Beth and he felt himself grow protective. *This is my family and heaven help whoever tries to harm them because I will defend them with my life.* But first he'd give Lanson's plan a try.

Early the next morning, rising before Bill and Davy were awake, Tom hastened to the doctor's office.

"She's gone. I advised her to wait for you, but she said she had too much to do," Doc explained, shaking his head. "Stubborn women these days."

Tom experienced a sickening sense of déjà vu as he hurried to Beth's place. He knocked on the door, waited, and when she didn't answer, he opened it himself. Somehow, he wasn't surprised to see satchels packed and standing by the door.

Beth came from the boys' bedroom, looked startled to see him there, but quickly recovered. She acknowledged his presence by saying, "I don't have time to talk right now," and then went back for another bag.

"What are you doing?" Tom asked when she returned.

"We're leaving, Tom." Her voice was void of expression.

Over my dead body, he thought. "Do you really think I would let you go when you're carrying my child?"

"I'm not pregnant," she stated emphatically. "Doc Fisher is

mistaken. I just had a touch of influenza."

"Beth, I don't buy it. You've been sick every morning for weeks now. I imagine there have been other changes,"—how could he say this without offending her?—"changes in your personal cycle to indicate you are pregnant."

Beth blushed to the soles of her feet. "Precisely! If anyone should know, I should. I am not pregnant!" she retorted.

Tom's eyes became lackluster. Not pregnant? It felt as if a piece of his heart had been pinched off. He sat in the nearest chair, the disappointment almost felling him.

"Thank you for keeping Davy with you last night. Doc Fisher told me what you did." She bent to resume her task of packing.

"Your fainting scared him pretty bad. Me too, for that matter. It must have been quite a shock for you to see your uncle get off the train."

She straightened up. "So, you know?"

Tom gently grasped her arm. "Bill told me. He told me everything, Beth. All about Mead, your Aunt Tilly. What it was like having to live with them. How you thought you'd killed him. Running away. Everything."

Beth sank into a chair, and tears that came so easily of late, traced down her cheeks.

Tom sat on his haunches before her and held her trembling hands. "He wants to take the boys back."

"I expected as much. That's why we have to leave immediately. He can't take Bill and Davy."

"Shhh. Listen, I talked to Aaron Lanson and he suggested—"

"You told Mr. Lanson about us?"

"He's a lawyer, Beth. He wants to help."

"Why? He barely knows us."

"Because I've retained him. He says we'll have to take Mead to court."

She stared despondently at her lap. "I doubt it will be that easy."

"No, probably not. Lanson figures the judge might favor your uncle over you because he at least would provide a male influence for the boys."

She gave a pathetic laugh. "A male influence? What good is his kind of male influence?" Her words were bitter. "He doesn't love them." She buried her face in her hands.

Tom ached to see her this way. He gathered her in his arms. "I have an idea, but before you make any decisions, I want you to hear me out completely and consider it carefully. Okay?" She didn't respond so he repeated, "Okay?"

She nodded, her face still hidden in her hands.

He pulled back. "I could be a male influence for the boys."

She let her hands drop to her lap, and blinked in confusion. "You want custody of Bill and Davy?"

"Yes . . . well, not just me . . . I want the two of us to have custody. Beth, we'd have a good chance of keeping the boys if we're married."

She gazed at him through liquid eyes. "You'd marry me just so Uncle Mead wouldn't get the boys?"

He smiled sadly. "You know I've wanted you as my wife for a long time. Mead's coming to Whistle Creek has only emphasized the need to hurry. I won't lose you, Beth. And I won't give up Davy, nor Bill. I want us to be a family."

"A family?" Hope flickered in her eyes and then disappeared. "But what if it doesn't work?"

"We won't know until we try." Tom placed a quick kiss on her lips. "Trust me?" When she nodded, he kissed her again. "Okay, here's the plan."

Tom left Beth minutes later, carrying Davy's Sunday best clothes slung over his arm. He hurried, stopping at Betner's long enough to briefly explain the situation and to ask Mary if she'd help Beth get ready, a task Mary readily accepted. Earl was in charge of notifying the minister that he'd be performing a wedding immediately following the morning service.

Davy, of course, was overjoyed to learn Tom was marrying his sister, and his excitement was doubled when Tom informed him they'd all be taking the train to Tannerville immediately afterwards.

Bill, however, remained stoically silent.

"Okay, Bud," Tom ordered, "take your clothes and set them out on the bed so they don't get creased."

Bill waited until Davy was out of earshot before firing, "Beth's only marrying you just to keep us together, you know."

"I hope to God she's marrying me for more than that, but you'll have to ask Beth her reasons yourself. As for me, I love your sister, and if she lost you two, she'd be heartbroken. I can't let that happen." Tom dragged the tub from the corner. "I'm trusting Lanson to know what he's talking about."

He started pailing water across from the copper boiler. "Listen, I want to get ready. I suggest you get a few things packed for Tannerville. We haven't got much time." Up the stairs he called, "Come on down and have a bath, Davy. I don't want no ball of dirt for a brother-in-law."

While Davy scrubbed in the tub in the kitchen, Tom rifled through his top dresser drawer in his bedroom. *It has to be here somewhere.* He started in the back left corner, feeling his way through folded sweaters and work shirts. Finally in desperation, he yanked the drawer from the dresser and flipped it over. The contents tumbled onto the bed. The last thing to fall with a soft clump atop the sweaters was a small carved, wooden box. Smiling, Tom slowly lifted the hinged lid, and his mother's wedding ring, its single diamond, twinkled at him from its bed of royal blue velvet.

His parents had been married just shy of fifteen years when the influenza took them and his sisters. That was many years ago and the pain had faded, but Tom still could feel the warmth and happiness they had shared as a family. In a few hours, he would be the head of his family, accepting responsibility for his wife and her brothers. Life would never be the same. He wanted to slow down, to sit and ponder these last minutes of bachelorhood, but there was no time to waste. He slid the ring onto his pinkie, and closed the box. He had a wedding to attend!

Chapter 22

Just as Tom had hoped, Mary took the situation into her own hands. She scurried over to Beth's, a large garment bag under one arm and a sewing basket hanging from the other. When Beth opened the door, Mary shouldered through, dropped everything onto the table and gave the girl a crushing hug. She ignored Beth's tear-stained face.

"Tom is always full of surprises, but this one beats all. I'm so happy, dear. I thoroughly approve of his choice of wife." She hugged her a few seconds longer and then set to work. "Now, we mustn't waste a moment."

She opened the garment bag, drew out a long white gown and held it up. "When God blessed us with our boys, I never thought I'd see this worn again. It was mine when I married Earl. I'd be so proud if you'd consent to wear it today."

"Oh, Mary—" Beth thought she had cried all the tears she had, but more threatened. How could she wear a white wedding gown, a symbol of chaste innocence? Yet, how could she refuse without raising suspicion?

Mary misunderstood her hesitation. "Oh, I know it will need a bit of adjusting in the bodice, but it won't take long. I brought my sewing things." She turned the dress inside out. "Quickly, dear, strip down to your pretties so you can try this on for a fitting."

In a daze, Beth passively did all she was instructed, turning this way and that, raising her hands above her head, dropping her arms by her side. Mary held the pins between pursed lips, pulling them out one at a time, fitting and tucking and pinning. Then she carefully lifted the garment over Beth's head, mindful not to scratch her with the pins. She threaded a needle and began to stitch.

"Do you have everything packed you'll need?" she asked as her fingers nimbly pushed the needle and thread in and out the silky fabric.

Beth nodded, then sank into a chair across the table, her hands clasped tightly on the tabletop. "Do you know why he's marrying me? What did he tell you?"

Mary's hands paused. "He told me about your uncle, may the devil take that cruel man's soul, but don't be thinking that's the only reason he wants to marry you. Tom loves you, plain and simple." She resumed her stitching. A minute later she bit off the thread, knotted it again, and started on the other side. Beth watched silently until Mary finished.

"All right, girl," Mary said, turning the dress right side out, "try this on again, and if it fits then we'll do your hair. How would you like it, up or down?"

"Down," Beth replied quietly. "Tom likes it down."

Mary gave an approving smile. "Good girl. You'll see. Things are going to work out just fine. I've got a good feeling about this marriage . . . a very good feeling." She raised the gown up high. "Okay, lift up your arms."

*

Whistle Creek's Methodist Church hadn't seen a wedding in more than a year and Reverend Harding was slightly peeved he didn't have more time to prepare for the ceremony. But Earl explained the couple was anxious to catch the Tannerville train immediately after the vows.

Harding smiled begrudgingly. Love was supposed to be patient, but he didn't suppose the good Lord would frown upon a couple so impatient to be man and wife.

Fortunately, Harding delivered one of his less inspiring sermons, and the minute the benediction was pronounced, the congregation filed quickly outside and scattered.

The wedding party assembled inside immediately, Mary and Earl on Tom's side, Bill and Davy on Beth's. Before commencing the ceremony, Reverend Harding took a moment to make eye contact with the bride and the groom. He prided himself on being able to read people's emotions through their eyes.

The bride's were puffy, but otherwise wide and expressionless. No tears of happiness or even those of trepidation as he might have expected, but eyes void of any emotion. Not knowing what to think, he turned to the groom. Tom's eyes were dark gray, like polished steel, full of challenge and determination. They stared back at him with an unsettling intensity.

This was not good, Harding fretted. *Where was evidence of their love?* He stared down into his Bible, asking God for some sign he should marry this couple. And he was given it. Out the corner of his eye, he saw Tom's fingers search out Beth's hand in the folds of her gown and give it a reassuring squeeze. Harding looked again into Tom's eyes. Ah yes! That was better. He turned again to Beth.

"Are you going to marry them or stare at them all day?"

The minister and the entire wedding party dropped astonished looks to the shortest attendant. "Davy!" Beth reprimanded quietly.

"Well, jeepers! We're gonna miss the train, if'n he don't hurry up."

Harding cleared his throat. "Yes, of course, I forgot. Let us begin then. Dearly beloved, we are gathered here this day in the presence of God and these witnesses to join this man and this woman . . . "

The wedding was performed without frills, and it was over quickly. Had she given her vows? Beth wondered. She vaguely remembered repeating the words the minister had spoken to her, so she supposed she had. And she recalled Tom sliding a ring on her finger and that she had the presence of mind to wonder how he'd acquired it on such short notice, but she remembered little else.

Tom kissed her cheek and backed away. In a daze, she looked forward. Reverend Harding was smiling at her. She turned to her right. Tom was smiling at her. Beyond him, Mary was smiling.

Everyone was smiling. Except Bill and he seldom smiled. In the presence of so many happy faces, Beth smiled, too. *I must be married*, she thought, her sensibilities numb.

The train whistle startled them all into action. "We'd better get going." Tom quickly thanked the minister and shook his hand, discretely paying him for his services. He faced Beth. "Ready?" She didn't reply. "Beth?"

Mary stepped forward. "You men go on ahead and hold the train. I want to speak with Beth before she leaves. Go on now. You too, Davy."

"But she'll miss the train."

"The train will wait a few minutes. Now shoo!"

Tom strode down the aisle, holding Davy's hand. They grabbed their luggage and exited the church. Bill and Earl followed.

Mary turned to Harding. "Reverend, do you mind if I have a few minutes alone with Beth?"

"Oh! Why no, not at all." Harding graciously made a hasty retreat, leaving the two women alone in the church.

Mary steered Beth into the front pew, sat her down and then pinched her pale cheeks firmly.

Beth jumped, and her eyes blinked wide and startled.

"Finally, a spark of recognition," Mary uttered with satisfaction, brushing her thumbs across Beth's cheeks, now blotchy pink. "Beth, I know everything has happened so fast you're in a state of shock, but you're going to have to pull yourself together. There are three people outside depending on you. It won't benefit anyone except your uncle if you fall apart now. Do you hear?"

Beth nodded.

"Fine. I want you to walk out of this church straight and tall and proud, and get on that train. You're Mrs. Tom Carver now. Show Tom you have the courage and spirit to be his wife."

Courage, Beth thought. The next few days would take all the courage she had, but now she had Tom to help her. Together they would face whatever the future held. Beth hugged Mary close. "Thank you, Mary. For everything."

The train whistle blew again.

"Hurry now," ordered the matronly woman. "The train won't wait all day."

Beth hiked up the long gown and ran down the length of the church and outside, meeting Tom coming up the steps to get her. Without a word, he swept her up into his arms and carried his bride across the muddy street, through the station and up the three steps into the train. Then, and only then, Mary allowed a single tear of happiness roll down her cheek.

They made quite a spectacle, and the onlookers cheered and waved, sending the handsome blacksmith and his new bride off with ovations of good wishes.

*

The melee outside the hotel woke Mead from his sleep. He rolled out of his bed (still dressed in the clothes he'd worn the night before) and rubbed his tender belly.

"Can't a body get some rest around here?" he muttered. His tongue felt like it was covered with dry cornmeal and his head hurt as if it had been split in two by an ax.

He staggered to the hotel window and peered outside. The train pulled away from the station and the jubilant crowd on the platform dispersed. Mead wondered what in hell could cause such a commotion. He bent over to pull his boots on, groaning more than usual. It was such an effort, he decided to go without. He snapped his suspenders up over his shoulders, dragged on his suit jacket he'd dropped in a heap on the floor, and headed downstairs to have cup of strong coffee.

When the waiter filled his cup, Mead asked, "What was all the hullabaloo a few minutes ago?"

"The blacksmith and the schoolteacher just got hitched."

Mead sipped the hot brew. *Gawd, all that fuss over a simple wed—* He spewed the coffee across the pristine tablecloth. "The teacher you say? What's her name?"

"Miss Patterson. Well, Missus Carver, now. It was quite a sight, really, him carrying her to the train. Ought to be some honeymoon, though. Took her two younger brothers with them. Tell you when I get married, I don't plan on taking company. It'll be just me and the missus."

Mead jumped to his feet, raced out the door and was halfway across the muddy street before he realized he wasn't wearing boots. Leaving a trail of mud through the hotel, he headed back to his room for his boots. He needed to talk to the lawyer right away.

On his way out a minute later, he stopped at the front desk to get directions to Lanson's residence. Mead arrived just as Lanson was heading out the door.

"Excuse me, sir," Mead accosted, winded from his short run. "I was wondering if I could have a moment of your time."

"I'm sorry, but I'm on my way out." Lanson closed the door.

Mead tagged along on his heels. "But this is important. I came to Whistle Creek to get my nephews, but their sister and her new husband up and whisked them away right from under my nose."

Lanson smiled as he continued down the street. "Tom Carver is definitely a man of action."

The comment made no sense to Mead. "I was hopin' maybe you'd help me get them boys back. I kin pay ya."

Lanson stopped and turned. "I'm very sorry, but I don't think I can be of any assistance to you."

"Why the hell not?" Mead asked.

"I'm afraid it would constitute a conflict of interest."

"What's that mean?"

"It means I have already agreed to represent Mr. and Mrs. Carver and her brothers, so I cannot possibly help you. Nor would

I want to."

"What!" Mead was flabbergasted.

"Yes, we plan to take this matter before the judge in Tannerville. When we're finished, I sincerely doubt you will be allowed to own a dog. Good day, sir!" With a smug smile, Lanson pivoted on his heels and continued down the street.

Mead growled. *Good day? Hell fire, it wouldn't be a good day until those boys were back on the farm slopping hogs and feeding chickens.*

Mead ran to the train station to buy a ticket for Tannerville. There wouldn't be another until tomorrow morning. He cursed his luck, but down the street, he saw the lawyer enter the bank. Good. Lanson would have to wait too.

*

The clerk at the Imperial Hotel in Tannerville sympathized with the man across the counter, but there was simply nothing he could do. "Perhaps if you had telegraphed ahead," he said in way of an apology.

Tom nodded. "Yeah, I guess I should have." He picked up the lone key, stared at it and dropped it in his pocket. "Thanks anyway."

"You're welcome. Enjoy your stay, sir."

Beth waited beside a large potted plant, looking very conspicuous in her wedding gown.

"They've only one room available," Tom explained, his voice tight and controlled.

"Oh," said Beth, and then "Oh," again, this time more emphatically when she realized the significance of what Tom had just told her. "What about another hotel?"

"There's the Regal, but it's not the sort of place we'd want to stay."

Beth glanced at Bill and Davy sitting in luxurious brocade armchairs. Their eyes were agog, absorbing the sights like two sponges soaking up liquid.

"But surely the Regal would be better than four in one room," Beth reasoned.

Tom smiled indulgently. "Beth, most people who go there pay by the hour."

"By the hour? What good is an hour's sleep?"

Tom stared at her, waiting for her to comprehend.

"Oh." Color rose in her cheeks.

Tom started picking up the baggage. "They promised to bring up a couple of cots for the boys later on. Come on, let's get settled in."

Their room was up the stairs and three doors down the hall. Tom unlocked and swung the door wide. Davy was the first through.

Tom contemplated putting the bags down to carry his bride across the threshold, but somehow with Bill and Davy staying in the same room, the custom seemed rather ludicrous. After all, this wasn't exactly what he'd call a conventional honeymoon, especially when he considered the reason the wedding took place so hastily.

"After you," he said, motioning with the luggage for Beth to enter.

Davy was on the bed, bouncing wildly. The joints of the old brass bed squeaked in objection. Something compelled Beth to look at Tom at the exact moment he looked at her. She glanced away. Suddenly it seemed as if the bed were the only piece of furniture in the room.

"Stop it, Davy!" she scolded. "Beds aren't made for bouncing on." *Especially this one. And especially when there's going to be four in the room.* She dared not look at Tom, but she wondered if he was thinking the same thing.

Mercifully, Bill broke the awkward silence. "Hey, Davy! Let's go see if they've got an indoor toilet somewhere. I bet they do, a fancy place like this."

"Wow!" Davy bounced off the edge to the floor.

Beth realized she was about to be alone in a room with her husband and a bed. Though she knew it was absurd, she felt anxious. "Wait a minute!" she erupted, then unable to think of a suitable excuse to keep the boys in the room, she ordered, "At least, take off your good jackets and ties." Within seconds, jackets and ties landed on the bed and the boys charged off to explore the facilities.

Tom laughed and set the luggage down, giving the door a kick behind him to close it. "Kids!" he chuckled.

Beth laughed too, more nervous than amused.

"Well, might as well unpack." Tom skirted around the foot of the bed to the armoire where he hung up his clothes. She tried to do the same, discovering too late there wasn't room along the side for both of them to stand.

"Oh, here, let me get out of your way." He carefully stepped around the bed as if touching her skirt might be lethal.

It took Beth all of one minute to hang up the clothes she and her brothers brought. She could feel Tom watching her and she wished she could crawl inside the closet herself and shut the doors. She needed time to sort through her emotions. With all the rush and confusion of getting married and catching the train, she hadn't given tonight any thought.

What would happen between them, she wondered. It was their wedding night. If the situation were different, if it were just Tom and her alone in the room, then she had a pretty good idea what they'd be doing in that bed. A tingle she now recognized as desire raced through her and she forced it to cease. Nothing would be happening tonight. Or would there, she wondered. What if he pressed her into performing her marital duties? What if the boys overheard?

She calmed herself. Tom wouldn't put that kind of pressure on her, she was certain, but still she worried. What if her nearness aroused him beyond the limits of common sense? What if his nearness aroused her beyond the limits?

Tom chuckled and she turned to see what entertained him so. He was looking at her.

"Isn't life funny?" he commented with a half-smile. "Here I am, in a hotel room with my beautiful wife, and she's acting as if she's afraid of me, and by God, if I'm not acting the same way. Somehow I imagined our wedding day would be a little different."

He had introduced the subject and she knew if she wanted to talk to him about what he expected tonight, it was now or never. "Tom, I know you must be disappointed . . . I mean . . . with the boys and all."

Suddenly there was a quiet knock at the door and her opportunity to speak frankly with him was gone.

"Guess who," she said, her brows raised in a sheepish apology.

"I think I already know."

It was Bill, looking embarrassed.

"Uh . . . me and Davy are going to explore around town." He nervously avoided looking Tom in the eye. "We won't be back for a couple of hours . . . at least that . . . maybe more. I thought I should let you know."

Tom smiled. The boy had the subtlety of a whorehouse madam. "A walk around town sounds like a good idea. We'll change and be down to join you in a couple of minutes. Wait for us in the lobby."

Bill looked surprised. "Ah . . . okay . . . good." He bolted down the hall as the door closed.

Chapter 23

"Well, Mrs. Carver, we've been invited to see the sights of Tannerville. I would be honored to be your escort." He bowed and presented his hand.

She placed her hand in his. "Mr. Carver, I would be most pleased to accept your invitation."

They laughed, glad to have the mood lightened even for a moment. "I guess we'd better change." Immediately the awkwardness returned.

Sensing her reluctance to disrobe in front of him, Tom suggested he wait outside for a few minutes. He stood in the hall, receiving some quizzical stares as people passed to go to the lobby. A minute later, Beth opened the door a crack.

"Ready?" he asked.

"Not exactly," she whispered. "I need your help. I can't undo all the buttons."

Twenty pearl buttons trailed down the gown's back and while she could unfasten most of them, she couldn't manage those centered between her shoulder blades.

Tom's throat constricted. He'd resolved there would be no intimate contact tonight, but his decision to remain celibate was much easier to maintain when his lovely bride was fully clothed. Sweat formed under his starched white collar as his fingers fumbled nervously with the buttons. If he was affected this much undoing her buttons, how was he going to be able to lie next to her all night?

"They're tight little suckers," he said, hoping she'd think that was the reason for his ineptitude. When the task was completed, Tom turned his back to face the wall. "If you don't mind I'll just wait in here. I feel kinda conspicuous standing in the hall."

"Oh . . . of course."

His ears strained, listening to the rustle of silk. What his eyes didn't see, his imagination did. In his mind he saw her clad in only a chemise and drawers. Delicate lace . . .

"Okay. You can look now."

She was already dressed in another outfit, neckline up to her chin and buttoned securely, sleeves full and cuffed tightly, bulking skirts adequately hiding her shape. Tom was surprised, and at the same time relieved. If she were just in her undergarments, as he'd imagined, he'd be hard put to meet the boys in the lobby in a few minutes.

Hoping she wouldn't notice he was fully aroused, he maneuvered around to the armoire to get a change of clothes. He glanced at Beth. She turned and stood with her back to him. Turning his back also, he peeled off his suit jacket and hung it up. He undid his trousers, let them drop, stepped out of them and then bent over to pick them up.

Beth had the uncontrollable urge to peek, but when she caught sight of his white underwear, she quickly turned away, her cheeks flaming. She tried to forget what she had seen, but it was too late. The image of him bent over, his behind toward her was burned into her memory, and even with her eyes closed she could make out the strong shape of his buttocks. Her heart thumped wildly in her chest. *Shame on you! What if Tom had peeked when you were dressing?* And then she wondered, had he? Her heart pounded louder.

"Are you almost ready?" she asked, anxious to escape her self-induced torture chamber.

"Just about."

A second later, he stood in front of her. Lord, but he was handsome, she thought. With or without clothes. Pushing her racy thoughts aside, she strode toward the door, saying, "We'd better get downstairs."

But Tom caught her and pulled her back against his chest.

"No, not yet," he whispered. "There's something I must know

first." He ran his hands gently down the front of her dress, over the swell of her pounding breasts to stop at her tummy. "Ever since we met there have been secrets. But there is no need any more, honey. We are husband and wife, 'til death do us part. Tell me," his voice was a breathless whisper, "is there going to be a child?"

Her answer was equally breathless. "Yes." She tipped her head back to gaze at her new husband, and he saw the truth in her eyes and she saw the love in his. "We're going to have a baby in December."

He came around her and bent to kiss her tenderly. "I am pleased beyond measure," he whispered against her lips.

*

Tannerville had a population three times that of Whistle Creek and a main street twice as long. Being Sunday, the stores were closed, all except the restaurant in the hotel. They stopped there first for some freshly baked pie before going window shopping. Davy dragged Bill ahead down the street, bouncing with energy and excitement.

They passed a brick building—the courthouse—and Tom glanced across at Beth. She was staring straight ahead, her head held proudly, but tears were glistening on her eyelashes. He knew what she was thinking. The same thoughts crossed his mind. What if they lost the boys? He wrapped a protective arm around her shoulders and left it there as they strolled down Main.

"We have to tell Davy," she said, her voice almost breaking.

"I know. But not yet." Their feet thudded on the boardwalk. It had a calming effect on them, almost like a mother's heartbeat. "Let's let him enjoy this day. We'll tell him tomorrow, right after breakfast."

Beth nodded, watching her brothers. "Bill's scared. He hides it well, but I can tell."

"We're all scared." This time Tom stopped. He turned Beth by the arm to face him, his grip tight. "Beth, I swear, even if we all have to move a thousand miles away, I won't let Mead have the boys."

They continued their walk in grim silence.

Three hours later, after having strolled up and down every street in Tannerville several times, they returned to the hotel. To pass the time before they went for supper, the boys played tic-tac-toe.

They went down to the hotel restaurant late, and after the main course, Tom lingered over a second and third cup of coffee while the boys ate dessert. Davy chattered nonstop, a welcome distraction for the rest of them, but the thought of what tomorrow might bring was never far from their minds.

When they returned to their room, they found two cots and extra blankets had been supplied. One was placed at the foot of the bed and the other on the side opposite the armoire, leaving very little floor space to move about in the crowded room.

Beth and Davy played I spy, while Tom and Bill stared unseeingly at the walls. The moment the room became dim, Tom suggested they get to bed, saying, "Tomorrow's going to be a big day."

"Why? What are we doing?" Davy asked, his interest piqued.

There was complete silence in the room. Bill's head snapped around to look at Tom. Tom, in turn, looked in Beth's direction, obviously at a loss for words.

She came over and pressed her face close to Davy's. "That's for me to know and for you to find out . . . tomorrow. Right now, it's bedtime. Out of your clothes, mister."

Davy stripped down to his underwear, causing her to fret about changing into her nightgown. Bad enough to have the first-night wedding jitters without having an audience. While Davy peeled, the other three in the room cast anxious glances at each other.

Finally, Tom suggested, his words coming out croaky, "How 'bout Bill and I go down to the lobby while you two get into bed? It's so crowded in here, we'll be tripping over each other."

She almost sagged in relief. "Oh, yes, that would be fine."

Ten minutes later, with Beth safely on the far side of the bed and the blankets tucked up to her chin, Tom returned.

"Where's Bill?" Davy asked, sitting up in his cot.

"He'll be here in a minute." Tom stole a quick glance across the room at his bride before extinguishing the lamp. Aided by the street's gaslights filtering through the curtains, he began to change.

She forced her eyes shut. Her ears strained to listen. The bed creaked, and Beth felt the mattress sink under his weight as he sat on the edge. She heard his shoes clunk on the floor, then the soft sliding sound of his pants coming off, first one leg and then the other. Presently, the bed creaked again, and his stocking feet padded around to the armoire. Its doors clicked open and coat hangers slid along the wooden bar inside. After a moment, she heard the door click again, follow by more footsteps.

"Ouch! Confound it!"

"What happened?" Beth's eyes flew open. Tom was in his underwear, looking like a ghostly apparition, standing on one leg and holding the other foot in his hands.

"I cracked my toe on this stupid cot."

"Sorry," Davy whispered in the dark.

"It's not your fault," Tom replied irritably. "It's this tiny room. We're crowded in here like fleas on a small dog. The hotel should make their rooms bigger."

But he and Beth knew it wasn't the room's size triggering his sour mood.

Cool air seeped under the covers as he slid in beside her. He stayed on his side and she on hers, keeping a proper distance between them as if they were strangers instead of husband and wife.

A couple minutes later Bill came along. He, too, undressed in the darkness, but dumped his clothes on the floor.

"Great," Bill muttered disgustedly, getting into his cot, "my feet stick out the end."

"You'll just have to make the best of it like the rest of us." Tom didn't feel much compassion for the youth. If anyone had reason to complain, he did. He was in for one uncomfortable wedding night, sleeping five inches from his bride and not being able to make love to her as he so desired.

"Are you all right, Davy?" Beth asked.

There was no answer, leaving everyone to presume he was already asleep, but a minute later his little voice piped up, "Boy, did I ever give God lots to listen to tonight! I had to thank Him for a whole bunch of things . . . the wedding . . . and the ride on the train . . . and the supper. Oops! I forgot to thank Him for the dessert."

Beth smiled in the darkness and Tom chuckled. "He knows, Bud."

"Do you say prayers, Tom?" Davy queried in the dark.

Beth waited in silence, realizing she didn't know how he would answer. In fact, she knew very little about her new husband or his daily habits.

"Ah . . . well . . . I used to. I guess I sort of let it slip." By God, if he wasn't blushing.

"You should say prayers," Davy lectured. "I prayed things would work out for us in Whistle Creek and they did."

The boy's confession tore at Tom's heart. "Well, I guess I'd better start again. Goodnight, Davy."

"Will everyone just shut up? How's a fella supposed to sleep with all this yappin'?" Bill grumbled, rolling over onto his stomach. His toes dangled over the edge of the cot.

"Goodnight, Bill."

"Hmph!"

Under the covers, Tom's hand searched out Beth's. Their fingers laced together, the only joining of their bodies circumstances would allow.

"Goodnight, Mrs. Carver," he whispered.

Her reply was barely audible. "Goodnight."

He rolled onto his side, facing away from her and she did likewise. Their worries about tomorrow were intertwined with their yearnings of the night and when sleep finally came, it was long overdue.

*

Breakfast was eaten with the solemnity of the Last Supper. Beth sipped on tea, discreetly adding what Doc Fisher had given her to curb the morning sickness. Tom watched her guardedly as he drank his coffee.

Bill ordered a big breakfast, but didn't eat it all. Only Davy did his breakfast justice, polishing off his own and then eating some of Bill's.

Later he skipped ahead back to the room, while the rest followed with heavy feet.

"So what are we going to do today? Can we go shopping?" he asked, once again bouncing on the bed.

Beth looked at Tom, but he seemed as reluctant to tell Davy as she was. "Maybe we'll go shopping later," she said, "but we have something we have to tell you first."

Davy gave one more hop and landed on his rump. He wiggled until he was sitting at the edge. Tom sat beside him and draped his strong arm around him as if to brace him for the news. Bill leaned against the wall for support.

"Davy, what we have to say is something none of us wanted ever to happen," Beth began.

"What do you mean?" His happiness disappeared, replaced with a worried frown. "What's wrong? You're scaring me."

The situation became too intense for Bill and he bolted from the room.

"Bill, come back!"

"Leave him be," Tom advised. "He doesn't need to be here for this." He shifted around, at the same time turning Davy by his narrow shoulders to face him. There was no easy way to do this so he came right out with it. "Son, your Uncle Mead is alive and has come to try to take you and Bill back."

Davy stared at Tom. Then his face twisted with rage and he slammed his fists into Tom's gut, pummeling him. He screamed, "No, no, no." Tom didn't try to restrain the boy. Davy had every right to feel angry, and better it was vented at him than at his sister.

Beth tried to intervene, but Tom raised his hand to stop her.

When Davy's rage was finally spent, he began to sob and Tom held him against his shirtfront.

"Don't let him t . . . take me," he wailed, sucking in big gulps of air. "Please d . . . don't let him t . . . take me."

It would have been easier to cut out his own heart than to listen to Davy beg like that. "I won't. I promise," he answered, vowing somehow he would keep his word.

Beth sat on the bed on the other side of Davy. Tom wrapped his arms around them both and the three of them clung together.

Davy wailed for a long time and then suddenly he wrestled back, pushing against Tom's chest to get free. Startled, Tom released him, allotting him just enough time to lean out over the floor before throwing up all of his breakfast.

And then he was crying about that, half choking as he vomited and wept. When it was all over, he ran into a corner, trying to hide from them.

It was the worst ten minutes of Tom's life and the ashen look on Beth's face told him it was hers too.

"I'll go get something to clean this up." He rose from the bed.

Beth nodded and went to the corner where she dragged Davy back into the sanctuary of her arms.

Tom found Bill in the hallway, staring out the window. Bill turned around. "How did it go?"

"Bad. He cried so hard he threw up. I'm going to get a mop."

"I couldn't stay."

Tom placed a hand on the youth's shoulder. "It's all right. I understand."

When Tom returned a few minutes later with a bucket and a mop, Bill was still staring out the window.

Beth was lying on the bed with her little brother's back cradled against her stomach. She hummed a soothing melody to him, and soon his sobs abated, and he laid on the bed, looking like a beaten pup.

Tom cleaned up the murky puddle on the hardwood floor, carrying the bucket and mop back to the bathroom. When he returned to the room, Davy was asleep, still held by Beth. Tom whispered quietly in her ear, "The train will be in soon. I should go meet Lanson."

She nodded.

"Will you be all right?"

She nodded again and he dropped a kiss on her temple.

In the hall, he stopped beside Bill. "Wanna come meet the train with me?"

"Sure," he answered, going first. His quivering voice told Tom he was close to crying.

Chapter 24

The train was late. As soon as the conductor put the step down, Aaron Lanson shot off the train like a bullet from a forty-five. Livid, his face, flushed with anger, and his gate, long and determined, Lanson crossed through the stationhouse to the main street.

Mead Parkerson, his face just as red, rushed along behind Lanson, giving him an earful. Finally the lawyer turned and, competing with the din of the crowd gathered to greet the train, yelled, "Listen, if you do not shut up, I will shove my fist down your filthy throat and pull out your voice box."

"Did you hear him?" Mead grabbed another passenger walking by. "He threatened me!"

"Yeah? Good for him! He'd be doing the world a favor if he could shut you up for five minutes."

"I want to see a lawyer. Where is the nearest lawyer?"

Lanson pointed down the street. "Last business on the left. I look forward to our time in court." Under his breath, he added, "I hope the judge throws you behind bars where you belong."

Parkerson snorted, did an about-turn, took one step and collided with Tom's chest. Mead looked up, surprised. "You again? What the hell was in that drink you had made for me last night? I darn near—" Suddenly he frowned. "What are you doing here?"

"I'm here to guarantee you never bother my wife and her brothers ever again."

It took a moment to register, then Mead huffed. "You? You married Beth?"

"Yup. Got a problem with that?"

He opened his mouth, about to say something, then clamped it shut, sidestepped around Tom and hurried down the street.

Lanson shook Tom's hand, then Bill's. "That old coot! All the way here I wanted to choke him."

Tom chuckled. "You look like you could use something to settle your nerves."

Lanson straightened his collar and shook out his tight shoulders. "Not a chance. I want to stay this way. It'll give me the instinct to kill when I get him in court. Speaking of which, I'd better stop by the courthouse and set up a time. Where are you staying?"

"At the Imperial. It's full, I'm afraid."

"I've got an aunt in town, lives in the brick house on Fifth Street. I can stay with her. As soon as I know anything, I'll let you know."

Bill had been silent, but just before Lanson left, he asked him, "Do you know the judge?"

"Not personally, but I've heard Judge Stone is a fair man. Don't worry."

Less than ten minutes later, Lanson knocked quietly on their hotel door.

"We can't see him today," he told Tom. "Apparently the judge has gone fishing and won't be back until tomorrow afternoon."

Tomorrow afternoon. That meant one more day worrying and another night of lying awake. Tom shook Lanson's hand. "Thanks for letting us know."

*

A loud rap on the hotel door brought Tom fully awake early the next morning. He dragged on his trousers and opened the door to find Parkerson there.

"You're up early," Tom growled, his mood sour partly because he had slept poorly, but more so because seeing Mead first thing in the morning was an unpleasant sight.

Mead pushed his way into the room and surveyed the sleeping quarters. "Well, ain't this a cozy set-up."

"What do you want?" Tom stepped in front of him, blocking him from intruding further.

"It's time to go to court. I was just talking to the judge and he said—"

"Impossible!" Tom spat. "Judge Stone has gone fishing and won't be back until this afternoon."

"Well, I guess fishing was no good, 'cause I run into him having breakfast at the Chinaman's Café. I told him all about the trouble them damn kids have caused me and he said let's get this settled once and for all. So you best hie yourselves on over to the courthouse right away." Mead looked so smug, Tom had to refrain from plowing his fist into his face. It took a great deal of self-control to merely guide him out the door.

Tom turned to face his worried family. "Okay, let's get a move on. You boys put on what you wore to the wedding." He took two strides to the armoire. "Come on, Beth. Get dressed."

"But the boys," she started to protest the lack of impropriety.

"You two dress facing the wall and we'll do the same. There's no time to waste."

Five minutes later, Tom was dressed and on the run to get Lanson from his aunt's house.

*

The courthouse was small, its furnishings consisting of two rows of wooden benches, a large oak desk, and a bookcase sagging under the weight of volumes of thick books.

Beth moved along the front seat, Davy following her, then Bill and Tom bringing up the rear. Except for the muted footsteps on the hardwood floor and their clothing brushing against the bench, the room was silent. Lanson took the center aisle seat. They waited. Their tension was so taut one could almost hear it zinging in the air.

Parkerson entered the courtroom, sans lawyer, and sat on the other side of the courtroom. Beth glanced sideways at him, but the sight of him only added to her already queasy stomach. Just before they left the hotel room, she had a sip of her medicine, but obviously it hadn't taken effect yet.

Davy saw his uncle and quickly crawled onto Beth's lap. She wrapped her arms around him. His trembling increased her anxiety.

A door opened at the front left and Judge Stone entered. He looked nothing like Beth had imagined he might. Somehow she expected his appearance to reflect his name. Instead Judge Stone was a short, skinny man, in his fifties, with thin mousey-gray hair. He slouched as if his beard, badly in need of trimming, was too heavy for his scrawny frame to carry.

She glanced up at Tom and the expression on his face told her he, too, had expected the judge to look different.

Lanson stood respectfully, indicating to Tom and Beth and the boys to do likewise. Judge Stone eased himself into his cushioned leather seat, placed his palms on the desktop and looked about his courtroom as if confirming the surroundings had not changed since his last appearance.

"Be seated," Judge Stone ordered, then picked up the gavel and rapped it soundly, causing everyone in the courtroom to jump.

Beth, so nervous her legs could barely support her, sank back into the seat. It seemed as if their entire future had come down to this one moment, down to the decision of this one man. She dared not allow herself to contemplate what would happen if he ruled against them for fear she would start crying. She promised herself she wouldn't break down.

"All right," the judge stated, "let's get this show on the road. Who wants to go first?"

Lanson glanced sideways at Tom and raised an eyebrow, apparently taken aback by the lack of judicial protocol.

Parkerson jumped to his feet. "I will, your Honor. As you already know, I am Mead Parkerson and those two boys over there," he said, pointing, "they are my nephews, and my legal wards. I got custody of them when their parents, my brother and his wife, were killed in an unfortunate accident." He pulled a grayish colored hankie from his suit jacket and dabbed his bloodshot eyes. "God rest their souls."

After an appropriate moment of appearing disconsolate, he sniffled and continued, this time pointing at Beth. "The boys' sister stole them away from our home, and I'm here to take them back home so me and my good wife can give them a proper upbringing."

Lanson stood immediately. "Your Honor, I object. Mrs. Carver did not steal her brothers. She was merely—"

The gavel came down hard, interrupting Lanson's objection. "Just you sit down. You'll get your turn."

Lanson complied, and Tom gave him a worried look.

Judge Stone turned to Mead. "You got anything else to say?"

"Yes, sir, I do." He reached inside his coat and pulled out a piece of folded paper and slapped it against his palm. "This here paper proves that me and my wife are the guardians. It's my brother's Last Will and Testament."

"Do you know about any will?" Lanson whispered to Beth.

She frowned and shook her head. She had always assumed Mead had custody because he was the closest living relative. Suddenly she felt physically ill and this time it had nothing to do with her pregnancy. Surely her father hadn't planned for them to stay with Uncle Mead and Aunt Tilly. Didn't he know what sort of man his brother was? She looked fearfully at Tom and he, too, looked concerned.

The judge reached forward. "Bring me that paper." He studied the documentation, seemingly unmoved.

Lanson stood again. "Your Honor, we have no knowledge of such documentation."

"Well, it's right as rain," Parkerson declared with a confident smile.

Lanson continued. "Judge Stone, I request Mrs. Carver be given the chance to verify the signature."

"I guess that's fair enough. Come and get it."

Parkerson frowned, but did not protest.

Beth set Davy from her lap and he crawled from the refuge of her arms into the waiting arms of Bill.

Lanson handed her the paper. Her hands shook and the paper trembled like an autumn leaf in a breeze. Tom leaned across in front of the boys. His hand supported hers to hold it steady.

"Check it carefully, Beth," he whispered. "He might have forged it."

Beth read the will and then carefully studied the angular penmanship and the signature. It had been over four years since she'd last seen her father's writing, but the signature before her looked genuine.

"Oh Tom." She knew, by verifying the signature's authenticity, she would lose custody of the boys. "What can we do?"

He didn't know. Oh, that he did. Tom stood. His knees knocked. "Your Honor, I'd like to say something." His Adam's apple seemed lodged in his throat. "Judge, the boys have everything they need in Whistle Creek . . . love, guidance, friends. If they went back to Duggan, they'd have none of that. I couldn't love Davy more if he were my own son."

Memories of afternoons spent with Davy came flooding through. *Davy, his little buddy. What would he do without him?* Tom swallowed hard. "And Bill, well, I've grown to respect him. He's got convictions and dreams. He may be only sixteen, but he's a fine young man."

Bill blinked at the unexpected compliment. Tom stared straight at him and a bond was forged.

"Sir," Tom went on, "words on a piece of paper shouldn't overrule what a person knows in his heart to be right. Please, don't take—" His throat constricted and he didn't know if he could finish. He closed his eyes, concentrating on forcing out the words. "Please don't take the boys from us."

Judge Stone stroked and pulled on his long beard in almost the same motion he might use when milking a goat. "That was one fine speech. Mighty fine indeed, and if this were an elocution contest, you'd get a red ribbon. But this is a custody hearing and not even a judge can dispute a will. I grant Mr. Parkerson custody of his two nephews."

"*No!*" A scream tore through the courtroom, and Beth realized it had come from her.

Davy sobbed against Bill's shoulder and, half crying himself, Bill consoled him, saying, "It's all right, Davy. I'll take care of you."

Tom felt like he'd been flattened by a forty-ton train. He sat speechless, stunned.

Lanson hastily approached the desk. "Your Honor. Surely—"

"My decision holds. This case is closed. Court is dismissed." One final hammer of the gavel and their future was sealed. Judge Stone exited through the side door.

Mead, jubilant with the ruling, danced a little jig over to Beth and snatched the will from her hand. "Too bad," he flaunted, "but the law is the law."

Tom jumped up and grabbed him by the collar, pulling him close. "Listen, you piece of pig manure, you'd better take good care of them. You harm one hair on those boys and I'll hunt you down and kill you. So help me, I will." Tom shoved him away, and Mead stumbled backwards.

Parkerson straightened himself and his clothing. "We'll all go back to Whistle Creek this afternoon, just like one big happy family. I'm giving you until tomorrow to get the boys' things ready. I think that's being fair, but I'll be takin' them home to Saskatchewan with me on tomorrow's train."

*

Beth remembered very little of the train ride home, except that she felt like crying the entire way and it was only by sheer will that she hadn't. But Davy cried, inconsolably, and by the time the train pulled into Whistle Creek, he was exhausted, both physically and emotionally.

Surprisingly, Parkerson remained at the opposite end of the train car and never once came near them. Beth decided it was because of Tom's menacing glare thrown at him every time he even glanced their way.

Mary and Earl were waiting at the station, Tom having telegraphed ahead with the dreadful news. From the train station they went directly to Betner's where Mary had supper waiting. Beth could not recall if she ate or not, nor what was said over dinner, if indeed there was a conversation. Her only thoughts were of tomorrow and how at this very same time, Davy and Bill would be gone, and she'd feel as if half her life had been torn from her.

Immediately following supper, Bill went to say goodbye to Annaleese. Tom and Beth departed soon after, taking a despondent Davy home to bed.

He was put in the guest bedroom again, in the bed that would have been his if things had worked out the way they should have. To Beth he seemed so much smaller this time, fragile almost, shrunk down under the covers so only half of his head poked out.

She sat on the edge, while Tom stood at the headboard, feeling about as useless as the bedpost. "It won't be nearly as bad this time, Davy." She fussed with his blankets to avoid looking him in the eye, certain she would burst into tears if she did. "Daisy will have had her calf by now. Remember how you got to bottlefeed the last one? The way he bunted at the bottle and just about knocked you on your behind?" Davy nodded. "Well, I bet you'll get to feed this one, too. That would be fun, wouldn't it?"

Davy shrugged.

"And the gophers will be out," she continued. "You and Bill can snare them again, just like you used to do." She chattered on, hoping to convince Davy living again at Duggan would be an adventure, yet all the while thinking this entire ordeal was a nightmare and how unfair it was that a few scribbles of a pen could bring about such grief.

Tom stroked Davy's brow gently. "And I'll have a look around to see if I can find my old slingshot. Then you can bean them right between their beady eyes." He gently drilled his finger into the bridge of Davy's nose. "Right there," he said, forcing a smile.

"But I'd rather stay here," Davy protested weakly.

"I know, sweetheart." Beth nearly choked with emotion and she looked up at Tom for support.

"And we wish you could too," he answered softly, "but for now you have to go."

There was an empty silence for a few moments and then Davy rolled onto his side, as if shutting them out. "I wanna go to sleep, now."

"Don't you want to say your prayers before you go to sleep?" Beth asked.

"Don't feel like it."

"But you always—"

Tom gently squeezed her shoulder, stopping her from further exhortation. He nodded silently towards the door.

She kissed Davy's head lightly, and the realization she might not have the opportunity to kiss him goodnight again for quite some time caused her eyes to burn with tears, and her throat to clamp shut. She sat there for several heart-wrenching seconds, loathe to leave her little brother's side. Finally, Tom grasped her arm and drew her away.

Outside Davy's room, he pulled her into his embrace, and they leaned on each other for support like two straw bundles in a stook.

And finally, in the privacy of their bedroom, Beth sank onto the large bed and succumbed to her tears. She'd never known a physical pain quite as raw or as agonizing as this feeling of hopelessness and loss and worry.

Tom rocked her back and forth, sharing her pain, and it was all he could do not to break down, too. But his love for her made him strong, stronger than he ever thought he'd need to be.

Minutes later, when her tears began to subside, he shifted her in his arms so they sat face to face. Her nose was red, her lips splotchy, and her eyes puffy. She was the most pitiful sight he'd ever seen, yet he never loved anyone more. He wanted to hold her, protect her and love her forever.

"All the way home I was thinking there has to be some way to make this better," he said.

"If only there was. I can't believe my father would give Uncle Mead guardianship. He couldn't have known what kind of man Mead had grown to be." A fresh flood of tears threatened, and Beth blinked them back.

"I'm going to get Lanson checking into the will. But in the meantime, I've got an idea. Since the judge won't let us have the boys here in Whistle Creek, maybe we should move to Duggan."

Beth was speechless. A tear rested on her cheek and Tom rubbed it away lightly with his big flat thumb. "Move? Tom, you've worked so hard to make your business successful."

"I know, but this is more important."

"But you've lived here all your life. All your family is here."

Tom brushed a strand of hair from her face. "Not all. Part of my family will be in Duggan too." He gazed at her with an intensity that burned right through her and kindled a small flame of hope. "Think of the advantages. If the boys need us, we'd be right there, not two hundred miles away. And don't you think Mead would go easier on the boys if he knew we were around?"

It was true. As much as Mead liked to flaunt his authority, Beth knew he was a coward.

Tom continued. "And you could see Davy every day on his way to school."

She brightened. "I could!" Suddenly she threw her arms around his neck and began planting soft sweet kisses all over his face. "Thank you. I can't believe you'd do this for me."

"Beth, I love you. My life wouldn't be worth a tinker's damn if you were unhappy. So call me selfish, but I plan on spending the rest of my life making you happy."

"You are the most generous man I have ever known, and I love you dearly and I promise to spend the rest of my life making you equally happy." With that end in mind, she kissed him fully on the lips.

Tom had all good intentions of tucking her into bed and then sleeping downstairs. The day had been long and tiring and she needed to rest.

But it seemed his new wife had a different intent. When he went to pull away from her, she held him tight. She kissed him again with a passion that surprised him.

His arousal was rapid and full. "Dear Lord, Beth," he said throatily, "what you do to me." He leaned her back on the mattress, his body half covering her. His lips crushed against hers, nearly bruising them against her teeth. She opened her mouth, accepting his delving tongue as it raked from side to side. He groaned. "I can't help myself. I love you so much."

Beth was too impatient for conversation. "Don't talk, show me."

He drew her to stand before him. Their hands frantically removed their own garments. Their breathing became labored with expectation. Tom's pants and underwear came down in a single push. He stood on one foot, dragged a pant leg off, then hopped wildly on the other foot to yank the other pant leg free.

Beth dropped her skirts, pulled down her cotton drawers and crinolines, and left them in a frilly heap on the floor. She fought with the tight buttons of her bodice.

"Leave them," he ordered gruffly. His eagerness to know her again was matched only by her desire for him. Too impatient for any preliminary touching, Tom laid her back on the edge of the bed, wrapped her legs around his waist and took her swiftly.

The bed frame squeaked and its headboard drummed a lively rhythm against the wall until it reached a thunderous level. But the only sound they heard was their song of love making.

They certainly didn't hear the small boy exit the bedroom across the landing. They didn't hear him tiptoe down to the kitchen to don his coat and shoes. They didn't hear him slip outside.

Chapter 25

By the light of a waning moon, Davy started running. He had to hurry if he was going to make Tannerville by morning. He had to talk to the judge one more time, convince him how important it was that he and Bill be allowed to stay with Beth and Tom.

He ran down the train tracks, slipping often on the frosty wooden ties. The moonlight reflected off the rails, two silver lines converging to a distant point on the horizon. Beyond the horizon was Tannerville. In between was the trestle crossing over the creek that Whistle Creek was named after.

*

Dawn was breaking when Tom heard the pounding on the door downstairs. He pulled on the pants, still bunched on the floor.

Beth was awake immediately. "Surely it's not Uncle Mead already!"

"If it is, I'll knock his block off. We have until this afternoon before he's supposed to come."

It was Lanson at the door, coat pulled up to his ears to ward off the chill of last night's frost. Beside him was a hefty man, a stranger. They both were grinning ear to ear.

"What's going on?" Tom asked, letting them in.

Lanson removed his gloves. "Tom, I'd like to introduce you to the Honorable Judge Stone, the real Judge Stone."

Tom was silent, stunned.

Judge Stone chuckled. "I can understand your shock. I have to admit I was rather surprised myself when Mr. Lanson met me when I returned from fishing and told me what had happened. It seems my janitor thought it would be fine and dandy to impersonate me. He is now looking out from the inside of a jail."

"I'm still afraid I don't follow."

"Follow what?" Beth asked as she joined the men in the kitchen. She pulled her robe tight around her.

Tom made the necessary introductions.

She shook her head. "If you're Judge Stone, then who . . . ?" She sank into a chair, confused.

Tom indicated the gentlemen should also seat themselves, and then quickly tossed some logs into the stove to chase away the cold.

The judge explained. "As I was telling your husband, Mrs. Carver, that charlatan was my janitor, Newly Jones. From what he told us, he met up with Parkerson in the saloon, and after a few free drinks, he agreed to help your uncle gain custody of your brothers."

"Why would he agree to do that?" Tom asked. "Just for free drinks?"

"Plus a tidy sum of four hundred dollars."

Beth huffed. "Uncle Mead barely has four dollars let alone four hundred."

"Apparently Newly is easily duped."

Tom turned to Lanson. "You suspected something, didn't you?"

"From the moment the trial started. Everything was so unconventional. So after the trial, I asked my aunt if she knew Judge Stone and she did, but the man she described was certainly not the man in court. I merely waited for the real Judge Stone to return from fishing."

"So now what happens?" Tom asked. "Do we have another trial?"

"We could," the judge answered, "but what would be the point? Parkerson will soon be sharing a cell with my janitor and will be otherwise engaged for several years."

For a moment there was silence and then Tom let out a whoop. Beth covered her open mouth with her trembling hand. "Does this mean . . . ?"

Tom picked Beth up and swung her once around the kitchen. "It sure does, darling. We have custody of the boys."

"But the will?"

Lanson was quick to answer. "It is of no consequence now, but I'm willing to bet my gold ring it was forged."

"It's over? We're safe?"

"Better than that, we're a family," Tom corrected, hugging his wife.

Judge Stone rose to leave first. "I think, Mr. Lanson, we ought to leave now. The Carvers have had a lot to deal with these last few days. I think they need some time to absorb this good news."

The moment the door closed, Tom swung her around the kitchen again. Then abruptly her put her down and announced, "Let's go tell Davy."

"Yes. Right away." They raced to the spare bedroom.

Their elation was short lived when they found an empty bed. Davy was gone.

"I don't understand it," she said, after having checked all around the house. Tom had just returned from checking the barn. "Where would he have gone?" she asked.

"He probably couldn't sleep so he went to be with Bill at the livery," he said casually, though the tense look on his face belied his calm manner.

Ten minutes later, they were inside the livery, waking up Bill.

Bill was immediately alarmed. "Davy wouldn't run away."

Tom took control of the situation. "Let's not panic, here. He's probably hiding somewhere. We need to take a good look around first before we jump to conclusions."

Just the same, the first place they checked was the Whistle Creek's boarding house where Mead stayed last night. The clerk told them that, not more than thirty minutes ago, Mr. Parkerson was led away by the authorities and Mr. Lanson and another gentleman were with him.

"Was Davy Patterson with them?"

"Little Davy?" the night clerk asked. "I didn't see him."

The morning sunrise was blocked by a heavy cloud, casting a gray pallor over the entire town. They checked the school, the smithy, and all the places he would most likely be, but found no trace of him.

"Tom, I'm scared," Beth admitted.

He looked solemnly at her. "I guess we'd better get a search party out."

Less than half an hour later, a large group of men and women gathered outside of Betner's store. The town was sectioned off into quadrants.

"Check everywhere," Earl instructed, taking charge. "Look in every building, barn, chicken coop. Check your root cellars, too. No telling where he might be hiding. Remember he's small and he could fit in any tight space. If anyone finds him, bring him back to the church and ring the bell. All right, let's go."

Over an hour later, searchers straggled back to the church, having turned the small town upside down. Nothing. Several men volunteered to search the outskirts of town.

"Maybe he went to Gordie's farm." Beth spun to face Tom. "He stayed overnight there once before."

"It's a thought. Bill and I will check it out."

"I'm coming, too," Beth stated.

Tom didn't waste precious time trying to deter her. "Fine." They rushed to the barn.

"There's no point in all of us going there," Bill said, as he tightened the cinch of his saddle. "We should split up."

"Right. You check Gordie's. Beth and I will go the other way."

"But the other way is the creek," Beth said. "Davy knows he's not supposed to go near there."

"Honey, he also knows he's not supposed to run away." Tom gave her a boost into her saddle, then went around to his horse, thrust his foot in the stirrup and swung his leg up and over. "We'll meet you back in town in . . . say a couple hours, if not sooner."

Bill mounted his horse and took off at a hard gallop.

When Tom and Beth reached the creek, they reined in their horses well back from the jagged banks. The water, considerably higher than when they'd crossed it on the train the day before, glided swiftly past. Murky whirlpools swirled along the edges, while small rocks and mud trickled down into the water. The banks were dangerously undercut and gnarled roots were exposed to the elements.

Rain fell, at first in a fine mist, then in a continuous drizzle, soaking their clothing. Tom gave his hat to Beth. "Here, wear this."

They road upstream along the bank's edge, calling out Davy's name, but the sound of rushing water drowned their voices. Often Tom would dismount, hand Beth his reins and walk along the craggy ridge, looking up and down the swollen creek, praying he wouldn't find him in the water.

At every farm along the way, they stopped. The farmers, up about doing their morning chores, hadn't seen any boy, but all promised to keep an eye out for him.

Disappointed and increasingly worried, they returned to the creek. Tom scoured the banks again. Then he saw something indistinguishable swirling in the eddy of a log jam.

"Wait there," he ordered.

"What do you see?"

"Just wait there!"

Tom slid down the bank, grabbing at roots and shrubs, scraping his hands on the sharp wet rocks. Whatever it was, it was small and dark, twirling around and around in the whirlpool. Occasionally, the passing current would grab at it, threatening to carry it further downstream.

Wading out into the frigid thigh-deep water, Tom grabbed for the object. It was a shoe and, upon closer inspection, he read Davy's name penned inside the heel. Staggering backwards, Tom fell against the bank, hugging the shoe to his chest. He groaned, fighting the pain in his heart as the drizzling rain ran icy runnels down his face. *Dear God,* he prayed. *Please, not Davy.*

"Tom, did you find something?"

Hurriedly, Tom dumped the water from the shoe and stuffed it inside his coat. "No, nothing," he hollered, and then scrambled up the slippery bank, glad for the rain which hid his tears.

"Maybe you should go back, Beth. It's starting to rain harder." He wanted to spare her the possible agony of finding Davy face down in some backwater.

"No! Two can search better than one." Strands of wet hair slashed across her cheeks and water dripped from her nose and chin. "We're wasting time. Let's go."

And time was important. Even now, the rain was turning to sleet. Spring snow storms could be surprisingly ugly.

"Lead my horse then," Tom instructed. "I'm gonna walk along the edge some more." As his eyes scanned the water and the banks, Tom told himself all he had found was just a shoe. It didn't mean anything. Until he found Davy's body, there was hope. There had to be hope.

Ahead, about a quarter mile upstream, loomed the train trestle, spanning the gully eroded deeper each spring by the rushing waters of Whistle Creek. Tom decided if he found nothing by the time they reached the trestle, he'd take Beth back and send some men to search downstream.

"Tom! I see him!"

"Where?" His heart stopped. *Please, not in the water.*

"On the bank by the trestle." Beth dropped the reins to his horse and spurred hers into a gallop.

He mounted and, from his higher position, saw Davy sitting on the bank, hugging his knees. "Thank you, God."

Davy saw them coming, stood on one foot as if he were playing hopscotch, and waved.

Before her horse had come to a full stop, Beth dismounted and scooped Davy up into her arms, crying. "Oh Davy, thank God you're all right. You gave us such a scare. What are you doing out here?"

"I was goin' to Tannerville to see the judge, but I was too chicken to cross the trestle. And then I lost my shoe and I was too chicken to come back home without it in case you got mad at me."

"Oh, Davy," she sobbed, setting him down, running her hands up and down his arms as if to convince herself he was safe and whole. "I don't care about a stupid shoe. I'm just so grateful you're okay."

"You're not mad?"

Beth shook her head.

"Maybe she's not, but I am," Tom boomed, dismounting. "I'm mad enough to tan your scrawny hide. Don't you ever pull a stunt like this again, you hear?"

"No, sir, I mean, yes, sir," Davy replied, standing free of his sister to bravely face Tom.

"Well, good then . . . fine," he said, his ire cooling off rapidly. "You had your sister beside herself with worry." He didn't dare admit how terrified he'd been.

He pulled the shoe out from his coat and handed it to Davy. "Here," he offered gruffly, "I found this downstream."

Davy took the shoe and put it on. When he stepped down on it, water oozed out around the sole.

Suddenly Tom's hands began to shake uncontrollably, and he stuffed them deep in his coat pockets. "I . . . ah . . . I thought you had . . . " He choked, unable to finish.

Beth went to him, touching his arm, and peered into his dark eyes. "He's fine, Tom. He's all right," she said in soft, reassuring tones. "He's just cold."

Tom nodded. "Right, and it's starting to snow. We'd better get him home where it's warm. Into some dry clothes." He lifted the shivering boy up into his saddle and then sung himself in behind. With a protective arm wrapped around the boy's small waist, Tom pulled Davy hard against him.

They rode silently until Tom felt enough control to scold gently, "What were you thinking of, Davy, running away like that?"

"I wanted to see Judge Stone. I need to tell him something he doesn't know."

Tom glanced at Beth. "What doesn't the judge know?" he asked.

"That I love you and so does Beth and that I want to stay here, and that it's not right a stupid piece of paper can make Bill and me live with a mean old man."

"We agree totally." Beth smiled at Tom.

"And I want to tell him that all my friends are here and that Bill has a girlfriend. And, Tom, remember you were getting a puppy this spring and I was gonna help train it? It's springtime now."

"You're right, it is, even if we're likely to have several inches of snow before nightfall."

"So you see?" Davy said confidently. "I'm sure if I talked to the judge, real polite-like, he'd let us stay. That's why I need to get to Tannerville so bad. Before Uncle Mead comes to get us."

Tom hugged Davy close. "You don't need to worry about your Uncle Mead ever again." While they rode back to Whistle Creek, Tom and Beth explained all about the deception.

"So we can be a family now?" Davy asked, squirming about in the saddle to face Tom.

"Yup!"

"Yippee!" Davy yelled.

Beth's heart swelled with happy emotions and her hand went instinctively to cradle the tiny bulge of her tummy. Yes, they were a family.

In the mood for more Crimson Romance? Check out *Rhianna* by Amanda L.V. Shalaby at *CrimsonRomance.com*.

CPSIA information can be obtained at www.ICGtesting.com
Printed in the USA
LVOW101556070413

327997LV00025B/1316/P